Path of the Tiger

CLEO CORDELL

BLACK
lace

Black Lace novels are sexual fantasies.
In real life, make sure you practise safe sex.

First published in 1994 by
Black Lace
332 Ladbroke Grove
London
W10 5AH

Copyright © Cleo Cordell 1994

Typeset by CentraCet Limited, Cambridge
Printed and bound by Cox & Wyman Ltd, Reading,
Berks

ISBN 0 352 32959 9

Chapter One

The sky was a bright and peerless blue and the sun overhead shone like a ball of molten gold. Cries of animals and the sounds of bustling humanity echoed on the still air.

Inside the army cantonment Amy Spencer looked wistfully towards the slats of the window blind which barred her from the exciting sights and smells of the Bombay street. In the colonel's drawing room the atmosphere was one of forced gentility.

Indian silks covered the small tables and exotic plants graced the carved rosewood mantelpiece, but here, as elsewhere in India, the British strove to recreate the society of London. A number of army wives were gathered together, taking tea and chattering to each other.

Amy lifted a hand and ran one finger around the inside of her high collar. In this heat it would have been sensible to adopt the native clothing, but she was aware that even to think such a thing was regarded as a sin verging on heresy.

Around her the air was thick with the smell of violet cologne, underlaid by the sharper spice of female sweat.

Amy stifled the urge to yawn and dragged her attention back to the conversation.

'And I said to her that eating the food from the street vendors was asking for trouble, my dear. All that spiced mess. It could be roast dog for all we know . . .'

Amy smiled politely and nodded. It was useless to protest that she would welcome the chance to sample the wares from the *khomcha-wallah* who advertised the delicacies he offered while wandering the street, a basket balanced on his head and a cane stool tucked in the crook of his arm. It would at least be something out of the ordinary.

She had never been so bored in her life. The conversation went on around her, the words slipping over her like water off a rock. Either it was gossip about the army wives on other cantonments in the area, or warnings about the dangers of going out unchaperoned and fraternising with the natives, the latter subject spoken of with hushed voices and the sparkle of shocked delight.

She looked around the room at the earnest faces, topped by drawn-back hair and neat ringlets. What dreadful hypocrites they were. They seized on the juiciest morsels of gossip, using them to brighten the boredom and sameness of their lives. If only they would allow themselves to see what was all around. India beckoned, offering a wealth of entertainments and delights.

Amy sighed and shifted position on the upholstered settle. She felt restless and ill at ease. The blood was singing through her veins and she wanted to be outside. In England she would have gone to the stables and ordered the lad to saddle her gelding. Galloping across the rolling downs towards the neighbouring estate where Magnus – the estate manager – waited, she had known true happiness.

The enforced inactivity was hard on someone like

herself. On the family's modest country estate in Sussex she had been allowed to run wild. She bitterly resented having to play the part of the perfect English lady here in India.

A trickle of sweat ran down the inside of Amy's bodice and soaked into the corset which seemed to grip her like a vice. She could feel the sticky heat gathering in the creases between her thighs, adding to the moistness and sensitivity of the little purse of flesh that was hidden there.

A tiny smile lifted the corners of her full mouth. Her quim, Magnus, had called that place, as he slipped his hand up her skirts and caressed her with his calloused but knowing fingers. She almost shivered at the memory . . .

Oh God that first time, when he had closed his hand around the mound of her sex. How thoroughly he had stroked her, pinching and spreading her virgin folds until she trembled against his broad chest, breathy little moans escaping her. The shame of being touched there had soon faded, turning instead into a sense of illicit delight. When the pleasure crested and broke she had cried out in amazement.

When Magnus showed her his cock and urged her to stroke it she had done so willingly, delighting in the hardness and potency of him. How fascinating was the male organ. Magnus had let her examine him, laughing when she held his heavy balls in the palm of her hand or stroked the dark bush at his groin. She loved to smooth back the cock-skin from the swollen purple head and tease the tiny slitted mouth with the tip of her tongue. An honourable man, Magnus had not taken her virginity, but he had pleasured her soundly in many and varied ways.

Between her thighs, Amy felt a hot and heavy pulsing begin, an echo of her body's response to the handsome estate manager. But Magnus was far away now. He'd probably married some country creature with a farm of her own.

The memory of the long hot hours spent lying in the thyme-scented grass at the side of the cornfield had the power to stir her still. She remembered the smell of Magnus's stocky body; the way his muscled arms felt, the touch of his surprisingly sensitive hands, and the taste of his stiff male organ.

Her body, having been awoken, burned for a lover's touch. Perhaps it was boredom which brought the recent dreams, so vivid and explicit in their sexuality. Or maybe it was the memory of that episode in England when she'd walked into the barn and heard the sounds up in the hay loft.

Amy let the memories surface in her mind, aware that her breasts were swelling and pushing against the confinement of her chemise. Unseen by the army wives, she linked her hands and pressed them into her lap, exerting pressure over the spot of pulsing heat at her groin.

For a moment, the drawing room faded and she was there again, climbing the ladder and peering through the trap door. Tom the carter was kneeling between Rosie, the housemaid's spread thighs, his great crested cock rearing up from his open breeches. Tom's cock was different to Magnus's. It was shorter and thicker and looked red and angry, the uncovered tip moist and red-purple in colour. Amy had watched with fascination as Tom plunged into the open and ready body beneath him.

Rosie moaned and gasped as Tom's muscular buttocks pumped away, his thick wet shaft pulling almost all the way out of her before slamming back in again. Amy bit back the little cries of empathy which rose in her throat. Magnus had never done that to her, too afraid that she might quicken and bring disgrace on her family. Her own intimate folds had grown swollen and

4

wet with wanting. When she returned to the house, she found teeth marks in her knuckles, where she'd pressed her hand hard against her mouth.

She'd ridden across to Magnus's farm and told him what she'd seen. That had been a special afternoon, Magnus making her recount the experience in great detail while he threw her skirts over her head, spread open her quim with his fingertips and licked and sucked her until she thought she might dissolve into pure pleasure. Afterwards he had just lain looking at her, her shapely white legs clearly displayed by her tumbled skirts. How he had admired the cluster of bright red curls which surrounded her quim.

'Your blood's as hot as your colouring, my lovely,' he murmured, unable to keep from stroking her. 'I've never known a woman so eager for loving.' And soon he'd begun to pleasure her again.

She had known that her liaison with Magnus couldn't last and had not been dismayed when her father had announced his imminent posting to India. The house was alive with excitement and the talk was of the strangeness and beauty of the land they were to travel to. Amy had imagined that she would meet many handsome officers and be able to continue her erotic adventures.

But the reverse was the fact. She met only married officers and their wives. India was something she glimpsed through windows or passed through on the way to a picnic or house party. The vibrant colours of saris, buildings and painted statues passed her by, the sights as elusive as butterflies.

Her father's duties took him away for long periods and her mother was deeply involved in the round of army social events. Amy felt that the English community was stifling her. She might as well have been shut up in a nunnery. No wonder she was plagued by explicit dreams. The worst thing was that she felt starved of physical pleasure. Her entire body: skin, breasts and most particularly the sensitive sex-flesh between her thighs, felt in a state of almost permanent arousal. The sultry Indian heat and the constriction of her Western clothes only made it worse.

'Are you quite well, my dear?' one of the wives asked her. 'You look a little flushed. You haven't been out in the sun without a hat, surely.'

'I'm just hot. That's all.' Amy forced herself to smile and picked up her paper fan.

'It takes a while to settle in,' the other woman said helpfully. 'It's barely two months since you arrived. You'll soon feel at ease out here. We do all we can to remind ourselves of home.'

Amy nodded. She had indeed found the army base to be a self-contained little England, with all the accompanying prejudices and small-mindedness. Social snobbery was somehow heightened in India. The list of rules about seemly behaviour were endless and the divisions between white people, their servants and the natives – however high-born – were carved in stone.

She recognised the fact that she was sinking rapidly into lethargy. It frightened her to think that there was not a single woman with whom she felt the slightest affinity.

I shall go mad, she thought, if I have to attend any more of these tea parties or listen to the brainless mutterings of Edith Taverner or the dire warnings of Maud Harris. Some of them were well meaning enough, but they were all as dull as ditchwater. She felt guilty for feeling so superior, but she couldn't help it. At least I know that I'm alive, she thought. And I won't allow myself to be pushed into a mould by them.

She knew that the stirrings within her were part of her need to stretch and try her wings. There were things to discover, interesting men to meet. But how was she going to meet anyone under the age of sixty-

6

five, when she was obliged to behave like a respectable memsahib?

Tears of frustration pricked her eyes. Lifting the china tea cup she took a sip of tea, making a conscious effort to subdue the turmoil which was rising within her. Another of the ladies began speaking and Amy balanced the tea cup and saucer on her knee and tried to pay attention.

'The thing is,' birdlike Maud Harris cut in, glancing at Amy, 'we must all keep up the team spirit. It doesn't do to flout convention. If we let standards slip, well, who knows what might happen.'

Amy winced inwardly. This most recent outburst had been prompted by the fact that she had insisted on going riding alone the day before. She tightened her lips, wishing a number of imaginative disasters down on Maud Harris. No veiled sarcasm or hints of disasters to come were going to stop her doing as she pleased.

Suddenly she had had enough. I shall scream if I have to listen to any more of this, she thought. The close atmosphere in the room seemed to be choking her. She had to get out into the garden where the sun was so vibrantly alive and the smells of dust and spices were carried on the breeze.

Glancing around she made certain that no one was looking at her directly. With a quick jerking motion of her arm, she upturned the cup and saucer, watching with satisfaction as a long brown stain appeared on the skirt of her white poplin gown.

'Oh dear! Look what I've done,' she said, bending down to pick up the pieces of china. 'Oh, Mrs Harris, I'm so sorry. I'm afraid I've smashed the cup. How very clumsy of me.'

Maud Harris's small mouth quivered and for a moment Amy felt like a monster. The tea cup was part of a set brought from England. Like the other women, Maud treasured anything which reminded her of her homeland.

'Oh, it's nothing really,' Maud said gallantly. 'But your skirt should be sponged immediately. The tea will stain if you leave it.'

Amy stood up. 'Yes. You're right of course. I'll attend to it at once. Will you excuse me ladies.'

It was all she could do to contain the spring in her step. She left the room with a light heart, all thoughts of the broken tea cup banished from her head. In her room she shrugged off the stained skirt and left it in a heap. The skirt was probably ruined but it seemed a small price to pay for freedom. Hurriedly she slipped a blue-striped muslin skirt over her petticoats and tried a blue sash around her waist.

Leaving the house by the French windows which opened onto a verandah, she hurried down the path and into the thick vegetation of the garden. In the wall at the bottom of the garden was a gate which led straight onto the main street. Amy intended to see if that gate was locked and, if it was, then she'd find another way of escaping.

She'd had more than enough of being inactive; the only excitement being that of waiting for the weekly post to arrive from Europe. How pathetic it was to find herself devouring the months-old newspapers and magazines, just like the other women. She despised the person she had become in India.

Then and there she made a decision. I want *real* life, she thought, not life lived at a distance. She wanted excitement too, even danger, and not the second-hand relating of other people's scandalous doings.

She also knew that she needed to feed the flame which Magnus had awoken within her. There had to be people out there who felt as she did. People who weren't afraid to take what India offered. It was only a question of finding them.

* * *

Madeline Jackson watched the young woman stride purposefully through the trees.

She smiled to herself. She'd been watching Amy since the day she arrived, having marked her out as different from the usual women who were attached in some way or other to the British army.

She hoped that Amy would be approachable. It was plain that the young woman wasn't the usual product of the ruling class of the British East India Company.

Madeline felt drawn to the red-headed woman. She herself was almost an outcast. Oh, they were polite enough to her face, though she despised their stiff-necked greetings and enquiries after her health. The fact that her father was an officer in the army, meant that they could not cut her dead, but she was aware of the whispers, the speculations.

Madeline's supposed sin was by way of an accident of birth, and Amy's . . . Well, one look at that flaming red hair, white skin, and the quick, graceful movements of her body and it was plain that she was heading for trouble. She looked so vibrant with her sensual little face and unusual colouring.

And now here was Amy, looking as charged as a flaming taper and set to storm right out of the garden and into the main street. Madeline felt concern. For a young women like Amy that could spell disaster. Amy must not be seen to be rebelling. Keeping up appearances was everything in the army.

Madeline was all too aware of the risk of being shunned by her peers. Amy's life could be made a misery if the army wives turned against her. She knew instinctively that Amy hadn't thought her actions through.

Before she could think better of it, Madeline took a step forward and emerged from the cover of a tall, clump of ornamental grass.

'Wait, please,' she called out.

Amy started in surprise. 'Who are . . .? Are you following me?' She stopped and recognition came over her face. 'I know you, don't I? I've seen you around the cantonment. You're that . . .' She stopped again, the colour rising into her cheeks.

Madeline smiled.

'Half-breed? You can finish your sentence. I know what they say about me. A popular description is that I've had a touch of the tar brush. Isn't that correct?'

Amy looked nonplussed by such straight talking. Her light-coloured brows drew together in a frown as she studied Madeline, the amber eyes measuring and weighing her. After a pause she answered.

'Yes. That is what they say about you. I'm sorry. I did not mean to offend you.'

Madeline smiled inwardly. Such honesty was refreshing and most unexpected. She liked Amy Spencer more with every passing second.

'Thank you for being so candid, and I'm not offended. I prefer the truth to dressed-up lies. May I ask you something?'

'If you like,' Amy said, her eyes narrowing with interest.

'Are you really intending to go out into the street dressed like that?'

Amy looked down at herself.

'Dressed like what?'

'In English dress and without a parasol. You look like a runaway. You're ill-prepared for the heat and the dust and, without a servant to guide you, you're fodder for bandits and beggars.'

'Bandits and beggars?' Amy said, her voice rising with alarm. Then, when Madeline smiled, her face relaxed although she still looked wary. 'You're teasing me.'

'Not entirely,' Madeline said. 'There are dangers for the unprepared.' She took a step closer. 'And do you

10

want the officers' wives to find out that you've been roaming the streets unescorted? They could make a lot of trouble for you.'

Madeline paused and saw the look of doubt flicker briefly in Amy's eyes. There was a most determined set to the full pale mouth and a stubborn lift to her chin. She sensed that Amy was going to do just what she wanted, whatever she said. She admired the English girl's spirit.

'I can see that you're set on your own course. Would you like me to help you?' Madeline said. 'I've found ways to escape the confines of army society, ways to indulge my appetite for life.'

Ways that would seem shocking to some, she thought, but somehow she sensed that in Amy she had found a kindred spirit. She felt a thrill of excitement at the thought of having a companion. She had no real friends, the Indian and English communities treated her with equal suspicion.

When Amy didn't answer, Madeline shrugged and made to turn away. She tried to hide her disappointment but failed.

'You think you don't need help?' she said bitterly. 'Then you don't care what the British women think of you. You are very brave or very foolish.'

'Wait! Don't go.' Amy said, her amber eyes glittering with some contained emotion. 'I'm sorry. I'm not used to someone speaking so freely. I'd . . . I'd like your help. I really would.'

Madeline turned back slowly, her mouth curving in a friendly smile.

'Then come with me. At my house I have clothes that are more fitting for exploring the bazaars and alleys. You're welcome to borrow them.'

For a moment longer Amy looked undecided.

'Tell me one thing before I go with you. Why do you

wish to help me? The army women haven't been kind to you. And you don't even know who I am.'

Madeline threw back her head and gave a peal of laughter.

'Oh, you British with your introductions! Indeed I know you. I've been watching you these past few weeks, although you have been unaware of the fact. I see a kindred spirit in you. Is it not kismet that we meet here in the garden?'

'Kismet?'

'Fate. Meant to be. Will you come with me to my house? We'll drink *lassi* and I'll tell you all about myself. Then you can tell me your story. Will that serve you for an introduction?'

Amy laughed, the sound of it was infectious.

'How stuffy you make me sound. I'm really not like that. It's just that the last few weeks have addled my wits. Yes, I'll come with you, and gladly.' She held out her hand. 'My name's Amy Spencer and I'm very glad to make your acquaintance. Very glad indeed. I think you might just have saved my sanity.'

Madeline clasped the slim hand which Amy proffered. Her own honey-coloured skin looked startling against the paleness of Amy's white skin.

'I'm Mobashira Khan Jackson,' she said. 'My Western name is Madeline. You might find it easier to call me that. And I too, am most pleased to meet you.'

Amy leaned back on the upholstered divan and made herself comfortable amongst the cushions. It was cool and dark inside Madeline's house, the air redolent with the smells of spices and sandalwood. The floor was tiled and coloured rugs were scattered here and there. Tapestries, embroidered and studded with tiny mirrors, were pinned over the doors.

While they waited for the drink to be prepared Madeline told Amy about her background. Amy listened attentively, unable to look away from her new-found companion. The details of Madeline's birth, her Indian mother – a proud and beautiful Pathan and her father, an officer in the British army, were fascinating.

Amy felt quite ordinary beside Madeline, whom she saw as exotic and enigmatic. And Madeline was so beautiful. Amy had never seen anyone like her. The combination of dusky skin, silky black hair, and blue eyes – picked up by the blue of her tunic and pantaloons – was quite devastating.

Madeline's voice was softly accented and her English was perfect. Besides English she apparently spoke Hindi, Tamil and a variety of other dialects.

Amy thought that she had never met a woman with such charm and vivacity. She felt savage at the thought of the young woman's treatment by the officers' wives. How dare they spurn Madeline just because of her mixed blood? Madeline had done nothing to offend them but she was not considered fit company for the British ladies of the ruling class.

Though she seemed unconcerned by that fact, Amy sensed Madeline's underlying hurt and anger.

'So, now you know all about me,' Madeline smiled as her mother entered the room carrying a tray with drinks and snacks.

Madeline's mother was tall and graceful. Her black hair was woven with silver ornaments and her sari was embroidered with silver thread. Pouring long glasses of the frothy *lassi* she handed one to Amy.

Amy sipped her drink, enjoying the coolness of the chilled yoghurt with its flavours of roasted cumin seed and mint.

Then it was Amy's turn to tell Madeline about herself. Madeline listened attentively until Amy finished.

'How different our lives have been. And yet we have both experienced loneliness.'

It was true Amy realised. She had never had a close

female friend, not even in England. And now this intelligent beautiful women was seeking her companionship. Amy felt a rush of emotion. Was it possible that the dull routine of her life was to change?

'Come with me,' Madeline said, when they finished their drink.

Amy followed Madeline down shaded corridors until they reached her room. The walls were hung with silken tapestries depicting Hindu myths. From a rosewood chest Madeline took dark green trousers and tunic and a peach-coloured scarf.

'These colours will look wonderful with your skin and hair.'

The clothes were beautiful. Hem, wrist and ankles were embroidered with birds and leaves. Amy looked longingly at them and then down at herself. Putting on and removing her dress, petticoats, chemise and corset took the combined efforts of herself and a maid.

'I can't undress alone . . .' She began. 'Perhaps you have a maid?'

Madeline patted her arms.

'No need for that. I'll help you,' she said, her fingers already loosening the sash at Amy's waist. 'Remember I'm also used to Western dress.'

In a few minutes the tiled floor was littered with a froth of skirts and lace. Amy stood self-consciously in her chemise and corset, aware that the front busk forced the top of her breasts to bulge upwards. Her breasts were a little too large for her frame and she was very aware of them.

Madeline suggested that she remove her corset as it would be noticeable under the softly-draped Indian garments and with reluctance Amy agreed. As Madeline loosened the tight lacing and the halves of the boned fabric parted, she felt a prickle of self-consciousness. Without the corset she felt naked and exposed, even though she was still covered by her cotton chemise.

'You have a lovely body,' Madeline said, glancing at the curves of Amy's body which were revealed by the fine cotton. 'Such rounded limbs and that rich swell at breasts and hips. In England you must have had many male admirers.'

Amy coloured and put her hands down to cover the dark shadow at her groin. She was not used to such directness. Women of her class did not refer to parts of the body.

Madeline's straight dark brows flew together. 'Have I offended you? Forgive me.'

'I'm not offended. I'm just not used to such straight talking. But I like it. Your candour's refreshing.'

She felt tempted to tell Madeline about Magnus but decided that it was too soon for such intimacies. For just a second Madeline's hand rested on her shoulder. The contact was so unexpected that Amy flinched and then smiled apologetically.

Madeline laughed. It was an infectious sound, deep and a little husky.

'I did not mean to alarm you but I have always loved touching beautiful things. Your skin is so pale and soft. It is so different from mine and it invites a person's touch. But you know that of course. It must give you great pleasure to stroke and caress yourself.'

Amy looked at the other woman blankly, quite forgetting to be embarrassed by her state of undress. She was horrified. How did Madeline know that she sometimes touched herself – there?

She recalled the time she had made the discovery that she could bring sexual pleasure to herself. She had been lying on her stomach on her day bed, thinking about Magnus, aware of the slickness between her thighs and wishing that she could go to him – but he was away for the day at the market.

Amy had begun squeezing her thighs together, the rhythmic pressure causing delightful flutterings which radiated outwards from the heated core of her sex. Investigating with her fingers, she found the pouting little flesh-lips had grown wet and puffy. Those familiar melting feelings had swept over her when she began to stroke and massage her quim, copying the movements that Magnus made.

She had spread her legs wide and rubbed at the moist, musk-scented folds, stroking the swollen little bud until it stood out as strongly erect as a tiny cock. As she rubbed and pressed, tugging gently at the little hood of skin which covered her bud, the pleasure had coalesced into wonderfully strong inner pulsings.

Whenever she was unable to meet Magnus, Amy pleasured herself with her fingers. In the last few lonely weeks in India she had often stroked herself to a peak of pleasure, finding comfort as well as release in the sensations that rippled through her womanly flesh.

And Madeline did that thing too, Amy just knew she did.

Madeline looked at her closely for a moment and Amy imagined that her new friend could see right inside her and read all her guilty secrets. She felt a thrill run down her spine and was swept by an agony of shame, but there was also a hot little core of excitement within her. Madeline understood, she too had experienced the stirrings of sexual arousal.

Oh, there were many things they would talk about, intimate confidences to share – things which she could never, ever talk about with any of the army wives. Madeline's very presence hinted at pleasures and sensations far beyond her own limited experience. In the lovely, almond-shaped blue eyes, there seemed a wealth of knowledge and sensuality.

Amy opened her mouth to speak again, but Madeline's thick black lashes swept down to veil her eyes.

'Forgive me,' she said hurriedly. 'I spoke out of turn. It was stupid of me. I ought to have realised that you have not had the benefit of such freedom as I. How could you have? Your culture does not revere the pleasures of the body as does mine.'

That was true enough. Amy knew that the culture of India was very different to her own. Madeline smiled enigmatically and, though Amy prompted her to say more, she would not be drawn.

'Now is not the time,' she said softly as she helped Amy put on the silk tunic and baggy trousers, then wrapped the peach silk scarf around her shoulders.

Standing back to admire her handiwork, Madeline said,

'There. With the scarf covering your head you could pass for a Northern tribeswoman. Their skins are pale like yours. But you'd best keep your hair covered. No one in the whole of India wears such a flame on their head.'

'That's true,' Amy said ruefully. She had ambiguous feelings about her red hair. Magnus had loved it but she'd hated it, having been teased unmercifully as a child at school.

Reaching out, Madeline curled a strand of Amy's hair around her finger.

'It is wonderful. So soft and shiny, like silk. The colour of the setting sun. You should guard its beauty well and not waste it on those who are undeserving. Pay no heed to the women who mock or look askance at you.'

Amy looked closely at Madeline to see if she was teasing. But Madeline was sincere, the admiration written plainly on her delicate features.

'You really like it? At school they called me "carrot-top" and "red-hackle". I had freckles and pale eyelashes too.'

Thankfully her freckles had faded as she grew older

but her skin was still as white as milk and her eyes were an unusually pale shade of her hair colour, like light-coloured amber.

How was it that Madeline knew that the army wives had treated her with suspicion at least partly on account of her startling colouring? Perhaps her new friend had the 'sight' – something which was spoken of in whispers amongst the wives. Amy felt intrigued at the thought.

'Now to your feet,' Madeline went on. 'I think my sandals will fit. Ah, yes. What pretty feet you have, narrow and high-arched. With henna patterns on the skin they would indeed be beautiful.'

'I have seen such designs,' Amy said. 'They are intricate and lovely. Indian brides wear them, do they not?'

Madeline threw her a look from the tail of her eye.

'There are other occasions, solely for pleasure, when hands and feet are so decorated, as you will learn.'

Amy longed to ask more about the henna designs although as before she sensed that Madeline was keeping things hidden from her, giving just enough information to prick her curiosity, but withholding the whole explanation. The words 'solely for pleasure' were mysterious and beguiling. Though she burned to know everything, she knew that it would do no good to ask. Even on such brief acquaintance she sensed that Madeline could be inscrutable when it suited her.

Reaching for an inlaid wooden box, Madeline laid out a variety of cosmetics.

'There is one last thing which will turn you into an Indian beauty. Will you permit me?'

Amy sat still while Madeline darkened her eyebrows and lashes and outlined her eyes with kohl, drawing the line up at the corners. She painted her lips a clear red and then handed Amy a mirror.

Amy stared at her reflection in astonishment. Gone

18

was the pale washed-out look to her face. The dark brows gave distinction to her features, drawing attention to her mysterious, shaded eyes. The kohl showed up the colour of her irises, making them glow a deep, rich gold and the elongated black line gave them a fetching tilt. Her red mouth looked sensual and inviting.

'I hardly recognise myself,' she said with delight.

Madeline looked proud of her handiwork. She handed Amy the little box of kohl.

'This is my gift to you. You can practise enhancing the beauty of your eyes yourself. Now that you are an Indian lady, what would you like to do first?'

Amy had no hesitation in replying.

'Can we find a *khomcha-wallah*?'

Madeline's straight black brows lifted in amusement and Amy felt embarrassed. Every day since she arrived she had heard the cries of the street vendors and her dreams of escape had become centred on them. Any Indian child would be familiar with the delicacies sold by the *khomcha-wallahs*. How foolish and gauche Madeline must think her to ask for such a pedestrian treat.

She was about to change her mind when Madeline spoke,

'If that is what you would like. We'll eat as much *chaat* as you wish. Then I'll take you to the bazaars and to the temples. And then on to – somewhere I know you'll find extremely stimulating. Oh, there's so much I want to show you Amy. We'll have such adventures.'

And, looking into her new friend's lovely, glowing face, Amy believed her. She didn't feel like she belonged to the army any more. In her Indian clothes she felt exotic, sensual and ready for anything. As she moved the cool silk caressed her skin. Her unfettered breasts swayed gently and she was aware of the slightest movement of the firm flesh of her buttocks. She had worn a corset since the age of eleven and it felt very odd to be without it. But she had to admit that her body's freedom exerted a powerfully erotic pull on her senses.

The mystical, sexually untamed India called out to her. She knew that this aspect of India terrified the army wives, but Amy was fascinated by the many gods. Their names were evocative, strange and thrilling on her tongue:

Shiva, Vishnu, Parvati, Kali, Shakti.

She felt a surge of excitement that seemed centred in her lower belly. With Madeline at her side, might not the unknown India open up for her?

For the first time in many weeks, Amy felt happy and hopeful of the future.

Chapter Two

*A*my took the plate of green banana leaves from the street vendor, her mouth watering at the spicy smells rising from the food.

She had told Madeline her preference and Madeline had ordered for her. On top of a pile of split-pea patties, was a dollop of creamy yoghurt with salt and spices, and topping that a dark, satiny swirl of tamarind chutney.

Following Madeline's example Amy began eating the food with her fingers. The patties melted in her mouth and the spices brought tears to her eyes. She ate every scrap with relish, licking the last of the sweet-and-sour flavours from her fingers. Her mouth burning, the spices singing in her throat, Amy asked for more.

Madeline laughed and teased her for her greed, then happily ordered again. By the time they struck out down the main street Amy couldn't eat another mouthful. With her appetite sated, she concentrated on the sights which seemed to crowd her vision with their vibrance.

Bombay was the most exciting place she had ever seen. It appeared different when viewed this way and not from the draped windows of a *palkee* – a small litter carried on poles, much favoured by the army wives. She felt the real India all around her. It was dangerous and thrilling.

A cooling breeze blew in from the sea dispersing the smells of dust and heat. The reddish dust stained Amy's feet, blowing in around the straps of the sandals which Madeline had lent her, but Amy didn't care. She was bewitched by the colour all around. Her eyes seduced by the yellow, ochre and red from the piles of spices; flashing gold and silver from buttons and hair combs displayed on stalls; and the hot pinks, oranges and crimsons of the womens' saris.

Soon she forgot to be self-conscious and no longer imagined that everyone was staring at her. In the milling crowds she was just another veiled woman.

Madeline led her down shady side streets where fine houses, washed with pink and terracotta, were fronted by mulberry and jackfruit trees. Naked children played ball in the gutters. Skinny dogs bolted down offal and rotting fruit.

They strolled under the porticos of ancient shady temples where people placed gifts of flowers and fruit on shrines. Red sandstone columns and carved wooden screens formed small gardens where people ate food in the open air. In the far distance, forming a brown and sombre backdrop to the chaos of noise and colour, were the undulating Deccan hills.

After they had been walking for some time, Madeline glanced sharply at Amy, as if gauging her reactions.

'Are you ready yet for something special?' she asked.

A dart of excitement went straight to Amy's stomach. There had been a sense of waiting for something since they first emerged out of the door of Madeline's house and onto the main street.

Something was going to happen. She just knew it.

Madeline hadn't brought her here just to look at the sights, fascinating though they might be.

Part of Amy wanted to turn around and flee back to the army cantonments, to the life she knew, but another larger part wanted to experience all the things that Madeline, and India, promised. Things that might turn her world around, change her beyond recognition. Things that would relieve her of the burning ache of frustration, the sweet heaviness of sexual arousal. She had been living a half-life these past weeks. She wanted to awaken, to really – be.

She looked at Madeline and nodded. A pulse beat steadily in her throat. Her voice when she spoke was faint and a little hoarse.

'Lead on Madeline. Show me those hidden things which so terrify the memsahibs.'

Captain Jay Landers looked towards the dais, where candles glowed in brass lamps suspended from fine chains.

The air was thick with the smells of tobacco and incense, and wispy threads of smoke curled towards the stage. Men spoke in hushed voices, some of them caressing partially-clothed women who were sprawled across their laps.

Jay yawned and unbuttoned the collar of his uniform, his handsome face drawn into lines of boredom.

He'd been coming to this place for some weeks, ever since the regiment moved to Bombay. There were always places like this, ready to cater for the tastes of those who could afford it. Sometimes the nautch dancers were good and the live sex shows could be entertaining, but it would take something special to draw him from his inertia today.

He rubbed at the slight trace of stubble on his chin and stretched his long legs under the table. No one would be able to tell from his otherwise immaculate appearance that he had been up all night, pleasuring the bored wife of a certain army colonel.

Jay smiled as he recalled the woman. She hadn't been young for a long time, but she possessed a not-too-faded attractiveness. Besides, she had two desirable attributes in full measure; eagerness and gratefulness. She had bounced up and down on his cock with gusto, sucking and fucking him with equal delight.

He hadn't had to do a thing but lie back and enjoy it. It had been like being submerged in a perfumed mountain of flesh, not a disagreeable sensation. He liked big breasts and the woman had made admirable use of hers, trapping his cock-shaft in her huge cleavage and milking him dry, while her tongue had flicked at his straining glans.

He'd make sure he remembered to send her some flowers with a suitably worded card. You never knew when you'd have need of such stimulation again.

Catching the eye of the serving girl, Jay motioned her over.

'Bring me another bottle,' he said.

It was difficult to get a decent drink in India. So many of the countless different sects and religions prohibited their followers from imbibing alcohol. Lucky he had found this place. They knew how to cater to European tastes and served wine and arrack – a drink distilled from coco sap.

Jay glanced around the room, peering through the haze of smoke. Two women entered by a side door and made straight for the stairs which led to a screened balcony at the back of the room. He was about to look away, assuming that they were dancers, when he looked again.

Something about them was different. The taller one dressed in blue was striking enough to turn any man's head. There was something familiar about her, but he couldn't place her. His interest faded. It was the other woman, wearing green and holding her peach-coloured veil closely about her head, who commanded his attention. This one didn't move like an Indian woman. She seemed ill at ease and kept glancing around to see if anyone was watching her.

Piqued by curiosity, Jay sat up and leaned across the table. If the women had come to this place they must be available. Confident of his charm and good looks, he called out:

'Hey! You. Won't you come over here and join me for a drink?'

The woman in the peach veil froze. She turned towards him and for a moment she lost her grip on her veil. The flimsy silk fell aside and, just for an instant he saw the pale oval of her face. Startled amber eyes burned into him. He found himself caught and held by them.

Jay gave her his most winning smile, charmed by the glimpse of white skin, small straight nose, and those unusal tiger's eyes. He couldn't see her hair for the veil, but he imagined that it would be dark and shining, with a reddish tint.

He felt a stirring in his groin and was amazed he had the stamina to react in that way. The woman swathed in the peach veil was certainly unique. Some of these Indian women were so pale they'd pass for European women.

Then the woman threw him a look of withering contempt. She whirled around and followed her companion up the stairs. Stung by her reaction Jay took a second to recover. He wasn't a man who women ignored. Both women had almost disappeared into the shadows before he managed to call out.

'Hey! Where you going? What's wrong . . .'

He shrugged. It was probably just as well. She hadn't looked like a whore or a dancer come to that, neither had her friend. And it didn't do to get involved with high caste women. There could be trouble from their families and the army frowned on that. Jay was puzzled. Those two weren't the usual clientele. What were they doing in such a place?

He was tempted to follow them, but there'd be a furore if the owner caught him sneaking up to the balcony. That area was forbidden to anyone but honoured guests, or those with a lot more money than he had.

Picking up a glass he sipped at the arrack, letting its fiery strength slip down his throat. Ah, the music was beginning, drums, sitar, and the promising sound of finger cymbals. A woman swathed in sparkling red veils and not wearing much underneath, undulated onto the stage. Silky black hair tumbled down her back and her big, round breasts thrust provocatively upwards from a skimpy halter.

Jay settled back to watch. He'd seen this dancer before and she was good. She had a lush curvaceous body and she offered certain specialities. Just what he needed to get his juices going after the exertions of the previous night.

He felt in his pocket and closed his fingers around the handful of coins there. Yes, he had enough to buy her favours. His cock twitched with gratifying readiness. She would provide good sport for later.

As the dancer swayed in time to the music, lifting one bent leg so that the light shone through the filmy red veil and revealed the rounded limb beneath it, he forgot abc .t the woman in the peach veil.

Amy peered through the carved screen, intent on studying the man who sat at the table nearest the stage.

For one heart-stopping moment she'd thought he recognised her, but she soon saw her mistake. Captain Jay Landers was at least half drunk and his perception was clouded by lust. She'd recognised him at once. Half he officers' wives flirted with him and the other half cut him dead. Jay Landers was a scoundrel but, she had to admit, a very good-looking one.

The fear of being found out went out of her the moment she stepped onto the balcony and she collapsed against Madeline, shaking with helpless mirth. Madeline put her arm around Amy's shoulders and joined in the laughter. It was a moment before they recovered, wiping damp eyes on the backs of their hands.

'Did you see his face when I rebuffed him? Oh it was priceless. He looked so shocked. Arrogant beggar. I suspect that there haven't been too many women who've refused his advances.'

'He is a very handsome man.'

'I suppose he is in a dissolute sort of way. But he's far too aware of his own charm. He has a dreadful reputation.'

'You know this man?'

'Oh yes. I know him. He's a captain in the same regiment as my father. I've met him at various dances and dinners but he's never looked twice at me before. That's what's so amusing about what just happened.'

Amy began laughing again. Madeline smiled.

'And now you've seen how he spends his time, you have the advantage over him. That could be useful to you. But this is most unexpected. How unfortunate that someone who might recognise you is here. We can leave this place if you wish?'

Amy was enjoying herself, the minor episode having added a spice of danger to the adventure.

'Oh, no,' she said. 'Not unless you want to. Didn't you bring me here for a reason?'

'I did indeed. Your new education is about to begin. Watch carefully and observe.

Again Amy felt that mixture of fear and excitement. But there was really nothing to harm her. They could

27

watch in safety. Madeline had explained that she often came to watch the proceedings, masquerading as a dancing girl who was hoping to perfect her craft. They would not be disturbed on the private balcony.

As the music floated up from the room below, Amy watched the dancing girl begin to gyrate. Light flashed from the embroidered red veils. The girl was lushly curved, with bulging breasts, wide hips and a small waist. A jewelled cord decorated the parting in her dark hair and she wore many bangles and a glittering nose-ring. Hooped earrings, hung with many tiny bells decorated her ear lobes. As she spun round, the filmy veils fanned out around her.

The occupants of the room had fallen silent and all the mens' eyes were on the stage. An air of expectancy hung over everyone. Amy felt the atmosphere in the room intensify as the dancing girl pulled off the first veil and let it float to the floor.

The dancer's finger cymbals chimed in time with her movements. Shoulders shaking, she leaned forward her breasts almost wobbling right out of her halter. The slight mound of her belly rose and fell as she tensed and released her muscles. Another veil fluttered to the stage floor, and another. The watchers cheered as each garment was discarded.

When only one large veil was left, the dancer fell to her knees, her hips circling round and round. Grasping the corner of the veil she pulled it free from her waistband and held it aloft. Apart from the breast halter, she wore only a scrap of fabric which covered her pubis. The silk was so thin that the night-dark plume that covered her sex was plainly visible.

The watchers began cheering and urging the dancer on. Smiling she threaded the veil between her legs and moved it back and forth over her thrusting pubis arching her back and moving her hips in a provocative manner.

28

Amy felt the heat rise into her cheeks. She had never seen any woman acting in such an openly erotic way. She was shocked that she found the sight and the audience's reaction very arousing. Her reactions confused her. Was she supposed to feel that way?

Jay Landers stood up unsteadily and approached the stage. At the look on his face, she felt a jolt of sensation between her thighs. Jay's eyes were intense and glazed with desire. His handsome face was flushed and there was a confident smile on his well-formed mouth. His tightly fitting army trousers were stretched over the muscles of his thighs. She could see the engorgement at his groin and suddenly she felt the urge to see him naked.

The dancer smiled and held out the veil, wrapping it round Jay's neck and pulling him close. Jay snatched out of her hands and buried his face in the cloth. The audience clapped and laughed.

Jay and the dancer kissed with wide open mouths, their tongues lashing together. Amy felt herself growing damp between her legs. A tingling heat was spreading outwards from her quim and finding an echo in the throbbing at the base of her belly. The passionate kiss spoke of hunger and wanting. Something within Amy resonated to that same need. It had been a long time since she'd been with a man and her body was squirming with remembered pleasure.

The dancer pushed Jay away, smiling up at him with shining dark eyes, she held out her hand.

Grinning Jay, reached into his uniform pocket and pulled out a handle of coins. Jangling them he held them out for the dancer's inspection. She nodded, took them, and dipped her head to whisper something in Jay's ear.

He's just paid for her favours, Amy thought, quite shocked but not really surprised.

The dancer put the little pile of coins on the floor

beside her and Amy realised that there was more to the transaction. Much more.

Jay regained his seat and poured himself more arrack. The dancer spread her thighs open more widely to balance herself and leaned back a little. Raising her hands she cupped her breasts in their halter – squeezing and rubbing them until the dark nipples thrust erectly against the thin fabric.

Her black hair streamed over her shoulders, brushing the floor behind her. As she moved her hips the thin strip of material between her legs was forced tightly against her pubis. The depression formed by the parting of her sex-lips could clearly be seen.

When the cries of encouragement in the room were frenzied enough, the dancer removed the halter. She caressed her breasts, lifting and offering them, her thumbs rubbing the rigid cones of her nipples. In the candlelight her nipples looked shiny and very red. They have been oiled and rouged Amy thought, excited at the thought of decorating her body with paint in that way. How exciting the girl looked. Her breasts looked so swollen, so sexual with their big red tips.

Amy's own intimate folds were growing ever more swollen and heavy and her nipples itched and burned. The whisper of the silk trousers against her bare legs, the looseness of her chemise against her breasts, were unique sensations. In her new clothes, she felt almost as naked as the dancer. The feeling prompted strange, perverse thoughts.

How shameful, yet how arousing it must be to have so many men watching, their bodies whipped to lustful frenzy by the display of female charms. In Amy's mind it was she who was kneeling on the stage; her legs that were spread open; her fluttering sex which pressed against the damp cloth slung between her legs; her breasts which were exposed, the nipples roused to hard little peaks. The watchers were waiting for her to

30

strip so that they could feast their eyes on the jewel of delight between her legs.

The dancer was obviously enjoying the power she projected. And Amy trembled with empathic delight.

The dancer's hands, slim with long, gold-painted nails swept down over the slight pout of her belly and toyed with the jewelled belt which she wore slung low on her broad hips.

The watchers began chanting. Amy needed no translation.

'Now. Now. Do it now. Take it off.'

Slowly the dancer untied the scrap of fabric which cupped her pubis and drew it free. She flung the filmy scrap into the room and the man who caught it cheered and waved his trophy overhead. Arching her back the dancer pushed her hips forward and opened her thighs as widely as possible.

Amy felt a fresh wash of heat flood her face as the dancer's pouting sex was spread open. The inner folds, fringed by a thick growth of dark hair, were red and moist; as enticing and intricate as a tropical fruit. Amy couldn't look away. She had never seen another woman expose herself in this way. She leaned closer to get a better look. Is this what Magnus had seen when he crouched between her legs and tongued her?

The dancer's vulva gaped almost obscenely. It looked fecund and exciting and Amy suddenly felt the urge to display herself in that way also, to glory in her own sexuality and to have a man look at her with desire. Just as Jay was looking at the dancer.

In the darkness of the balcony, which was pierced by pinpoints of light, she pressed her hand between her legs, trying to ease the burning and throbbing of the firm little pip which was imprisoned between her swollen sex-lips.

Next to Amy, Madeline moved restlessly, and Amy

31

knew that her new friend was also affected by the scene below.

'The woman is famous for this,' she whispered to Amy. 'The men vie with each other for the honour of buying her favours. Her inner muscles are strong. Watch and you will see proof of that.'

The dancer picked up the pile of coins. She smiled, her wide mouth curving in a confident smile. She held one coin aloft, so that it glinted in the candlelight, then, reaching between her legs she brought the coin close to her wide-spread sex.

As she pushed the first coin past the fleshy seal of her body, the watchers began counting. One after the other, the dancer inserted the coins into her vagina. Finally the whole pile of coins were all inside and the watchers cheered.

Rising to her feet the dancer strolled around the stage. She swung her hips and moved her feet in the intricate movements of a classical Indian dance.

'She's good. Very good,' Madeline whispered. 'She must be a classically trained nautch dancer as well as an entertainer.'

And what muscle control, Amy thought with awe. The whole pile of coins remained in place as the dancer spun and whirled. No wonder Jay wanted the woman. What delight he would have in her honed, dancer's body.

After a few more turns around the stage, the dancer squatted, knees apart and ankles together, facing the audience. Holding her arms above her head, she pressed her palms together and closed her eyes. Her head moved in a jerky sideways movement, as if it was unattached to her neck. Her long black eyes slid back and forth. The movements were timeless and hypnotic.

The audience grew quiet. The dancer looked like an Indian goddess, the embodiment of all desire and beauty. Then, into the silence came a sound, a coin fell onto the stage with a chink, plink. Another followed, and another, as the dancer used her internal muscles to bring forth the whole pile of coins.

The cheering was deafening and no one applauded louder than Jay Landers. Walking to the stage he held out his hand and the dancer took it. Quickly she scooped up the coins, then stepped down and stood at his side.

Jay slipped off his uniform jacket and draped it around the naked girl's shoulders, then, curving his arm around her waist possessively, he led her away. She smiled up at him with gleaming brown eyes, looking unexpectedly demure after her performance.

Amy felt oddly moved by Jay's gallant little gesture. A libertine and a scoundrel he might be, but she couldn't deny that he had charm. And he was very arresting to look at.

She found her gaze following him until he left the room, disappearing through a curtained archway. He and the dancer would take pleasure with each other now. Amy envied the dancer and wished that she could be party to the pleasures she would enjoy. How would it feel to have Jay Lander's hands stroking her? Doing those things to her body that Magnus had done. Things which caused waves of sensation to spear her swollen sex?

'Have you seen enough for now? Or do you want more?' Madeline asked, breaking into Amy's thoughts. Her light blue eyes glinted with satisfaction.

Again Amy felt that Madeline knew what she was thinking. It was most disturbing. For a moment Madeline looked wholly Indian. It seemed wrong to call her by her Western name. With the pattern of the pierced screen superimposed on her lovely face, she looked mysterious and like something carved on the pillars of a temple. Amy felt a little in awe of her new friend, but she was wise enough to realise that that was part of Madeline's charm for her.

'I've never seen anything like that. I know I really ought to be shocked and outraged, but instead I'm just . . .' She broke off, searching for the words.

Madeline supplied them.

'Intrigued, fascinated, aroused?'

'Yes. All those things. And more.'

Madeline smiled, showing just the tips of her perfect white teeth. Amy sensed her friend's relief.

'Good. So you do you want to see more?'

'Yes,' Amy whispered, without hesitation, her voice hoarse. She thought she knew what Madeline was going to show her – indeed she hoped she was right. Her pulses quickened.

'Then come with me,' Madeline said. 'There is a way into the back room from this balcony. We can watch your captain with his dancer. And when you next meet him, you will have him at your mercy.' She smiled, her eyes gleaming wickedly. 'That is, if you so wish.'

And as she followed Madeline, Amy thought what a novelty that would be. Captain Jay Landers was going to get a surprise the next time they met.

Chapter Three

The small back room of the club was lit by the light of one hanging brass lamp. The walls were ochre coloured and the floor was bare earth, packed hard and swept clean. The only furniture was a wooden table and chairs. Tapestries covered the far wall.

Madeline motioned to Amy to be silent and showed her the small eyeholes which were cut into the wall. A piece of thin gauze hung over the holes and Amy realised that they were able to watch the occupants of the room without being observed.

Jay Landers and the dancing girl were embracing, their mouths pressed tightly together. One of Jay's hands slid up the girl's sides and cupped a breast. Grasping the erect nipple he rolled it between his finger and thumb. A little mewling sound of pleasure came from the girl's mouth as Jay pinched and twirled the red-brown peak.

She strained against him, lifting one leg so that she could rub her pubis against his muscled thigh. Jay's hands strayed down to the girl's buttocks and began squeezing them, lifting the rich globes and moulding them together.

Amy's breath came fast as she watched. There was something primeval about the scene in the room. Flashes of yellow light illuminated the entwined bodies, glinting off the brass buttons on Jay's uniform and imparting a golden glow to the dancer's dusky skin.

Now Jay's hands moved to the dancing girl's shoulders, exerting a gentle pressure to that the girl sank gracefully to her knees. Madeline and Amy had a clear view of the dancer's profile and her naked body. Slim dark hands found the buttons of his trousers and unfastened them deftly. She parted the dark cloth and Jay's erect cock sprang free. The column of thick, veiny flesh looked pale against his clothes.

Amy bit into her full bottom lip as the girl's hand encircled Jay's stiff shaft, moving back and forth so that the moist glans slid free of the cock-skin. When the dancing girl bent forward and took the swollen bulb of Jay's glans into her mouth, Amy felt a potent spasm of lust.

All the sexually dry days, the craving for a lover's touch and the incomplete pleasures of self-love over the past few weeks seemed to boil up inside her. Her quim was already soft and swollen. The internal pressure of her arousal was mounting, dissolving into a pearly wetness which seeped down and bedewed her silk trousers. She could feel that she was getting wetter and the throbbing point between her flesh-lips was hot and strong.

She had to touch herself. She just had to. The erotic tension inside her was almost unbearable.

Unseen by Madeline in the darkness, Amy slipped one hand under her tunic and into the waistband of her trousers. With the other hand she encircled her breast, squeezing and teasing the swollen teat just as Jay had done to the dancing girl.

Her questing fingers found her quim and slid past the curls of her pubic hair. Shifting position she opened her legs, so that she could penetrate her folds. She was burning hot and swollen and her pleasure bud was strongly erect. Her body's moisture felt silky to the touch. Stroking gently up the sides of her engorged bud, she drew down the pleasure from inside her body.

The sexual heat spread down to Amy's tensed thighs as she watched the couple in the other room. The dancing girl's cheeks bulged as she drew Jay's cock into her mouth, then slid it out again. Jay's head lolled back and his eyes closed as she worked at him. His mouth was open and his breath came fast. His expression looked almost pained. Amy expected him to surge against the dancing girl's mouth at any moment, but instead he pulled away.

She watched as he motioned to the girl to approach the table. The girl nodded, her big red mouth curving into a smile. Amy's fingers continued their pressing circular motion as the girl leaned over and pressed her belly flat to the wooden surface. As the dancer arched her back, the full rounded globes of her buttocks were pushed up and out. The dark red valley between them was partly visible. Jay fell to his knees and began kissing the soft golden flesh. Holding the girl's buttocks apart, he licked and mouthed the moist inner surfaces.

Amy held her breath as the sensations of pleasure grew within her, seeming to concentrate layer upon layer. She imagined how it would feel to have Jay treating her in that way, the roughness of his unshaven cheeks against her sensitive bottom-flesh; the hot stabbing of his tongue, the feeling as he circled her anus with its sensitive, questing tip.

Her quim pulsed as her fingers stroked and massaged, smoothing her creamy wetness over the tiny hood of flesh which contained the hard, throbbing little bead. Her legs trembled and she feared they might give way. She sagged against the wall, resting her upper

37

body against the cool surface, her cheek crushed to the side of the gauze-covered eyeholes.

Oh, she was near. So near.

Jay rose to his feet and she saw that his mouth glistened with the dancer's juices. His cock was standing straight, rearing up potently from the nest of dark curls at his groin. The tip was uncovered and the cock-skin formed a tight collar under the swollen glans. The flaring purple tip looked ready to burst. She saw one drop form and hang there, a clear viscid drop.

Amy felt a strong urge to capture the drop on her tongue. She imagined how Jay would taste. Salty and rich perhaps, or clean and subtle, like rain. Magnus had tasted rich and gamey. The musk-rich smell of his pubic hair had driven her wild.

She'd like to circle the pronounced ridge around Jay's glans, then suck him, as Magnus had taught her to do. She wanted Jay to spurt into her mouth, groaning as he did so, his warm seed flowing down her throat.

At that thought Amy's womb seemed to rise up within her. The pulsings of her climax were strong and deep. She screwed her eyes shut, opened her mouth in a silent rictus of ecstasy and allowed the intensity of the sensations to riot through her.

On the other side of the wall, Jay pushed the head of his cock towards the dancer's buttocks. She pressed back against him, opening her thighs wide and lifting herself so that her distended anus, collared by a ring of tiny black curls, was pushed out lewdly and made available to him.

Amy watched with fascinated horror as Jay stroked the wrinkled little orifice with his thumb, while sliding his organ lower down and into the dark red shadow of the dancer's vagina. With a grunt Jay began thrusting against her rump. His buttocks contracted as he pumped away at her, gripping her around the waist with his free hand to get more deeply into her.

Amy stroked herself gently now, almost lazily and was amazed to feel her passions rising again. After she brought herself to a melting peak, she was usually satisfied, but it seemed that her body was more demanding today. Her fingers were awash with her juices and the lips of her quim felt extraordinarily thick and fleshy. She pinched her clitoris between finger and thumb, welcoming the sharp spice of pain mixed with pleasure and began to work the scrap of erect flesh back and forth.

The dancing girl was giving hoarse guttural cries as Jay pounded into her. He had his thumb buried inside her anus now, his four fingers splayed out across her honey-coloured rump. His hair had flopped forward onto his forehead and the sweat on his face gleamed in the lamp light. When he drew part way out of the girl and began rimming her entrance, Amy saw his wet red shaft.

She wished that it was her he was surging into, her warm dark cavern that he was filling with his rampant flesh. Oh God, she lusted for the illicit pleasure of his thumb inside her tight forbidden orifice, turning and thrusting as he was now doing to the dancer. She imagined the delicious shame of being filled by his thumb, of the awful pleasure of that questing digit as it slipped inside, probing deeply and stroking the satiny inner walls.

Didn't the dancing girl want to bear down? Free herself from that wickedly intimate caress? Amy could almost feel the dancer's fight with herself. The girl threw her head from side to side, her dark hair lashing them both in her passion. Animal moans and grunts came from her. With a series of high pitched little screams she reached orgasm, surging back against Jay's muscled belly, her hands clawing at the rough wood of the table.

Jay screwed up his face as his climax approached.

'Oh God. Yes, yes,' he moaned, his voice hoarse and

strained. 'You beautiful, hot little bitch. Squeeze me. Milk my cock. Oh, yes. That's it.'

Jay's words acted on Amy like a spur to her senses. The tension within her mounted again. Her fingers stroked, probed and tweaked with almost bruising force. Her sore flesh sang as she coaxed it unwillingly towards another shattering climax.

With a sudden movement Jay withdrew both thumb and cock from the dancer and jammed his pulsing shaft upright between the girl's cleft buttocks. His hips pumped as his creamy fluid spurted into the air.

Amy imagined that she could hear the drops as they spattered onto the girl's golden back. Her quim convulsed and she closed her legs, trapping her hand in her hot, wet crevice as another climax washed over her. A moan rose in her throat, but she caged it behind her teeth. It was quiet now in the other room and she daren't risk detection.

After a few moments Amy caught her breath and sneaked a look at Madeline. She could only see her dimly but she could tell that Madeline too was slumped against the wall and Amy knew that she had also stimulated herself to orgasm. She felt a rush of emotion, almost sisterly in its strength. How amazing that they had shared this intimate moment, both so intent on granting themselves relief that they had been unaware of each other's presence.

It was hard to believe that just a few hours ago she and Madeline had been strangers. Amy felt as if she had been through a religious experience. She felt cleansed and liberated. It was as if she had *found* herself in India for the first time. Perhaps it was possible for her to be as free and independent of spirit as she had been in Sussex.

She returned Madeline's smile and reached for her hand. Threading her fingers through Madeline's she squeezed them gently. They needed no words. The erotically charged experience had united them as nothing else could have done.

In the next room, Jay was pulling up and buttoning his trousers and the dancing girl was beginning to stir. Madeline pulled at Amy's hand.

'We should leave now,' she whispered. 'Follow me.'

Amy allowed Madeline to lead her back to the balcony and down the stairs of the club. They hurried along the narrow alley and back into the heat and bustle of the street.

Madeline stopped in the spreading shade of a pepul tree. While the silvery leaves danced overhead in the baked breeze, they brought freshly-pressed fruit juice from a vendor and then sat on the stone steps of a well, where a street artist was painting the colourful image of Shiva onto a square of palm leaf.

The sun was low in the sky and the silhouettes of fairy-tale towers and minarets were a deep red against an orange background. As Amy's eyes met Madeline's over the rims of the clay cups, they exchanged conspiratorial smiles. Suddenly Amy started to laugh, but it was a nervous response. Deep inside she had begun to quake with delayed reaction.

'I can hardly believe this!' she whispered. 'What am I doing here? Dressed like this? For the past two months I've been buried alive and now I've just experienced the most provocative, exciting few hours of my entire life. It's due to you, my friend. I'm truly grateful. But . . . I . . . I just don't know . . .' She finished lamely.

Madeline laid a hand on her thigh. It felt cool and reassuring against her heated skin. Despite the earlier excitement, when she had been as aroused as Amy, Madeline was calm now and once again in control. Knowing that, steadied Amy. She felt the rush of panic begin to subside.

'You're completely overwhelmed, aren't you?' Madeline said gently. 'I understand that. It would not be

41

natural if you were unmoved by what you saw. Do you want to stop now? To go back to being a daughter of the army? You can do so if you wish. I would understand if you made such a decision.'

She paused and gave Amy a searching look, her blue eyes glittering with that mixture of knowledge which was both discomfiting and very appealing.

'When you have had time to think, you will feel different. I suspect that you will want to experience more sensual delights,' Madeline went on. 'And there is much to discover. Many things which are not available to those of Western blood. Do you want them, Amy? I sense that you do.'

While Madeline was speaking Amy had been recovering her composure. She was once again certain of what she wanted.

'Yes. Oh, yes. I do want those things, Madeline. I couldn't go back to being half-alive and sitting through long dreary days with a needle and thread in my hand.'

'I thought that would be the case,' Madeline said, throwing Amy a brilliant smile. 'You *are* like me. I knew it the moment I saw you. We are greedy for life you and I. And we both love to take risks.'

'Perhaps that's true,' Amy said softly. 'I hadn't realised it was so obvious.' She paused for a moment. 'Can I ask you something?'

'Anything.'

'What if I had been horrified or outraged by what we have just seen? I might have fled and never wanted to see you again.'

'I considered that,' Madeline said. 'And decided that I had to take a risk in bringing you here and shocking you. I had to prove to you, and to myself, that we were alike. Oh, Amy such times we shall have. I will make an offering to Shakti and ask the goddess to watch over us. We shall be like sisters. I swear that I shall never let harm come to you.'

42

Amy touched Madeline's shoulder. She already trusted her new friend implicity. At that moment Madeline seemed to embody all the sensuality and mystery of India. She was an enigma, able to live in two worlds and she spoke of things which Amy did not understand but was willing to learn.

'I believe you,' she said. 'I feel as if I have known you all my life. I want you to take me on this journey with you. I only have one thing to worry about now.'

'What is that?'

'How on earth I'm going to think up enough excuses to get out of all the engagements and invitations to tea over the next few weeks!'

Amy sat on a colourful woven rug next to Maud Harris, watching the British officers play polo.

Across the carefully tended playing field she could see the white walls and the shuttered windows of the officer's club, to which later, everyone would repair for tumblers of weak whisky and soda. For the ladies there would be tiny glasses of milk punch and chip potatoes and parched gram to nibble.

She twirled the ivory handle of her parasol, positioning it to shade her face more effectively. The wives and other unmarried women called out encouragement to the players, waving gloved hands in delight when their favourite gained a point.

Amy tried to concentrate. Polo could be quite exciting and some of the officers exhibited great skill on horseback but her mind was full of the prevous day's experience. She couldn't wait to meet Madeline again. The two of them had so much in common. In her Indian clothes she had felt at ease; anonymous amongst the bustling crowds of India's many races and at the same time more herself.

In fact it seemed very odd now to be sitting amongst the women, dressed like them in a gown of pastel-dyed

43

muslin and wearing a broad-brimmed straw hat. She felt oddly imprisoned by her British persona.

The layers of camisole, corset and petticoats under her gown seemed even more uncomfortable than usual. Madeline had given her the tunic, pantaloons and scarf and they were hidden in the bottom of a tin trunk in her room. She thought longingly of the comfort of wearing her Indian clothes but she wasn't brave enough to flaunt them amongst her countrywomen.

She would dearly love to shock them all. Oh, what a sensation that would be. Her lips curved in a secret smile as she pictured the horrified looks and gasps of outrage. She would be condemned as 'unsound' – a favourite term for anyone who didn't fit in – and put into the hands of the older married women for character training.

She shuddered at the prospect, hating all the pettiness and prejudice. But she was wise enough to know that it was impossible to rail against the tide where conformity was expected and being too clever was seen as a flaw in women.

Amy resolved to act demurely and not attract attention to herself. That didn't seem so bad now – now that she had an outlet for the secret, more sensual side of her character. She would only be playing the part of the perfect Englishwoman abroad; something which appealed to the streak of drama in her temperament.

At heart she would continue to be wild and daring and hot for all that life offered. She could be as independent as she had been in Sussex, as long as she played by the rules.

She felt as gleeful as a child with a new toy. The secret was hers alone. No matter how dreary her life was, or how much she must repress her high spirits, she had her other life with Madeline to look forward to.

A raised voice at her elbow made her start guiltily. She was so far gone in her reverie that the polo field, the grunts of the players, and the thudding reverberation of horses' hoofs had quite faded away for a moment.

'Oh, very good, Bravo!' called out Maud Harris, clapping her small hands as two horses thundered past, their riders hanging down low over the sides of their mounts to strike the ball with their long-handled mallets.

Maud turned to Amy, her face wreathed in smiles.

'Isn't this too thrilling?' she said, her small features more animated than Amy had ever seen them. 'Oh, look over there. I do believe that Captain Landers is about to take to the field.'

Amy glanced at the playing field with new interest. Jay Landers was indeed mounting his horse and riding towards the players. She smiled inwardly. It appeared that he could number dried-up little Maud Harris amongst his admirers.

Whatever would Maud say if Amy told her about Jay's exploits with the dancing girl? She would have loved to see Maud's sharp features dissolve into lines of outrage, the already tight mouth grow even more pursed as she told her that she had watched Jay plunge his cock into the dancer's body.

Amy hugged her secret knowledge to herself, feeling a glow of remembered pleasure seep into her limbs.

'Captain Landers is a fine player,' she said evenly, surprised that her voice wasn't shaking with barely-suppressed mirth. She felt the urge to provoke Maud and couldn't resist it.

'He's very handsome too, isn't he?' she said innocently, her eyes opening wide and her face assuming an expression of blandness. 'Do you not think so Mrs Harris?'

'Oh yes,' Maud breathed, forgetting herself for the briefest moment. Almost at once her tone hardened. 'Handsome is as handsome does, my dear young woman. Looks can deceive. I advise you to stay well clear of the captain. Young innocent women like yourself are creatures of impulse and too easily influenced by men like Landers.'

Amy allowed her eyelashes to sweep down demurely.

'I'm sure you're right, Mrs Harris,' she said. 'Thank you for your advice.'

Maud's thin lips curved with self-satisfaction. She patted her neatly coiled hair, pushing imaginary stray strands under the flounced brim of her straw hat. Reaching one gloved hand towards Amy, she tapped her wrist in a proprietorial gesture.

'I think you're settling down quite well after all. A few of us had doubts about you, my dear, I don't mind telling you. It's one thing to be fun-loving, even a little pert and boyish – you're young after all. But one must remember to toe the line. Our main function, as women, is to support our men, help them further their careers. It really doesn't go down, to be too forward in India.'

'Yes, Mrs Harris,' Amy said.

Lord, but the woman was insufferable. Amy would have liked to slap her pompous face. She seemed to think that it was her personal duty to instruct Amy in every way.

Maud, having had her say, settled down to watch the game, her eyes straying constantly to the striking figure of Captain Landers.

His broad shoulders and muscled arms were visible under his cotton shirt and the muscles of his thighs strained against his jodhpurs. He wore his white topi – or pith helmet – at a rakish angle, pushed far back on his head so that a lock of his hair flopped forward onto his forehead.

Amy watched Jay Landers too, her thoughts far more

daring, more informed, and more calculated than Maud Harris could possibly comprehend.

Madeline sat on a low, individual red platform called a *paat*. All around her the celebrations of a wedding were in progress.

The bride was one of her mother's many relatives. Madeline had lost count of the number of people her mother visited or who came to visit their house. The extended families of India meant that scores of people were crowded into the modest dwelling on the edge of town.

Joyful music filled the house and the air was filled with voices praising the beauty of the bride and wishing good fortune on the young couple.

The bride wore a Pathani sari of royal-blue silk, edged with maroon and gold. Golden jewellery decked her hands and feet and a black dot of kohl marked each cheek – to deter evil spirits.

Madeline too wore her best silk clothes in shades of yellow. Her long black hair had been woven with hibiscus flowers and gold rings covered her slim hands. A nosering glittered in one nostril, connected to her dangling earrings by a fine golden chain.

While she smiled and joined in the festivities, her mind wandered free, dwelling on the shared experience of the previous day. What was Amy doing now, she wondered? Certainly she wouldn't be in such stimulating company. Madeline imagined that she would be bursting to talk about what she had seen, but she was forced to keep her secret to herself.

All the better for their new friendship; it would thrive on their shared confidences. Madeline could hardly wait until she saw Amy again. Her flame-haired companion was like a newly-opened bud; a little more warmth and she would blossom fully.

They were to meet in the garden of Amy's house, in

the afternoon, when the memsahibs took their rest. The wedding celebrations were to go on late into the night but Madeline would make an excuse and leave within a few hours.

With an effort she dragged her attention back to the present. Her mother looked happy and at peace. Catching Madeline's eyes, she smiled. Madeline felt a rush of warmth towards her. It was her mother's influence that had shaped her into a strong, independent woman. It had not been easy for her mother to exist with a foot in two worlds, but her grace and intelligence charmed everyone who came into contact with her.

One of the relatives engaged her mother in conversation and Madeline looked away. She was hungry having fasted before the wedding feast. She studied her portion of food.

The floor in front of each diner had been decorated with curlicues made with red, green and white powders. Large metal plates of food were set down in the centre of each pattern. Incense smoke rose into the air spiralling upwards along with the sound of happy chanting.

Madeline dipped a *papadum* into a dish of coconut chutney and transferred it to her mouth. Chewing slowly she savoured the spicy relish. Small bowls held a variety of food, some savoury like the *dhal* cooked with cumin seeds and lime juice, and lima beans flavoured with a black spice mixture. Other dishes were sweet, made of semolina and boiled milk. Her favourite were the *jalebis* – luscious syrup-filled fritters.

Madeline's full mouth curved in a smile as she recalled Amy's delight in eating spicy snacks from the street vendor. Her new friend was a delightful mixture of childlike innocence and simmering sensuality. She wanted to show her so much, to open up her eyes to the glory all around her.

And she knew what the next adventure was to be

48

One of the *chuprassis* – or messengers, attached to the cantonment had let slip the information that Captain Jay Landers was giving a private party in his quarters. The *chuprassi* had rolled his eyes, signifying that it was to be a special kind of party and Madeline knew what that meant.

Madeline had seen the way Amy looked at Landers. It was plain that she desired him, but in the cloisterlike atmosphere of the army quarters she was not likely to meet him alone. The private party would be a good opportunity for them to get acquainted.

Madeline wished to please her new friend and if Amy wanted Landers, then Madeline was happy to help her get him. She was confident that Amy would come to no harm. She would be there to see to that. If the party became too rowdy, the officers the worse for drink, they would slip away into the night.

The experienced and dissolute Jay Landers couldn't help but be captivated by Amy's air of innocence. But Madeline suspected that Jay Landers would find Amy a very different prospect from the women he usually associated with.

Her tilted blue eyes glittered with laughter. Amy certainly had the advantage over Landers. Madeline wondered how her friend would put her knowledge to use.

Chapter Four

*I*n the near distance, light poured from the open windows of the bungalows which made up the officers' quarters. The sound of voices raised in laughter floated on the still night air.

Amy leaned out of the little horse-drawn carriage as they approached the officers' quarters. It was after ten o'clock and the air was cool and redolent with the smell of jasmine and lilies. She felt nervous and excited. The fact that she was flouting convention by coming to a bachelor's house unescorted added the thrill of danger to the escapade.

She only hoped that they wouldn't run into any of the army wives as they returned from calling on friends. The late evening was the time when most people made social calls. Reaching out her gloved hand she squeezed Madeline's fingers. Madeline returned the pressure, giving Amy one of her devastating smiles.

'Almost there now,' she said. 'You haven't changed your mind?'

'Oh, no. I'm looking forward to seeing Jay Landers on his home ground.'

Amy smoothed the lace ruffles around the neck of

her dove-grey, tarlatan evening gown. The rounded tops of her breasts were just visible above the wide scoop of the neck which was so low that it also left a good deal of her shoulders bare. Her neat waist was accentuated by the shaped bodice and the full skirt, worn over a wide-hooped petticoat.

She had dressed with care, choosing the daring gown which she had worn only once before. Madeline looked beautiful in a Western style evening gown of dark-blue taffeta. Her gleaming black hair was looped over her ears and then swept into a chignon on the nape of her neck. Only her honey-coloured skin and small straight nose, betrayed her Indian blood.

Madeline ordered the driver to pull up behind the bungalows and to wait in the shadows of a grove of tamarind trees for their return. Alighting with care they shook out the folds of their gowns. Before they set off Madeline gave the driver some money.

'I'll pay you the rest when we return,' she said, ensuring his reliability.

The driver nodded and settled down happily to sleep until he was needed again.

Linking arms the two women walked through the thick vegetation until they came to the swept gravel path which led to Jay Landers' bungalow. The noise of laughter was louder now, interspersed with the chink of glasses and raised female voices. As Amy stepped onto the verandah she could see into the brightly-lit room.

Groups of people sat at card tables, others sat in pairs on low sofas or were dancing to the sound of a trio of musicians. Amongst the colourful silks and satins of Western evening gowns there were a few saris. Obviously the distinctions of race and class were loosely adhered to on these occasions.

The officers all wore dress uniform; belt buckles and buttons gleaming in the golden lamp light.

Amy hadn't expected to see so many people or to see them engaged in such ordinary activities. Somehow she had imagined that Jay Landers would be lounging on a silk-draped divan with a half-naked woman on either side of him.

She smiled at her own naïvety. This wasn't a bordello after all and Jay Landers might be a rogue, but he appeared to be a cultured one. She caught sight of him across the room. He was studying a hand of cards. His fair hair was slicked back from his broad forehead and he had a slim cigar clamped between his white teeth.

Amy hung back a little, unwilling to stroll boldly into the room full of people who all looked as if they knew each other. Perhaps it had been a mistake to come. They hadn't been invited. What if Jay turned them away? She turned to Madeline to voice her fears but Madeline had seen the look on her face.

'Courage my friend. We're not turning back now,' Madeline said softly. 'This might look like a genteel soirée, but the night's young. The real entertainment won't start for a while yet. Come along. No one's even going to notice us.'

Madeline slipped her arm around Amy's waist, propelling her forward towards the open doors.

A *chuprassi* in a spotless white jacket and turban came out to meet them and escorted them into the bungalow. It was as Madeline had said. One or two heads turned in their direction and a stocky officer with greying hair lifted his glass appreciatively, then turned his attention back to the card game.

To Amy's disappointment, Jay Landers didn't even look up. Madeline moved across the room to where a table, draped with a white cloth, held a huge crystal punch bowl. An Indian servant ladled punch into glasses and handed them to Amy and Madeline.

In no time at all the two young women were surrounded by officers asking them to dance or inviting

52

them to play cards. Jay Landers might not have noticed them, Amy thought, but every other man in the room had.

Madeline was so beautiful that she was bound to attract attention, but Amy had never been so spoilt for male company. A judicious use of the cosmetics which Madeline had given her helped her confidence. She knew that she looked striking with her hair swept into a coronet of red-gold plaits and her emerald ear-bobs swinging against her neck.

She looked around the room. This was all very different to the stiffness of the formal dances she was used to. The easy atmosphere spoke volumes about Jay Landers's reputation as a relaxed host.

For a while, she drank punch and engaged in animated conversation. She studied the occupants of the room, noticing that most of the women were strangers to her. Some of them were beautiful and she saw that a few of them were of mixed birth. One or two of the officers knew her and spoke a few, polite words before melting back into the crowd of guests.

She smiled at the look on their faces. Each without exception had looked shocked and embarrassed to find her there.

'Why Miss Spencer. This is indeed a surprise . . .' Seemed to be the stock comment. After which the speaker tailed off and made his excuses.

Amy was enjoying her notoriety. She didn't think she need worry about anyone betraying her presence to her family. Every person in the bungalow knew that this was a very private party and no one would want to admit to having been present.

During the evening she saw Jay Landers moving amongst his guests. She did not approach him or attract his attention, having decided to pick her moment before she made herself known to him.

Before long Amy became aware that the atmosphere

was changing perceptibly. She couldn't have said when she first noticed it but she saw that many of the card players had quit their tables. Some of the guests had disappeared, perhaps to some side room or had gone out of the open doors to sit with female companions on cane sofas in the garden. She noticed too that there were fewer women in the room. Squeals and screams of laughter seemed to be coming from the far end of a corridor which led off the main room.

Madeline was nowhere in sight. Knowing that her friend was more than capable of looking out for herself, Amy decided to investigate the bungalow further. The sounds of screams and laughter was growing more frenzied with each passing moment and Amy felt a flutter of anticipation along with her curiosity.

She walked across the room, making for the door which led into the other rooms, her dove-grey tarlatan skirts whispering across the polished floorboards.

There were only a few couples dancing now. The oil lamps had been turned down so that the room was suffused with a soft rosy-gold hue. Amy sensed the tension in the slow-moving couples. There was an air of expectation in the breathy giggles, the tossing ringlets, and the graceful movements of the women.

Amy saw male arms steal around waists and heads bend to place kisses on bare, creamy-skinned shoulders. Her eyes widened slightly as she saw a tall, slim officer with brown air and a pleasant face, slide his hands up the bodice of his partner's dress and stroke the exposed tops of her breasts.

Amy expected the woman to put up a token resistance at least, but she only laughed and flung back her head, thrusting the firm globes towards the officers face. With a groan he squeezed one breast, causing it to bulge almost free of her gown and bent his head to suckle the big brown nipple.

The mood of mounting eroticism acted like a heated

wine on Amy's already heightened senses. She had never seen her peers acting in such an uninhibited fashion. She was fascinated and eager to see more.

Moving swiftly into the corridor, she made her way towards the back of the house. A door to a small side room hung open and Amy glanced in as she passed. She caught a confused image of a draped dais, topped by a huge bed. Pale, naked figures were writhing on a dark coverlet. It was difficult to see in the gloom but she could make out at least four people.

Amy checked her step, not quite able to believe her eyes. The people on the bed continued their activities, only the occasional cry or moan floating towards Army. One of the figures sat up and she heard a husky laugh. Her pulses quickened as she realised that she must be silhouetted in the doorway.

'Come in. Come and join us,' a male voice called. 'There's room for one more, m'dear.'

Amy beat a hasty retreat, putting a hand over her mouth to muffle her giggles. In fact she was a little shocked at her composure. She ought to have been appalled but she only felt amused and titillated. She realised also that she was a little drunk. The punch must have been stronger than she thought.

The alcoholic glow was pleasant and gave her the courage to continue down the corridor to the double-doors of the room at the end. Stretching out her hand, she pushed the door open a crack and peered inside.

A crowd of people were standing around a large table, laughing and shouting encouragement. Amy couldn't see what was happening for the crush of bodies. Silently she slipped into the room and melted into the shadows. Apart from two silver candelabra, which blazed with light, the room was dark.

A number of people moved away from the table and Amy had her first clear view. What she saw excited and shocked her. Two women were sprawled on the table.

They were stripped to chemise and corsets and were spread out, their skirts raised and the loose necks of their chemises pulled down to expose their breasts. Their clothes looked wet and clung to their rich curves; whatever liquid they were soaked with had turned the thin cotton transparent.

Both of the women were laughing and kicking up their legs, their rounded thighs and pubic hair exposed for all to see. One of the women was past her first youth and her huge, pear-shaped breasts lolled one to either side of her ribcage. The other was younger and well fleshed. Her hips and thighs were stout and her breasts were large and round. She had a big fleshy bottom, which she waggled enticingly at no one in particular.

As Amy watched, one of the crowd of men around the table poured a bottle of wine over the exposed breasts of the larger of the two women. Another man poured a second bottle over her lower belly, trickling it between her spread thighs while she wriggled and spread her legs for him.

'Ooooh. Me too,' the second woman crooned, arching her back and thrusting her uncovered pubis into the air.

Her quim was covered with a thatch of wiry brown hair. Amy could see the red thick-lipped sex, moist and streaming from an earlier application of wine. As the woman spread her legs lewdly, Amy was shocked to see the dark funnel of her vagina.

She's totally shameless, Amy thought. Somehow it seemed different to the display by the dancing girl, although she couldn't have said why.

One of the men obliged with a stream of red wine, pouring it directly onto the woman's spread sex and laughing as it splashed inside her.

'Lovely. I'm all sticky again,' the woman said, squeezing her big breasts together with her hands so that the wine could be directed down her cleavage. 'Who's going to clean me up then?'

With a great cheer, the watchers bent forward and began lapping up the wine. Eager, questing mouths sought out the sweetly-sticky nipples and fingers probed between the sturdy thighs, scooping up mouthfuls of the musk-tainted wine. The other woman received similar treatment. Then, suddenly, as if a signal had been given, two men dropped their trousers and climbed onto the tables.

The cheers doubled in volume as the larger woman lifted her knees into her chest and thrust her spread sex towards the nearest man. With a shout of triumph he buried his cock inside her and began to thrust for all he was worth. The older woman turned onto her belly, presenting everyone with a view of huge dimpled buttocks and a man mounted her from behind.

Amy watched for a while, then drew away from the table. She found such an open display of debauchery hard to take. It was one thing to watch the sexual act in all its intimacy – she had been very aroused by watching Jay with the dancer – but there was a hearty, almost sideshow quality to the tableau being enacted on the table. She found the sound of slapping flesh, the squelch of wine-wet mouths as they mashed together and the grunts and theatrical squeals all vastly amusing.

Distanced from it as she was by humour, she did not find the sight of the overblown women and their drunken paramours at all erotic.

It was very hot in the closed room and she moved towards the window, meaning to take a breath of air. Only then did she become aware of the man standing in the shadows and watching her closely.

It was Jay Landers. She saw the flash of his teeth as he smiled.

'You don't look too impressed,' he said.

'I'm not,' she said evenly. 'It's really rather . . . silly, don't you think?'

He threw back his head and laughed. 'I do indeed!

How refreshing to have someone say so. Everything palls given time, the pleasures of the flesh included. Were you going into the garden? I'll come with you. I need a breath of air.'

Jay opened the French doors and Amy preceded him onto the verandah. She had never been so close to him before and was surprised by how tall he was. He had taken off his dress jacket and wore only a collarless white shirt. It was open at the neck and she saw the light brown curls of his chest hair and the faint outline of his developed pectoral muscles.

'So. How do you come to be here in my quarters, Miss Spencer?' he said. 'You're the last person I'd expect to come visiting. Shouldn't I have received your card and returned it with one of my own, inviting you, and your chaperone, to tea?'

Amy laughed. 'Yes. If I had wanted a proper introduction, but I didn't. I thought it would be far more interesting to meet you here, like this.'

'You wanted to meet me, alone? Your independence astounds me, Miss Spencer . . . What is your first name? I think we can dispense with formalities, don't you?'

Amy felt a little dart of disappointment. He wasn't even aware of her first name. It was just as she thought. Up until now he had been completely oblivious of her. She might not have existed for all he cared. Well that was all about to change.

'You may call me Amy,' she said, sparkling up at him.

'Well, Amy. How is it that I never noticed you before? I cannot believe that I have passed you by.'

'Perhaps you didn't look hard enough,' she said pertly. 'Or perhaps you were too busy playing the field and throwing over all your other young women. You have the most dreadful reputation Captain Landers.'

His eyes glittered with interest and humour. 'Call me

Jay, please. You're an astonishing young woman. I've never met anyone who is quite so plain speaking. And yet I sense that you're not a shrew. You are fascinating Amy, as well as beautiful. What a fool I've been to waste my time on brainless ninnies. Come, let's walk a while. There's an arbour just off the main path. We can sit in the moonlight. I have a feeling that we're going to get on famously.'

The arbour he spoke of was a few mintues walk away from the bungalow.

The jointed branches of a casuarina tree swayed in the warm breeze, the limbs resembling gigantic horse-tails. Bougainvillaea both white and red clambered over neem and pepul trees, forming a sweetly-scented shelter away from prying eyes. A cast-iron seat was placed under the trees. Amy sat down next to Jay.

He slipped his arm along the back of the seat and Amy was acutely aware of the warmth of him through the thin fabric of her grey gown.

'I'm sorry there aren't any cushions but the white ants eat everything out here,' he said smiling. There was an attractive off-centre tilt to his mouth when he smiled.

'It doesn't matter,' Amy said.

It seemed natural to lie back in the crook of his arm and she did so. She felt his lips questing through her hair and pressing against her temple and that seemed natural too. Her stomach cramped with longing. She could smell Jay's clean male body smell. Overlaying that was the sandalwood scent of his hair oil.

'The lack of cushions might matter, if we wanted to lie down and make ourselves comfortable,' Jay said, lifting her chin and looking directly into her eyes.

Amy returned his gaze unflinchingly. She knew what she wanted him to do and it was obvious that he was more than willing. In the moonlight his eyes looked very dark, almost black. She knew them to be a deep brown, like chocolate, an unusual combination with his suntanned skin and fair hair.

She lifted her mouth to him, a little groan rising in her throat as his lips came down hard on hers. His fingers stroked her throat as his tongue pushed strongly into her mouth, tasting and exploring.

She returned his kiss with passion, turning into his embrace and clutching at his shirt. Her fingers roved over his strong muscled back and moved down to brush against his narrow waist. His tongue was hot and demanding against her own. He pulled away and she felt his mouth trace a burning path down her throat and across the white skin of her chest.

Her heart was thudding and her breath came in shallow gasps. With each breath the tops of her breasts rose up and out of the low neckline of her dress. Her nipples were erect already and she felt the lace of her chemise chafe them into more prominent peaks.

She bit back a little cry when Jay brought his hands up, took a hold on the deep neckline of the dress, then with one sure movement jerked the dress down, freeing her shoulders and breasts, but jamming the froth of fabric around her elbows, trapping her arms against her sides. The warm night air caressed her bare skin and whispered against her straining nipples.

'Oh, nooo . . .' She breathed, curling inwardly with shame, her voice hardly a whisper. 'Don't . . . look at me like this, please.'

She dipped her chin, her sandy lashes veiling the expression in her eyes. Part of her was appalled to be sitting there with her bodice pulled down and her breasts thrust up high by the top of her corset, but another deeper, darker part of her exulted in the wanton picture she presented.

'God but you've got lovely breasts,' Jay said thickly.

'You've no need to feel ashamed of them. They're so inviting I can't resist them.'

He slipped off the seat and fell to his knees in front of her. Leaning forward he linked his arms around her slender waist and began suckling her nipples, taking each into his mouth in turn. Amy bit her lip as the tender, pulling sensations rioted through her.

She felt a heavy, deep throbbing begin between her thighs as Jay bit gently at her stiff jutting peaks. Now and then he sucked hard and the pleasure-pain was almost unbearable. Was it possible to reach a climax from this caress alone? The sexual tension coiled in her stomach, leading Amy to think that it might be.

While Jay pleasured one nipple with lips and teeth, he took the other between finger and thumb, pinching and rolling until Amy couldn't still the breathy little groans that rose in her throat.

Jay laughed huskily.

'What a hot little bud you are. Ripe for the opening, aren't you? Is this why you came here tonight?'

'Yes,' she said, without hesitation, although her cheeks flamed with shame at the way she reacted so wantonly to him. 'I want you to do everything to me. Do whatever you like.'

'I've a feeling that you'll like it too, very much,' Jay grinned. 'How refreshing you are. There's no false modesty about you. I think I'll free your arms. You might want to use your hands.'

She sat still, her eyes downcast, unable to look at the heat of desire in his eyes as he turned her around and unfastened the back of her dress. Just looking at her that way, he had her trembling with lust. Jay was quick and did not fumble with the hooks. Plainly he was used to helping women out of their clothing.

The thought excited her. She liked the fact that he was experienced and appreciated women's bodies. It was also obvious that Jay actually *liked* women. She had learned early in life that that was unusual amongst men of her class. To most of them women were an irksome but necessary inconvenience.

In a few moments she had struggled free from the dress. Her hooped petticoats followed and soon she wore only her corset, chemise, her knee-length grey silk stockings and shoes.

'Leave them,' Jay said as she reached behind her back for the laces of her corset. 'You look wonderful.'

Bunching her gown under them, they lay back on the seat. Jay's hands found her breasts again and continued with their stroking. Amy writhed against him, her legs parting as the sensations from her nipples flowed down and centred in her loins.

Covering her mouth with his, Jay moved one hand down to her knee. He stroked the tender spot at the back of her knee, then smoothed the fabric of her chemise up her thigh, caressing the soft white skin as he did so. When his fingers reached the apex of her thighs, Amy moaned against his mouth. She felt him smile as his questing fingers closed over the slitted fruit of her sex.

Amy opened her legs more widely and raised her hips to allow him access. Jay's fingers stroked up her parted folds, rubbing gently on either side of her pleasure bud. The pressure of his two fingers exerted a sort of pinched caress which forced her strongly erect bud to stand proud between his moving digits.

'You're wet already, sweetheart. Are you ready for me?'

'Yes. Oh yes,' Amy breathed. The longing to have him inside her was squirming in her belly like a living thing.

Jay raised himself up beside her and the firm column of his erect cock pressed into her thigh. For a moment he looked down at her and there was a question in his eyes. Even while he still stroked her quim, causing her to shudder with the pleasure of his touch, she saw his doubt.

'Perhaps I should just frig you until you spend. Then you can do the same to me.'

'No! No . . . I want you inside me. Please. Do it to me Jay.'

Some part of her rational mind was still able to work though her body was a prisoner of the sensations which sapped her reason. She thought she knew why Jay was hesitating at almost the last moment.

'Oh Lord. Don't stop that. It's heavenly,' she stammered. 'I . . . promise you . . . that I'm not some . . . pallid virgin who's dying for you to relieve her of a burden. I . . . won't regret any of this . . .'

His eyebrows rose, while his expert fingers stroked and probed and – oh, God – entered her a little.

'Really?' he said with admirable calmness, given the circumstances. 'That's exactly what I did think. I was wondering how you'd feel in the morning and whether I'd feel like a cad for taking advantage of your innocence.'

Amy moaned and tossed her head. Hardly innocent. If only he knew. How was it possible that she could answer him? All she could think of was the pleasure his fingers were drawing out of her, the fact that her quim was so wet and slippery and fertile and dying to be filled with his hot, hard, man-flesh.

'You surprise me,' she whispered. 'Oh, Lord . . . That's so good. I . . . I thought you'd welcome the chance to add another conquest to . . . your tally. I didn't . . . expect you to have a care for my . . . feelings.'

It was almost too much to concentrate. She'd break soon, she knew it. The pleasure was building, cresting and his damned infernal touch was so knowing. He was pushing a finger inside her and the slight soreness felt wonderful. She felt his knuckle press against the tight closure of her vaginal flesh and knew that he'd partly breached the seal of her virginity.

Jay stared down into her eyes, which were half-closed with passion. His voice was soft, self-mocking.

'In truth, Amy Spencer, I did not expect to care about you at all. I surprise myself. But it seems that you're truly set on your course. Now – where were we . . .'

Amy surged against his hand, half-maddened by his finger that was inside her deeply now, rotating, smoothing around her tight inner walls, opening and readying her. But she was ready, had been since the moment he kissed her. She half raised herself and her amber eyes blazed into his.

'Damn you to hell Jay Landers! Will you shut up and push your cock into my quim before I explode with wanting you!'

He chuckled and his lips brushed teasingly against hers.

'Never let it be said that I disappointed a lady.'

Positioning himself between her thighs, Jay pushed his swollen cock-head into the entrance of her vagina. Although she had been expecting, longing for it, Amy tensed and held her breath. His cock-shaft felt so much bigger than his finger had done and her flesh seemed to have to stretch to encompass him. Surely it wouldn't all go in, her flesh walls couldn't give that much.

Pressing forward slowly Jay slid inside her by degrees, gauging his progress by her reactions. When she felt his pubic hair against the base of her belly, Amy let out her breath.

'You're . . . so big. So wonderful. I feel . . . completely filled by you,' she whispered, emotion bringing tears to her eyes. She twined her arms around his neck. 'Now do it to me, Jay. Complete my education.'

Jay took her at her word and began moving slowly in and out. As she relaxed and began to match him, thrust for thrust, he went into her with more force.

Amy surged against him, lost in the primeval rhythm of the mating dance. She reached a climax twice, loving the feeling of being possessed, torn into. It was violent, something of the body alone. Jay was dominating her senses and she wanted it that way.

When Jay withdrew and spilt himself against her belly, she made a little sound of protest in her throat, feeling bereft without him inside her. She wanted to do it again, as quickly as possible. Jay's heart beat fast. She could feel it against her chest, as strong as a drum. She wrapped her arms around him and held him close.

They remained still for a long while. She stroked his face, while he pressed his cheek to the soft mound of her breasts. After a while they made love again and then again, a third time. Amy lost all track of time. I've become a glutton for pleasure, she told herself, and I don't care.

It was only when she noticed that the shadows were shrinking in the arbour and the sky was turning paler, that she realised how late it was. She sat bolt upright, rousing Jay who had fallen into a doze

'I have to get back,' she said, kissing his cheek and rubbing the slight shadow of stubble along his strong jaw line with the back of her hand. 'And I must find Madeline. Will you help me dress?'

She struggled into the creased gown, exclaiming in dismay at the state it was in. She would just have to hope that no one saw her creeping back into the house.

'When will I see you again?' Jay said.

'I'll send you a message,' she said, kissing him hurriedly. 'We can meet up when I go out riding.'

As she raced back along the gravel path, lifting her hooped skirts high, she saw Madeline standing on the porch of the bungalow, a look of strain on her lovely face.

'There you are! Where have you been? I've been out

of mind with worry. I thought something had happened to you.'

Amy grinned.

'Something did. Something wonderful. I'll tell you all about it.'

'There's no time now,' Madeline said, her tone unusually sharp. 'We have to hurry back and think of a way to save your skin.'

'What do you mean?' Amy stared blankly at her friend.

Madeline sighed with exasperation.

'Don't you realise what time it is? It's six in the morning. The time when the memsahibs take their morning rides before breakfast. We've been out all night, Amy. If I can't think of a way to smuggle you back into your house, you're ruined. And if you're disgraced I'll never forgive myself for leading you here.'

Chapter Five

*A*my sat on the edge of the carriage seat looking out anxiously at the sky which was growing lighter by the second. There was a peachy tinge to the horizon and the shapes of trees and houses were clearly visible.

Madeline had ordered the driver to take them directly to her house. Now she sat in silence, threading and unthreading her fingers in agitation.

'Can't you go a little faster?' she called out to the driver. 'Oh do hurry.'

Amy knew that she was the cause of her friend's concern. She felt guilty for upsetting Madeline, but couldn't help the feeling of elation which bubbled up and brought a smile to her mouth. Jay Landers had been everything she had hoped for.

With an enormous effort she dragged her thoughts back to the present. There was no denying the fact that she had landed herself in a pretty mess. She had better do some quick thinking, otherwise the rosy future she had imagined for Madeline and herself would evaporate like mist before the sun.

'Madeline?' she said in a small voice. 'I'm sorry if I behaved thoughtlessly. I know it's my fault that we're in trouble. You're . . . you're not still furious with me, are you?'

Madeline turned to her and for a moment her lovely face was stern. Then Amy saw that her slanting blue eyes were sparkling with humour. She felt relieved. How awful it would have been if Madeline turned against her.

Madeline reached over and embraced Amy.

'Don't look so worried. Of course I'm not still angry, you silly goose! It was concern that made my tongue sharp, but I'm still annoyed with myself. I ought to have realised that you would lose track of time once you reeled in the dashing captain. Was he worth it?'

'Oh, yes,' Amy breathed. 'He was just wonderful. Not at all like I expected. He was gentle and sort of hesitant, as if he didn't want to offend me. He wasn't going to actually . . . to compromise me fully, if you get my meaning. But I made him do it.'

Madeline laughed with delight. 'Really? It sounds as if you made quite an impression on him. You actually told him what you wanted? Captain Landers is probably used to wilting young ladies who are ignorant of all but the most basic bodily functions. No doubt they swoon under his caresses. What a change you must have been.'

Amy smiled. She hadn't thought of it like that, but she suspected that Madeline was right. Jay *had* been surprised when she was so forthright with him.

'You must tell me all about it sometime,' Madeline went on. 'I want to know everything, in detail.'

'Oh I don't think I could tell you . . . everything. I've never spoken of such things.'

At Amy's look of shocked surprise, Madeline's full mouth curved in a teasing smile.

'We're best friends now, Amy. And friends share everything. Isn't that so?'

After a moment Amy nodded. Secretly she wanted to tell Madeline all the details. There was no one else in whom she could confide, but to tell *everything* and in detail – just the thought of it made her blush.

'What did Captain Landers say when you told him about the club and the dancing girl?' Madeline asked.

Amy smiled. 'I didn't tell him. It didn't seem appropriate to talk about that. Perhaps I'll tell him the next time we meet. I'm to arrange a meeting when I next go out riding.'

Madeline patted her hand. 'I'm glad you're happy, but you must take care. It wouldn't do to lose your heart to such a rogue.'

'Oh I won't,' Amy said at once. 'I know perfectly well that men like Captain Landers aren't the type to settle down. I'm quite set on treating any liaison with him as a dalliance alone. It ought to be perfectly possible to enjoy each other's bodies without complicating things by falling in love.'

Madeline looked searchingly at her, her black brows drawing together in a frown. The way she was studying her disconcerted Amy.

'What is it?' Amy asked. 'What have I said?'

'Oh nothing. Just that I think I've underestimated you. You have it all worked out, don't you? You're set to be a heart-breaker, Amy Spencer. Do you know that?'

Amy rested her head on Madeline's shoulder and tucked her fingers into the crook of her arm. She yawned.

'All I know is that I'm ready to fall straight into my bed. I just want to lie still with my eyes closed and think about what happened tonight.'

Madeline moved her shoulder away gently, urging Amy to sit upright.

'Come on, sleepy head. We have to think up a plan. There'll be no rest for you for some hours yet, so you'd better rouse yourself and try to look wide awake. You won't be able to sneak into your house unseen at this hour. There will be too many people about. The only way we're going to save you from certain disgrace is if you're seen to be making your way *back* to your house, having been out on some legitimate activity.'

Amy saw the sense in Madeline's reasoning. She yawned again and stretched, resigning herself to staying awake. She would be able to rest for a few hours between luncheon and dinner which was taken around seven in the evening.

'You mean,' she said thoughtfully, 'I'm to act as if I'd gone out early and was just coming back? It's a good idea, but I'll have to change. I can't walk boldly up to the front gate wearing this gown.'

'I have it!' Madeline said. 'You've been out riding. I have a spare riding outfit. You can change at my house and borrow my brown gelding.'

'But won't someone notice that my horse is still in the stables?

'You'll have to hope that that's been overlooked. The plan isn't foolproof, but it's the best we've got. Prepare yourself to do some pretty quick thinking if necessary. Ah, here we are. Now, you hurry inside now. I'll pay the driver. There's not a moment to waste.'

Amy sat back firmly in the saddle as Madeline's gelding cantered along the dusty track. The horse was a finely bred intelligent animal. A single white mark on his forehead gave him his name of Blaze.

The riding habit of black velvet with white piping at the collar and cuffs fitted her well over the waist and hips but was too tight across her bust. She was conscious of the way her breasts swelled against the shaped jacket and hoped that she didn't run into Maud Harris or Edith Taverner.

The sun was already high and it beat down on her head. She was glad of the wide-brimmed hat which matched her outfit. As she rode, the warm breeze brushed past her face and rippled the flowing skirt of the habit which she had looped up over the gelding's withers.

Amy urged the horse into a gallop, skirting around the edge of a field of mustard. People from a nearby village were already up and at work. She could see the bright oranges and reds of saris against the yellow-green of the mustard plants. A sweet scent blew towards her from a field of beans in the near distance.

Despite the fact that she was terrified that the plan wouldn't work, she found herself enjoying the sense of freedom which riding always gave her. Most of the women rode before breakfast, riding for miles across country, stopping in the villages where they might be offered a drink of milk or some fruit. It was the one time of day when they were able to explore an India outside the confines of their own milieu.

Amy decided not to hurry back. This was too good an opportunity to be out and about without the gimlet eye of one of the senior wives on her. Besides she needed to work the horse into a sweat before she returned. At the moment he looked as if he'd only just left the stable.

Leaning over she patted the horse's neck.

'You're going to save my skin, Blaze,' she said, smiling when his ears twitched back and forth. 'Good lad, aren't you now?'

By the time she headed back towards the cantonment both she and the horse were sweating and streaked with dust. She had passed other women out riding and exchanged a few words or a wave. If she needed to verify her story she had witnesses. Confident now that she could slip into the stable without attracting undue attention, Amy slowed the horse to a trot and navigated the gate which led into the stable yard.

She left Blaze with a groom, having given instructions that he was to be stabled next to her own mount. As she walked the short distance to her house she saw that

71

her mother and a group of friends were sitting on the front verandah. They were gossiping, sewing, and drinking long glasses of soda and lime.

With a sinking heart Amy saw that Maud Harris was sitting next to her mother.

She had hoped to avoid speaking to anyone before she had entered the house, but there was no chance now of slipping unnoticed into the back entrance. One or two of the women looked up and smiled as she approached. Arranging her features into a smile Amy walked boldly up to the little group.

'Good morning,' she said brightly. 'I enjoyed my ride so much this morning, that I quite lost track of time.'

Her mother smiled. 'I did wonder where you could be. The morning's well advanced and breakfast was an hour ago, but I'm glad you enjoyed your ride.' She turned to Maud Harris and smiled, saying: 'Riding is such good exercise for a young woman, don't you think?'

Maud's small mouth curved. 'Oh yes indeed. But it doesn't do to overexert oneself. I hope Amy won't be too fatigued for the rest of the day. We must all be at our best for the special occasion this afternoon.'

Amy didn't understand Maud's comment for a moment, then she remembered. They were all to attend a garden party at the governor's residence. It was to be a formal occasion. Normally she would have welcomed the break in routine.

She groaned inwardly. The preparations for dressing would begin soon after lunch and there would be no time for her to rest until late evening. Well, she'd just have to make the best of it. After a meal and a bath she'd feel a lot better.

'As it's so late, I'll take breakfast in my room Mama,' she said, bending down to kiss her mother's cheek.

For just a moment she felt guilty for deceiving her. Her mother had accepted her explanation without com ment, never dreaming that Amy might lie to her. But a moment later, Amy dismissed such thoughts. She had to be true to herself and her nature demanded that she follow her own path in life. She was just not the type to sit sewing cross-stitch samplers or making quilted birthday cards.

She was about to go into the house, when something Maud Harris was saying caught her attention.

'I don't suppose we can do anything about it, her father's an officer and he'll be expected to attend the garden party along with his family, but I for one don't intend to speak to the woman. You may do as you wish of course. I'm afraid that I don't approve of friendships with women of that type.'

There was a flutter of laughter and a few comments in the same vein. One of the other women, an elderly woman with a face like a bloodhound said, 'I couldn't agree more. What's the place coming to? Euro-Asians I've heard these creatures called. To my mind they'll always be half-breeds!'

Amy felt her temper rising. They were discussing Madeline and others like her. She glared at Maud who had begun the conversation. What a poisonous little object she was. One day she'd take her to task for her comments, but not today. She didn't want to attract any more attention than was strictly necessary.

Her mother seemed to have noticed her 'new' riding habit for the first time. She was peering short-sightedly at her and was about to comment.

'I must go inside and change,' Amy said hastily. 'I do confess that the dust seems to have lined my throat. I'll get the ayah to make me some tea.'

Maud's voice rose above the others as she continued to give her outspoken opinions. Her brittle laugh grated on Amy. She bit back the retort that rose to her lips.

Clenching her fingers around the folds of her skirt,

she picked up the train of her habit and swept into the house.

Captain Jay Landers, resplendent in full dress uniform, stood with the other officers sipping from a glass of gimlet – gin with Indian tonic.

The governor's residence was an imposing stone building, its towers and turrets resembling a stately home in Scotland. It had a white facade and stone pillars either side of the front door. The formal gardens were immaculate, the flower beds a blaze of colour. On the lawn, a number of *shamianas* or marquees had been erected. A military band played softly in the background.

Jay's eyes swept over the crowd of women, all wearing afternoon dresses and huge hats, looking for one face in particular. It shouldn't be too difficult to pick her out, that flaming red hair was like a beacon. He had never much cared for the colour on a woman – until now.

He couldn't seem to get Amy Spencer out of his mind. That was unusual for him. Once he'd lain with a woman she passed quickly out of his memory. There had been so many. Sometimes they seemed to be all muddled up together, just so many breasts and thighs and quims.

But Amy was different. She had captured his imagination. He had never met anyone like her: a young woman who knew what she wanted and didn't mind asking for it. That was so rare amongst the British women as to be shocking. Jay couldn't forget the way she had ordered him to pleasure her.

He almost laughed aloud. There he was, going slowly, treating her like the untried virgin she appeared to be, and she had told him in no uncertain terms to get on with it! Oh she was priceless. Where had a young

74

lady like her gained such experience? He must be sure to ask her.

He remembered her body too. Such lush breasts, big and firm, surprising in such a slim woman. She had tiny pink nipples, a sweetly curved waist and lovely generous hips. When he slid his cock into her quim, she was hot and wet and smooth as silk. What would her quim taste like, he wondered? Would she be sweet and musky or salty and rich?

He imagined her sex-flesh against his mouth, the pink lips so tender and delicately formed. He'd smooth the little hood of flesh back from her pleasure bud and lick her until she shuddered and came. He wondered if she had red-gold curls around her sex.

Just thinking about it made him hard. It was a good thing that his uniform jacket was long enough to hide the tumescence at his groin.

Amy had said she would send him her card, but he couldn't wait for their next meeting. In fact, he didn't intend to wait. He wanted to know if she had managed to get back into her house without attracting attention. It would be disastrous if she was confined to the house, or worse still sent packing. He felt an actual pain at the thought of not seeing her again.

That was another new sensation; Jay had never given a fig for anyone else's feelings but his own. The fact that he cared about what happened to Amy Spencer was a little alarming but he was amused by the change in himself. Perhaps it was time he settled down and thought of marriage. Unable to believe that he had actually allowed the word 'marriage' into his thoughts he drained his glass. You must be getting soft, he told himself, as he helped himself to another drink from the tray being carried by a turbanned servant.

But he still kept looking for Amy. His eyes roved over the faces, shaded by wide hat brims decorated with

75

flowers and ribbons. She had to be here somewhere. No one stayed away from one of the governor's parties.

Walking over to one of the long tables, draped with a spotless white cloth and holding plates of sandwiches, curry puffs, scones, and little iced cakes, he helped himself to some food. One or two women smiled at him, the invitation in their eyes quite brazen. Normally he would have flirted with them but he had no heart for that today. They were all so . . . easy.

Nodding and smiling at the prettiest women, he moved across the lawn, ignoring their looks of disappointment.

He saw Amy standing on the terrace, deep in conversation with Madeline. His pulses quickened immediately. Amy looked lovely in a white muslin gown and a large picture hat trimmed with white feathers. She saw him at the exact same moment he saw her. Jay was gratified to see the hectic colour rush into her cheeks.

Executing a small formal bow he said, 'I hope I find you well, Miss Spencer.'

Amy smiled, her full lips parting to show pearly little teeth.

'I am very well thank you, Captain Landers,' she said.

Anyone listening would assume them just to be following the expected code of politeness, but Jay deduced from Amy's answer that she had managed to keep her escapade a secret.

'I'm glad to hear it. You look very fetching today, if may say so.'

Amy smiled. 'You may say so Captain Landers. Any woman is pleased to accept compliments from dashing young officers.'

Jay turned to Madeline.

'Would you permit me to monopolise your companion for a while? I thought we might take a turn around the gardens.'

Madeline nodded, threw Amy a friendly warning glance which said plainly – be careful this time – and turned away in a flurry of pale rose muslin skirts.

Jay smiled down at Amy. Her pale skin looked almost translucent in the shade of her hat and her amber eyes were sparkling and mischievous. He hadn't remembered her mouth quite accurately. She had lips like a rosebud, full and soft.

As they moved out of earshot of the others, Amy said softly,

'A turn around the garden? Is that really what you want?'

Jay leaned as close as he dared. Reaching out one finger he caressed the gloved back of her hand. Her perfume and the slight warmth of her skin through the white kid glove was intoxicating.

'You know damned well what I really want, you forward minx! But I don't see how I can get that here.'

She smiled and he noticed that she had a tiny dimple in one cheek. Lord but she was adorable. He knew then that he was besotted with her and he didn't care.

'I've been thinking about last night too,' she said. 'And I can't wait to have your hands on me again. I know how we can be alone. But only for a little while. Come this way.'

Amazed by her daring, Jay allowed her to lead him from the terrace. No other woman of his acquaintance would have taken such a risk. Her recklessness delighted him.

The lawn, terrace, and all the rose-covered walkways round the house were thronged with people, all of them awaiting the arrival of several dignitaries. Women in pastel-coloured gowns spilled out of the open doors of the house itself or sat around on cane furniture, flirting with handsome officers.

Amy walked slowly across the lawn, making towards shrubbery, and he kept pace with her. They made

77

light conversation about the weather and the results o the latest polo match, but he knew that she was a aware of him as he was of her.

Was her adorable little quim getting wet with excite ment? He was bursting to kiss her, to tip back her hea and grind his lips down onto her soft mouth.

His eyes kept flickering hungrily from her mouth t her breasts and he saw, with immense satisfaction, tha she was breathing hard. Her wonderful full breast were rising and falling, as if she had just run a race He imagined how they looked under her gown, th prominent pink nipples pressing against the softness c her chemise.

'You have a very bold gaze, captain,' she sai teasingly.

'Are you offended by it?'

'Not in the least. I'm flattered that you find m attractive.'

'I find you bewitching, tantalising and a lot mor besides,' he said. He had said as much to wome before, but this time he meant every word. 'As soon a we're alone I intend to take you. You're not safe wit me. Do you realise that?'

'Yes,' she said and her voice was hoarse and a littl breathless. 'I don't want to be safe. I want you to d what you did last night and I want a lot more besides. want everything.'

Jay steeled himself to be patient as they picked the way slowly through the crowds until they stood at th neatly trimmed edge of the lawn. A few steps awa there was a high, clipped box hedge – a testament the efforts of the governor's Indian gardeners.

Amy stood with her back to the hedge and Jay stoc beside her. When she spoke her voice was caln although there were two slashes of colour across h pale cheekbones.

'The governor and Lord Gilbert, preceded by an aid

de-camp, will arrive at any moment,' she said. 'They'll create a diversion and when everyone is taken up by the ceremonies we'll get our chance to slip behind the hedge.'

Jay grinned in open admiration.

'Well I do declare, Miss Spencer, you're quite the schemer. You amaze me. Have you always been so decisive, so set on getting what you want?'

'Always,' she said simply. 'I take after my father.'

Before he had a chance to answer her, the band struck up *God Save the Queen* and the men bared their heads. Everyone turned in the direction of the house, where the governor and his retinue stood in the doorway.

Jay looked around. All eyes were on the governor and Lord Gilbert, who walked slowly onto the terrace, leaning heavily on a silver-topped walking stick, as they began to descend the curving stone steps. The officers formed themselves into an avenue through which the governor and Lord Gilbert passed on their way down to the largest *shamiana*.

Jay grabbed Amy's hand and pulled her quickly behind the hedge. She gave a muffled sound, halfway between a protest and a giggle.

Without preamble he encircled her waist with his arms, tipped her back and kissed her soundly. She tasted sweet and fresh and he pushed his tongue right into her mouth as if he could possess her in that way alone. He pushed his throbbing erection against her thigh, knowing that she'd feel it through the layers of thin petticoats.

Amy made a little sound of eagerness and longing in her throat which drove him wild with lust. With trembling hands he began to unfasten the buttons on her bodice, but she covered his hands with hers.

'No, not here. There's no time for that,' she whispered. 'Unbutton your trousers and take out your cock. I want to suck you.'

79

He was too shocked and aroused to argue. God what a woman. No one had ever said such a thing to him. Amy used words like a carter and looked like an angel.

She was already sinking to her knees in a flurry of white muslin. Her hands, clothed in the long white kid gloves, reached for him. She caressed the bulge of his cock through his trousers. The pressure was maddening, making his cock twitch and buck against his underwear.

His fingers shook with eagerness as he fumbled with his buttons. Amy smiled and brushed his hands away.

'Let me do that,' she murmured.

Jay realised that she was much calmer than he was. She seemed to be in control of the situation and the novelty of giving himself into her hands inflamed him anew.

Deftly she opened his fly and reached inside. Her gloved hands were warm and exciting. He was so hard that it hurt. She took out his organ and held it around the shaft. It was incredible to think that this beautiful young woman was kneeling before him, stroking and admiring his stiff member. He watched her slim white fingers moving back and forth along his length and the pleasure cramped in his loins.

Amy's wide-brimmed hat cast a deep shadow over her face. He wanted to see her expression, to read the lust in her eyes. For he knew that he had found a woman who enjoyed the pleasures of the body as much as he did.

'Look at me,' he whispered thickly.

Amy tipped up her chin. Holding his gaze, and widening her incredible golden eyes, she put out her tongue and dabbed playfully at his cock-tip.

Jay swore under his breath, longing for the feel of her hot mouth enclosing him. There wasn't time for this teasing, but he sensed that Amy wouldn't be hurried. She, like him, was enjoying the risk of being discovered.

The tip of her tongue moved lightly across the slitted mouth of his penis, gathering up the clear juice which seeped from him.

Jay tensed his thighs as the ticklish pleasure spread down his shaft. Now her fingers had moved down to encircle the base of his cock. He saw the dark-blond curls of his pubic hair pushing through her gloved fingers. Then she bent her head and her hat hid her face from his view.

'Ah god . . .' he gasped, as he felt her use her pursed lips to push back the skin around the head and then encircle the big moist glans with her tongue.

The pressure of her lips as they scraped over the ridge of his phallus was delicious. He reached forward and cupped her face with both hands, holding her gently, almost reverently as she sucked him. Curling her tongue she licked around the bulbous glans, making tiny sounds of pleasure, and he knew that she was savouring the taste of him.

Knowing that she enjoyed sucking him and wasn't doing it to please him alone added a new dimension to his pleasure. His balls twitched and tightened. God, he was going to spend in her mouth. He tried to hold back, wanting the feelings to last, afraid that she might be revolted if he spurted into her throat.

But Amy gripped his lean hips and worked her mouth down onto his shaft, urging him to give up his jism. Her throat was so relaxed that he was able to plunge into the hot wet depths of it. Dimly he wondered where she'd learned to pleasure a man this way, but he was fast approaching the time when rational thought ended and there was only sensation.

Mindlessly he stroked her soft cheeks, feeling how they bulged as she sucked him, slid down onto him, drew him in. Then he bit his lip and came. His buttocks clenched and he emptied himself into her mouth with great, sweet, tearing jerks.

'God. My God . . .' he grunted, through clenched teeth, his eyes screwed shut.

For long moments he seemed locked into a private world where his soul was laid bare and there was nothing but the concentration of pulsing heat at his groin. He'd never experienced a climax like it.

Amy rose to her feet. And, while he sagged weak-kneed against the sturdy bulk of the hedge, she deftly put his clothes to rights. Then she put her arms around his waist and kissed him, thrusting her tongue deep into his mouth. He tasted the musky saltiness of himself on her lips.

Christ, but he wanted more of her. He wanted to pleasure her like she had done him, but there wasn't time. Already she was edging away, pulling at his hands. He was reluctant to let her go.

'Jay. Come on. We have to get back before we're missed.'

Oh she was cool, he thought. She looked fresh as a daisy, not a hair out of place. No one would ever know that she had just fellated him and loved every moment of it.

'Wait! Just for a second more. When will I see you again?'

'I don't know. I can't think about that now. Come on. We must go.'

'No! I'm staying here until you tell me when and where you'll meet me.' He grabbed her wrists, holding her pressed up against his chest.

'Jay please! Let me go!' Her amber eyes flashed with excitement. 'Oh, very well. The day after tomorrow then. I'll go riding extra early in the morning – at five o'clock. You know the place across the paddy fields? There's a patch of bamboo jungle. I'll meet you there.'

'I'll be there,' he said, bringing her gloved hands to his mouth and kissing them.

Feeling elated, now that he knew when they'd meet

again, Jay brushed himself down and hazarded a look through the branches at the corner of the hedge. Incredibly the governor and Lord Gilbert had only just reached the *shamiana*. All eyes were still turned away from the place where he and Amy were hiding.

Had it all really only taken a few minutes? It seemed incredible. His climax alone seemed to have gone on and on. Already the sensations were becoming a memory. He wanted to recapture those few moments of ecstasy as soon as possible.

He turned back to Amy and brushed his lips against hers.

'It's safe to go back out. You go first. I'll follow in a moment. If anyone is looking this way it'll seem less suspicious.'

Amy nodded. Just before she stepped out from behind the hedge she turned and blew him a kiss. He almost laughed aloud. How like her to tempt fate right up to its limit.

He felt that he had been waiting for a woman like Amy Spencer to enter his life for a very long time. This was only their second meeting, but he already had her measure. She was reckless, a risk-taker – just like he was.

And she was an enigma; behind the sweet face and girlish body, there was a full-blooded woman. He knew that he wanted everything that Amy had to offer. He knew also that, this time, *he* would have to do all the running.

Amy certainly took after her father – there was something almost masculine in her temperament, in the way she went after the things she wanted. Coupled with her feminine charms the mixture was potent, absolutely devastating. Jay knew that he was unable to resist such a woman. He knew also that everything had changed for him. For the first time in his life he was truly hungry.

No matter that other women were more than willing to slake that hunger, his appetite was for one alone.

Chapter Six

Amy and Madeline stood with the other women watching the military parade. A brass band struck up a jaunty note and Amy's heart swelled with pride as she watched the men march past.

The massed ranks were a sight to see. There were the shining brass helmets and leather breeches of the artillery officers, the black horsehair plumes of the dragoon guards, and the scarlet coats and white collars of the native infantry – the sepoys. The sound of marching feet, horses' hooves, and jingling harnesses added its own beat to the strident sound of the band.

Amy held a handkerchief to cover her nose and mouth as plumes of dust rose from the parade ground. It was early morning and already so hot that many of the watching women were fanning themselves. Amy wore only light petticoats under her gown, but she felt as if she was burning up. She longed to get inside, out of the hot sun and lay down in her shady room, but first she wanted to see Jay Landers ride past.

Her mouth curved in a smile as she wondered whether he'd be able to resist acknowledging her presence. Army rule was strict and the men would be

84

ordered to 'eyes right' as they approached the women, but no other sign of respect would be given. Somehow she suspected that Jay Landers would tip his cap to her if he felt like it. There were always those who could bend the rules with charm and verve.

The band changed its tune and orders rang out. Amy saw that the soldiers were being paraded to form the three sides of a square and her pulses quickened.

Something was about to happen.

A small procession appeared from the guard room. The provost marshall rode in front, followed by two files of soldiers – one of them led by Jay Landers. Amy realised why she hadn't seen him before now. He had official duties to perform. Behind the soldiers walked two prisoners, followed in turn by a number of privates and a corporal in charge.

'What's happening?' Madeline whispered to Amy.

Amy shook her head. 'I don't know. But it looks serious. I think the prisoners must be from Jay's regiment.'

The procession made a circuit of the square and stopped on the open side. Two privates moved forward and placed two shaped wooden blocks in position.

'Oh no! There's to be a flogging,' Amy gasped. 'I don't think I can watch. It's too brutal.'

She turned around and spoke briefly to her mother, making the excuse that she felt unwell.

Her mother patted her arm. 'I understand dear,' she said mildly. 'It's probably a touch of the sun. Find a spot of shade to sit in. This will all be over before too long.'

Amy began to make her way through the crowd. Edith Taverner put out her arm to halt Amy's progress, her long, melancholy face set into lines of disapproval.

'So faint-hearted Miss Spencer?' she said. 'You surely appreciate that discipline must be maintained. Flogging is merciful compared to a court martial.'

Amy pulled her arm free, her eyes blazing angrily.

'That may be so Mrs Taverner. But I do not have to be a witness to it!'

She had the satisfaction of seeing Edith's face blanch and was glad that she had been so short with her.

As she passed Maud Harris, Amy saw that the older woman was watching avidly as the coats were stripped from the prisoner's backs and they were forced to kneel. The look on her face, the almost feverish brightness of her eyes, made Amy feel sick. Maud's pointed tongue darted out to moisten her pinched mouth as her gaze roved over the prisoners' broad shoulders and muscular, bent backs.

As the first blow fell, and the prisoner gave a cry of pain, Maud gave a tiny sigh. Amy realised that proper, repressed little Maud was going to enjoy watching the flogging. In fact she seemed to be getting a distinct sexual thrill out of it.

Many of the other women were also watching as if spellbound, the same look of intensity on their faces. Lord, but she wouldn't have been surprised if they hadn't started to cheer – except that that would be considered very bad form.

Amy bit back a cry of disgust and continued to make her way back to her bungalow. She knew that Madeline was following her and felt glad that her friend was not given to such ghoulish pleasures. Those dreadful women, so pious and proper on the surface, were nothing short of monsters.

She knew that she would be condemned by them all if her own sexual escapades were to become common knowledge but, in her opinion, what she had done with Jay Landers – and what she intended to continue doing – seemed clean and wholesome by comparison with Maud Harris's blighted passions.

She decided that she had made the right decision

when she planned to forge her own path to enlighten-
ment – sexual and otherwise.

'Amy, wait!' Madeline called out, breathelessly.
'Where are you going?'

Amy slowed down so that her friend came abreast of
her.

'I . . . I was going back to my house to bathe and
change. I couldn't stay and watch that.'

'But you'll be in terrible trouble. Protocol demands
that you stay until the most senior army wife leaves.'

'Oh drat protocol!' Amy said. 'It's time that such
ridiculous antiquated customs died out.'

Madeline grinned and then began to laugh; she
slipped her arm around Amy's waist.

'I couldn't agree more. I wish that everyone was as
brave as you. You're like a breath of fresh air. Just what
we need to bring some life into this place. Since you've
time to spare, won't you come to my house? We'll have
breakfast there and then we'll spend the day together.
I've wanted to have a long talk with you, but there
hasn't been the time.'

Amy smiled, her spirits lifted by the thought of a
whole day spent with Madeline. She would have to do
some juggling to cover her tracks but thought she could
manage that.

'That sounds wonderful. I'll just call in at my bungalow and leave a note for mother to tell her that I'm
feeling better and have gone visiting. She won't remember whether I've received a visiting-chit from you or
not. Her memory's not what it was, poor dear. I'll need
to bring along an ayah for appearances sake.'

'Very well. I'll think of a way of persuading your ayah
to keep out of our way. You're sure she won't expect to
dog your footsteps all day?'

'Oh no. Tara's happy to do as she's told. As long as
she has something special to eat, she'll be content.'

'That's settled then. I'll go on ahead and get everything ready.'

Madeline bustled around giving orders to her household staff. She wanted special dishes prepared and everything made comfortable for when Amy arrived.

Her liking for her friend was increasing daily and now, added to that, was respect. Amy's integrity amazed her. She was so bold and outspoken on some counts, while retaining her freshness and that endearing gloss of innocence.

It was no wonder that she had captured the attention of Captain Landers.

Madeline had noted the way he'd looked at Amy at the governor's garden party. They had disappeared into the crowd and Madeline hadn't seen them again for some time. She had a suspicion that something had happened between the two of them and was itching to ask Amy about it.

The intimate tête-à-tête she had planned was long overdue. It was time that she told Amy about some of her own secrets, and now seemed a good time.

After taking a cool bath, she dressed in loose red silk trousers and a flowing green tunic. Drawing back her thick dark hair, she wove it into a single plait and tied it with a red ribbon. Heavy earrings of jade with gold tassels hung at her ears.

In her own room, which looked out onto a small courtyard garden, Madeline filled a hookah pipe with fragrant tobacco. Small dishes laid out on silver trays held a variety of finger food. There were cubes of spiced fish, rubbed with a coconut paste; kebabs on wooden sticks; and a variety of grilled vegetables and tasty dips. In a huge jug, packed all around with ice, was freshly squeezed mango juice, laced with cinnamon and lime.

Settling down onto a pile of silken cushions, Madeline drew deeply on the mouthpiece of the hookah. The tobacco smoke, cool and fragrant, filled her lungs and imparted a pleasant lightness to her mind.

Soon Amy would arrive. Madeline looked forward to entertaining her friend and sharing intimacies with her. She had never told anyone about the man who had taken her virginity. Even the memory of it brought a flush to her olive cheeks.

She had been so naïve, so trusting. Only later did she realise that she owed the man a debt for, despite his sternness and the coldness of his nature, he had awoken her to her own sensuality.

The shaded coolness of Madeline's house was exquisite after the heat and dust of the streets. Amy stepped into the hallway and then ducked under the archway which led to Madeline's room.

She and Tara had chosen to travel the small distance on horseback, Amy having taken the chance to return Blaze to Madeline. Riding even a short distance in the heat was exhausting and she was glad to sponge her face and wrists with rose-scented water before settling down beside Madeline.

Tara was settled happily in the kitchen, chatting to the other maids and eating heartily of the sweet carrot halva which Madeline had specially prepared. Amy felt peace steal over her as she sipped a glass of cold mango juice, relishing the sharp-sweet flavour of lime on her tongue.

Madeline's lovely blue eyes were heavy lidded and she realised that her friend was lightly intoxicated by the tobacco she was inhaling. Blue-grey tendrils of smoke wreathed upwards, mixing with the other smoke from perfumed incense sticks which smouldered in a shallow, punched-brass holder.

For a while they spoke of inconsequential things, like the fact that the hot season was fast approaching and then it would be unbearable to set foot out of doors until late at night or the small hours. Or that the shop of a Parsee, named Muncherjee, had just received consignments of finery from London and Paris.

Amy nibbled on the delicious morsels of food and accepted the mouthpiece of the hookah when Madeline proffered it. At first she coughed as the smoke reached her lungs, but she found she liked the taste of the cool tobacco and the swimming sensation in her head.

She grew even more relaxed, although she was aware that the atmosphere in the small room was charged with tension. Madeline's eyes glowed like fiery coals and there was a rose flush to her olive cheeks.

'We are the best of friends now, are we not?' Madeline said softly.

'I feel as close to you as a sister.' Amy replied, surprised by how difficult it was to speak. Her tongue felt too big for her mouth. She wanted to giggle, but Madeline was very serious and she sensed that she had something important to say.

'And friends share things, don't they?' Madeline said.

'Oh yes,' Amy said. 'I'd share everything I have with you.'

'I know this. But it isn't what I ask. Will you allow me to share my memories with you?' Madeline asked, her eyes intense and fathomless. 'You might find pleasure in the retelling and I . . . I would gain freedom from guilt and distaste.'

'But what have you to feel guilty about?' Amy began, then stopped, moved by the look on Madeline's face.

Madeline's fine eyes glinted with tears and her full red mouth trembled.

'Listen if you will. And decide for yourself.'

She lay back against the cushions, her dark plait like a shining, twisted rope against the embroidered silks. In the smoky gloom of the room her skin glowed softly like ivory.

Amy too, snuggled down into the cushions, lulled by

the hookah's spell and by the softly accented tones of Madeline's voice as she began to speak. Pictures formed in her mind and she saw the young Madeline, seventeen years old, slender and beautiful, her school books clasped in her hand as she made her way towards the missionary school . . .

'My feet had dragged that morning, long ago. Try as I might I could not force myself to hurry.

'There had been a break in the rains and every leaf glinted with a diamond of dew. There were so many shades of green; too many to number. The freshness of the morning called out to me and cast a spell over my unawakened senses which made me late for the second time that week.

'It was only as I reached the school and attempted to slip into the crowded classroom, that I experienced the first pangs of dismay.

'"Have you an explanation?" Father George Starr asked me, loudly.

'I dipped my chin and blushed hotly as every eye in the room was focused on me. I stammered out an apology, mortified to have been singled out by Father Starr.

'His handsome face was pale with anger and his thick, dark hair was awry where he'd pushed it back from his forehead in agitation. Just looking at the missionary made me feel hot and weak-kneed. I didn't understand why he had this effect on me. He was cold and remote, with never a friendly or encouraging word for anyone.

'But he was devastatingly good-looking, with broad shoulders and a slightly stooped gait. Most of the girls in the class were sweet on him. A fact of which he seemed totally unaware.

'"Speak up, girl, I can't hear you," Father Starr said, causing me to jump in terror. "That's the second time this week. You had better stay on after the others have gone. I'll deal with you later."

"Yes Father," I said meekly and took my seat.

'The threat of being kept behind after school played on my mind and I couldn't concentrate on my lessons. For some reason my mind was full of lurid thoughts, all of which were centred on Father Starr, and there was a hot, throbbing sensation between my thighs.

'I must be bad, I thought. I shouldn't have these wicked thoughts. Father Starr is a good, God-fearing man. If he knew what I was thinking he'd be terribly shocked.

'The day passed quickly and soon it was time for the other young people to leave for home. I sat behind my desk, waiting for the last of them to file out of the room. One or two of them cast me pitying glances, but others smiled gloatingly. My good looks had made me as many enemies as friends.

'"You'd better come through to my office," Father Starr said.

'I stood up and followed him. The small back room held a table and chairs and bookcases. Father Starr seated himself on a chair, sitting with his back very straight. There was a strange look on his face, an expression which I had never seen before.

'I felt a flutter of alarm in my belly, but also a sort of excitement which seemed centred in that secret place between my thighs.

'"Come here, Madeline," Father Starr said gently.

'His square face was high-coloured and there were beads of sweat on his top lip. His fine, dark eyes were glittering with some inner emotion.

'I was afraid. I shook my head.

'His eyes hardened, but he said softly. "There's nothing to fear. You know that you must be punished. So let's have the matter done with, shall we? No – come here."

'I moved forward slowly, my knees were trembling so much that I could hardly walk. In my heart I knew that something was going to happen. I could have run to the door and darted for home. My mother and father would not tolerate me being punished and would take my side against Father Starr. But something inside me wanted him to punish me. I wanted to feel his cool, strong hands on me. I knew what to expect. He often used the cane. Once across each palm. It wouldn't be so bad. I stopped in front of him and held out my hands, palms up.

'Father Starr smiled and I saw that his well-shaped mouth was moist, as if he'd licked his lips.

'"Oh no," he said. "I think a stronger lesson is called for. I've noticed that you have become very lax lately. You're too spirited, too wild. I shall have to attend to that."

'He patted his knees and reached out to grasp my wrist.

'"Come on now. Let's have you across my knee."

'I could hardly believe it. He actually meant to spank me! But through the haze of shock, I found myself moving forward, standing to one side of him and bending forward obediently.

'"That's it," he said, his voice breathless and a little hoarse. "Stretch right across me. Hands and feet on the floor and head down."

'I did as he asked, my cheeks burning with shame. I felt the roughness of his dark cloth trousers under my bare midriff and was aware of something hard pressing into me, something which twitched and jerked against my belly. I could smell his body. He smelt of fresh exertion and lemon soap.

'Stretched out as I was my small, tight buttocks were tipped up and presented to him with dreadful prominence. I felt his hand rest lightly on my bottom, stroking

93

and massaging it for a moment. It felt nice. Soft ticklish sensations spread out from under his palm.

'A little moan escaped from my lips. I couldn't help it and prayed that he hadn't heard. Then the palm of his hand came down hard. The stinging pain brought tears to my eyes. It hurt far more than I had expected. I writhed and bucked as he spanked me, his free arm locked behind my knees to hold me still.

'I began sobbing as his punishing palm crashed onto my buttocks, time after time. I had no time to catch my breath between slaps. As the pain of one slap rose into a crescendo, another new slap connected. I pushed against the floor with my fists, trying to get up but his grip was implacable.

'I hated him then. He seemed to be enjoying humiliating me. And the worse thing was that, in an odd kind of way, I was enjoying it.

'Then he stopped abruptly and I realised that he was trembling. I could feel his knees shaking under me and the thing that was pressing into my belly was hot and hard.

'Father Starr's palm returned to my flaming buttocks, but now his touch was gentle. He stroked me, using circular movements, which tormented but at the same time seemed to ease the bruised and tender flesh. I stirred against him, aching for his light touch.

'"I may . . . have been . . . a little harsh," he croaked. "I'd best inspect the . . . damage."

'And before I could protest, he took hold of the waistband of my baggy trousers and drew them down to my thighs. The thin fabric was bunched just under the place where the swell of one's buttocks joined the thighs. I cried out, mortified at being so exposed.

'Father Starr's cool, strong hands played over my bare skin and although I resisted, I couldn't help the little tendrils of sweet sensation which came in the wake of his touch. The pressure and heat between my thighs, which I had been aware of all day, grew stronger and now there was a new sensation of wetness there.

'I squirmed in an agony of shamed arousal as Father Starr soothed and stroked my hot buttocks. The pain and soreness was fading and only a stinging heat remained. Then I felt another, even more shocking sensation. Father Starr's hand was sliding down into the cleft of my buttocks, probing and opening as it moved deeper into the parting between my legs.

'"No! Oh no!" I cried out, biting my lip as the shameful pleasure grew, layer upon layer.

'His fingers had found the warm, wet place between my thighs. The secret place which had known no man's touch and he was stroking so gently, urging me to part my legs and I found myself obeying him.

'My belly cramped with terrible pleasure as his cold, strong fingers parted my fleshy folds and pushed inside me. I felt a slight sharp pain and then my flesh enclosed him. I wriggled and moaned as he thrust his fingers into me, moving them back and forth, his thumb stroking at a place where my hard little nub seemed to have become a second heart, so sweetly did it throb.

'Shaking my head from side to side, and pressing my palms against the baked earth floor, I worked my hips against Father Starr's knuckles. I no longer fought the pleasure, but instead welcomed it, embracing him deeply into my body and melting at his touch.

'He was breathing hard and making little sounds of encouragement.

'"That's it, my dear. Take your punishment. Surrender to me," he said.

'And I did, my secret place spasming against the tips of his invading fingers. Slowly he withdrew his hand and released me. For a moment I lay still, stunned by the sudden absence of his touch. There was more to experience though, I sensed it, and a great yearning rose up within me. I turned my face up to him and mouthed a single world.

' "Please . . ."

'Father Starr's fine dark eyes closed briefly. He seemed to be at war with himself, then the tight line of his mouth relaxed. He dragged his fingers through his thick dark hair and gave a single nod.

' "Up on the table with you," he said, his voice hardly more than a croak.

'Keeping my chin down, my face burning with heat, I rolled off his lap and stood up. My trousers were still lodged around my upper thighs, and I took hold of them and began to pull them up to cover myself.

'Father Starr lifted his hand.

"No. Take them off, right off now," he ordered.

'Slowly, I did so, watching with satisfaction the look that came over his face. I was wearing only sandals and my top, which covered my breasts. From the waist down I was naked and I must admit that I felt a sense of power as I saw his gaze flickering to the plume of dark hair between my thighs.

'Walking slowly towards the table, I lifted myself up and sat on the edge, my legs swaying gently.

' "You young Jezebel!" Father Starr whispered as he stood up and approached me. I then saw that the front of his dark trousers had a prominent bulge.

'His fingers moved down to his buttoned fly. In a moment he had reached into the opening and pulled out his organ. My eyes widened, but I only had a glimpse at the thick reddish stem as he moved swiftly towards me. Putting his hand to the centre of my chest he pushed me down until I fell onto my back.

'He stood between my legs, slid a palm under each one, and lifted me bodily towards him. My back scraped across the wood as he pulled my hips up towards his manhood. The warm, blunt head of his cock pressed against my parted sex. I felt it begin to enter me and I let out a little moan of fright and eagerness.

'Father Starr's eyes bulged as he looked down at me. A lock of his dark hair flopped onto his forehead and a drop of sweat fell onto my lips. Snaking out my tongue I lapped at it, savouring the strong flavour of salt.

'"Oh you Jezebel. Daughter of Evil," he whispered, over and over. "I am tempted and I cannot resist."

'His lips moved and I realised that he was praying silently for release from sin.

'I wanted to laugh, but the feeling of his hard male flesh sliding into me was so strange, so delicious that I threw my head back and let the feelings spread through me.

'Father Starr's cock pushed all the way into me, filling me, stretching me and sending ripples of glorious sensation to my very core. The feeling that had been building earlier came back, more strongly than before.

'I cried out as he moved inside me, gently at first and then more strongly, plunging in and out in a deep, strong rhythm. I raised my buttocks and pushed up to meet him, thrust for thrust. Without being told to, I would my legs around his waist and held him close, urging him to surge into me, deeper, harder.

'My first ever climax took me by surprise. My eyes opened wide in shock as the internal ripples spread and spread.

'My flesh convulsed around the rigid shaft and then Father Starr gave a great shout and drew out of me.

'Spurts of creamy fluid shot onto my belly. It lay like milk on my olive skin. But I was breathing hard and reached for him, so grateful for what he'd shown me, and I was certain that he'd take me into his arms. But he turned away without even looking at me. His mouth was twisted by something verging on disgust. Furtively he pushed his cock into his trousers and buttoned them up.

'"You'd best get home now," he said. "Go straight home, mind. And tell no one about your punishment. If you do, you'll go straight to hell. D'you hear me now!"

'I saw that his hands were trembling and he was close to tears. So I got down from the table, wiped myself on my handkerchief and pulled my trousers on.

'Suddenly, I was angry with him. He had enjoyed it too. What right did he have to make me feel small and dirty? I wanted to hurt him and I said the first thing that came into my mind.

'"I won't tell anyone," I said coolly. "But only if you'll do it to me again. I liked it. All of it. And I don't care if I do go to hell for saying so."

'His eyes widened in horror. "You wicked girl! Get away from me. Temptress! Harlot! Whore of Babylon! Oh I've been weak and foolish. God forgive me," he wailed.

'He wrung his hands and I saw that his eyes were indeed bright with tears.

'Suddenly he didn't look so glamorous to me after all. He wasn't even all that good-looking with that pathetic expression on his face. I felt a mild contempt for him and was sad that my illusions about him were shattered, but I wasn't sorry that we'd done that thing. I *had* liked it and I intended to do it again as soon as possible.

'At the door I looked back. He was sitting slumped with his head in his hands.

'"I'm going to be such a bad, bad pupil that you'll have to punish me often," I said softly. "And if you don't, I'll tell on you. My father would take his dress sword and cut you into little pieces if he knew what you'd done to me."

'He groaned theatrically and I laughed. I was still laughing when I reached my house.

'So you see,' Madeline said to Amy. 'I used the poor man. I made him spank me and then do it to me, time after time. He lived in fear that I'd tell someone and his nerves were in shreds.'

Amy chuckled. 'Good for you! The hypocrite. He started it and then couldn't face up to the fact that he was responsible for his own lust.'

'Do you really think so? I've regretted tormenting Father Starr all these years. It was as if a dam burst inside me when he spanked me that first time. I'd discovered a pleasure I never knew existed and I couldn't get enough of it.'

'I know how that feels. The man who showed *me* what pleasure was, was called Magnus. He was an estate manager on a nearby farm. I used to ride to meet him whenever I could. We spent hours in the barn or lying in the ripening corn, kissing each other, stroking and caressing. Magnus had a magic touch. He really knew how to pleasure a woman and he never once . . . pushed his cock into me.'

The last part of the sentence came out all in a rush. After listening to Madeline's disclosures, and the earthy terms she used to describe everything, it seemed natural to use similar terms. She smiled at Madeline, glad that her friend had trusted her with such a confidence. The air around them seemed to vibrate with intimacy.

'And Captain Landers?' Madeline said. 'Does he have a magic touch too?'

'I've only the one occasion to judge him on, but there'll be others. He compares very well up to now.'

'But what about the other day at the governors's garden party? I know you two were planning something.'

'Oh that,' Amy said, reaching for the hookah pipe once again. 'We hid behind the tall box hedge and I . . . took him into my mouth and sucked him until he spent in my throat.'

Madeline gave a scandalised giggle. Her blue eyes were round and gleaming in the soft light.

'You did that? When there was such a risk of being discovered? Oh, Amy Spencer, you are the limit! The very limit!'

Amy smiled happily.

'Do you think so? I'm just finding out how to be myself. And I'm loving the way I feel. Oh there's more to come, Madeline, I just know it. We'll have such adventures. And we must continue to share everything with each other. It makes it all twice as much fun!'

Chapter Seven

The bamboo jungle was a shifting curtain of green, as luminous as jade in the shadows and as bright as citrine where the sun shone through the tall stems.

Amy dismounted and led her horse in amongst the greenery. Paths wove through the plumed fronds which reached above head height. Now and then the jungle thinned out and there were clearings where stunted trees surrounded patches of soft grass.

She tied the reins loosely to a tree, so that her horse could crop the sweet grass. She was preparing to sit down and wait for Jay, when, without warning, two strong arms encircled her.

Amy cried out, her breath leaving her in a gasp of alarm. Whoever had hold of her did not realise his own strength. The pressure against her corseted waist and ribcage caused her heart to beat fast and a wave of faintness swept over her.

She staggered backwards and almost fell. The man holding her loosened his grip, supporting her weight easily against his body. She realised that he didn't mean to harm her and stopped struggling.

'Did I startle you?' Jay said, his lips close to her ear.

'Forgive me, darling. I couldn't contain my delight at seeing you.'

Amy relaxed against him, aware of his warmth and the solid muscles of his torso against her spine. She caught the scent of him, spicy cologne, tobacco and clean skin.

'Oh you,' she said, laughing with relief. 'You did give me a fright.' Turning into his embrace, she hit him lightly on the chest with one gloved hand. 'You have no business going around assaulting decent young women!'

Jay smiled and bent his head and his mouth covered hers, his lips insistent, demanding. She responded eagerly to his kisses. The taste and texture of his mouth made her tremble with desire, the tactile warmth of it prompting her to recall another of his body's tastes.

His cock had tasted warm and rich and salty – delicious. But this time she didn't want to fellate him. It was a shock to admit it so readily, but she wanted him inside her, his hard manhood pounding into her red wet heat.

Jay pressed her close, the buttons of his uniform digging into her through her dress. She felt the cold metal brushing the swell of her breasts where they bulged free of her corset. She was also aware of his strong muscled thighs moving against her muslin skirt and the ready tumescence at his groin which pressed into the softness of her belly.

It seemed as if every inch of him was being imprinted on her flesh, sensitising her skin and leaching a response from her. The barrier of their clothes between them seemed to be no hindrance. Amy's skin burned and tingled, aching for the feel of his hands on her bare flesh.

A moment later Jay broke away and looked down into her face.

'The thing I love about you is your eagerness. There's

no pretence at false modesty or the irritating game-playing which most women indulge in. You enjoy being pleasured and you're not ashamed to let me see that.'

'Should I be ashamed that my body responds to yours Jay Landers?' Amy said boldly. 'I see no reason to pretend. Is that so unusual?'

'Christ yes. It's unusual in gentlewomen like yourself. Most of them aren't aware of what's beneath their own skirts! And if they are, they don't know what it's for.'

Amy gave a peal of laughter. 'Tragic, isn't it? But it's their own fault. Pleasure is there to reach for.'

'Do you know that I'm mad for you?' Jay said hoarsely. 'Mad to have you, to possess you, to watch your expression as you reach your peak. I've thought of nothing but you since the garden party. You're on my mind when I wake and you're the last thing I see before I sleep.'

He grinned, his handsome mouth lifting in the crooked smile which she found so attractive. When he spoke again there was a hint of self-mockery in his voice.

'I've even had to resort to using the five-fingered widow to ease myself. And now look at me. I'm like some village lad who's hankering after the milkmaid! I've been here since five o'clock because I wanted to be certain that you weren't followed. What are you doing to me Amy Spencer? You're quite destroying my reputation as a rake. I fear that I'm becoming a changed man and it's all your fault.'

Amy smiled up at him, warmed by his concern for her welfare. The way he made a joke of everything charmed her. He seemed embarrassed to find himself acting honourably. In truth she hadn't expected Jay to be so thoughtful. His devil-may-care reputation had led her to expect him to be selfish and manipulative.

Could it really be that he was so affected by her? She had not endeavoured to capture his heart. Oh dear, how awkward it would be if he was to become too attached to her.

She looked directly at him, squinting slightly against the white glare of sunlight. His face was lean and tanned. Faint white lines radiated out from his eyes.

For his part, Jay was transfixed by Amy's ethereal beauty. Her skin was so white that he could see the tiny bluish veins beneath its surface. And, in the harsh morning light, her eyes looked a brilliant light gold.

He bent towards her slowly, his parted lips just brushing her pale forehead where a curl of her bright red hair had pushed free of her white-veiled pith helmet. That hair colour against her paleness was startling. Although he wasn't given to romantic fancies, he thought of marigold petals floating on milk. Reaching up he took off her hat, and laid it aside.

Gently he ran his fingers through her pinned-up curls, twining a gleaming coil around one finger. The backs of his fingers brushed against her cheek. Her skin felt smooth and cool.

Amy held her breath, as absorbed by Jay's slow sensuous movements as a cobra swaying to the pipe of the snake charmer in the street bazaar. The tension between them was palpable, but Jay seemed unwilling to give in to the passion which was evident in every line of his soldier's body; evident also in the slight trembling of his fingers and in the cadence of his breathing.

There was a moment of calm, of complete silence, when Jay just looked at her. The lambency in his deep brown eyes made her breath catch in her throat. The strength of emotion in his expression frightened her a little. Couldn't they just enjoy each other without getting all emotional about it?

To lighten the moment she said softly, 'We're alone now, for the first time. Are you going to spend the next two hours just looking at me?'

'Why not?' Jay said. 'I can't think of anything more delightful. I've lain awake at night imagining how you would look under all those layers of clothes.'

Amy gave him a pert glance from under her lashes.

'And now, I suppose, you expect to find out if the pictures you conjured up were accurate? Do you want to see me naked? Spread out before you like a feast?'

The thought of it excited her. No man, not even Magnus, had seen her completely unclothed. She remembered Magnus's fascination with her red-gold pubic hair. No doubt Jay was wondering about the colour of her maiden hair too.

'I know what you want to know. And the hair on my quim *does* match the hair on my head,' she said grinning. 'But I expect that you want to discover that for yourself.'

Jay cursed softly and ran his fingers through his swept-back fair hair.

'Forward minx! Do you never employ subtlety of speech?'

'Never if I can help it. I hide behind the necessary hypocrisy of my class, but I've never felt as if I had to pretend with you.'

'Just be yourself, your absolutely captivating self,' Jay said earnestly. 'and I'll never ask for anything more of you. Let's waste no more of these precious minutes. Will you permit me to act as your maid and help you disrobe?'

Amy turned around and presented her narrow shoulders and slim back to him. Jay's hands were deft in the unfastening of her white, ribbed-cotton riding outfit, which consisted of a separate boned bodice and skirt.

Under the bodice she wore only a fine white silk chemise and a light summer corset. Jay loosened her skirt and Amy stepped free of it. Her petticoats joined the other garments on the ground. Then she felt Jay's hands on the laces of her corset. When he had loosened them sufficiently, she unhooked the front busk and peeled the boned garment away from her body.

She felt naked and exposed without her corset, even though the fine silk chemise covered her from neckline to knee. The silk was so thin that the shape of her breasts and her nipples were visible through the fabric.

'Turn around,' Jay said, and slowly, she did so.

Bending down, Jay took hold of the hem of her chemise and drew it up over her thighs. Slowly he lifted it clear of her hips and up over the fullness of her breasts. Amy held her arms over her head, so that he could lift the garment free.

She heard Jay's inrush of breath as he peeled the garment from her. In a moment he dropped the chemise onto the heap of clothes on the grass.

She dipped her chin and stood with her hands clasped loosely together at her groin, aware of Jay studying her closely. Oh let him find me attractive, she thought in a moment of vulnerability. Perhaps my hips are too large and my legs too short . . .

Jay reached out and touched the column of her neck, trailing his fingers gently down between her breasts and stroking lightly across the slight mound of her belly.

'You're more beautiful that I imagined,' he whispered, his voice sounding awed. 'Will you lie down here, my darling? I want to just look at you.'

Amy lowered herself onto the froth of lacy petticoats, feeling the softness of the crumpled fabric against her naked back. She lay looking up at Jay, one arm curved behind her head for a pillow and one leg bent in a gesture of artless seduction.

Jay knelt down beside her and began unbuttoning his jacket. Keeping his eyes on her all the time, he divested himself of his other clothes, until he was naked.

Amy smiled at him, her eyes ranging over the plains

of his body. He had a superb physique. The army training had honed every trace of surplus flesh from his body and he was strongly muscled. A sprinkling of light brown hair covered his limbs and was clustered at the base of his flat belly.

Amy's eyes lingered at Jay's groin, admiring the darkly flushed column of flesh that reared up from its nest of hair. He was strongly erect, his rigid cock-stem lying almost flat against his belly. Between his legs, his sac looked heavy and potent. Jay glanced down at himself and then back up at Amy.

Her glance did not falter. She let him see that she enjoyed looking at him. It was a powerful stir to her senses to see a man so ready and responsive. Jay was like a handsome animal, a prize stud. And all that contained male sexuality was for her alone.

'So you like what you see?' Jay grinned.

'Oooh yes,' Amy said, arching her back and stretching like a cat.

The feeling of being naked in front of a man was so unique, so shocking, that she felt a rush of excitement to her belly and her sex seemed to tense and flutter. She knew that she was growing wet between her legs and could hardly wait for Jay to discover that fact for himself.

She parted her legs a little so that her lightly-furred sex opened and displayed a tantalising glimpse of wet pink flesh. She was gratified to see Jay's eyes follow her every moment. Kneeling in front of her, he reached out and placed a hand on each of her rounded thighs. Exerting a little pressure, he urged her to part her thighs more widely.

'I like what I see too. Very much. Open yourself to me, my darling. Let me gaze fully upon that adorable place which I so desire.'

Amy's cheeks grew hot as she did as he asked. The sun poured down onto her quim as she felt her flesh-lips part further and pout open for him. Now she was fully exposed to Jay's hungry eyes. He could not help but see that she was swollen and dripping and she felt a mixture of shame and arousal – a potent mixture which stirred her to an even greater state of sexual readiness.

Jay's fingertips brushed against the tangle of silky curls which surrounded her sex.

'Your sex hair really is bright red. I've never seen such an enticing little quim,' Jay said in wonderment. 'You're neatly made, my darling. So pink and new looking. And all wet and ready for pleasuring.'

Although Amy squirmed at his words and put up her hands to cover her blushing cheeks, she drew in her breath on a moan as he began stroking the puffed-up folds of her sex. Jay watched her reactions as he frigged her, running the pad of his thumb up over the little bud which was growing erect and beginning to throb sweetly.

Oh God, what must she look like? All spread out so wantonly, her legs open wide and Jay's knowing fingers playing her like a musical instrument. The sensations which radiated outwards from the hot liquid centre of her were exquisite.

'Bend your knees up, sweetheart,' Jay said hoarsely, adjusting the pressure of his fingers. 'I want to watch as you melt and dissolve with pleasure.'

He circled the firm little nub within its hood of flesh and smoothed the scrap of flesh upwards towards her belly. Dipping a finger into her vagina, he spread her creamy wetness up over her hard bump which seemed to pulse and tick as strongly as a miniature clock.

Amy lifted her hips, pushing herself against his hand. She didn't care if she did look shameless. She was enjoying being pleasured and admired by such a handsome and experienced lover.

She saw herself as he must see her. All she wore

were her embroidered white cotton stockings, held above her knees by ribboned garters, and her laced-up leather riding boots which reached to mid-calf. Above her stocking tops, her firm thighs looked even more naked than if she had been totally nude.

Her body was as white as milk, except for her tight pink nipples and the slash of colour under her arms and between her legs. She knew that her roseate sex, in its nest of red-gold curls, must look especially shocking against the paleness of her body.

Jay seemed to be entranced by her quim. He was still gazing rapturously at the moist, pale pink shape, the sacred female flesh; that place which Madeline had told her was also called a yoni and was venerated by the Hindu peoples.

Ah, God, Jay was stroking her gently, so gently, and the ripples of ticklish pleasure were spreading up inside her. Her womb pulsed and seemed to grow soft as she rocked against Jay's moving fingers. Everything within her was concentrated on that one burning spot between her legs.

She was so wet that his strokes slid and slipped against her fleshy lips. Her pleasure bud was hard and hot as a nut now. She almost cried out when Jay took hold of it between finger and thumb, pinching and tweaking in a firm, seemingly oiled rhythm.

As Amy's flesh convulsed and she rode high on the crest of pleasure she was aware of the morning sun, pouring hotly down onto her skin. It seemed to seep into every curve and crevice of her unclothed body, seeking out the last hidden throb of her climax.

Even as her first climax was fading, she felt the hot wetness of Jay's mouth as he enclosed her quim in a passionate kiss. His tongue darted back and forth across her still erect bud and little stabs of almost hurting pleasure built swiftly up to a new crescendo of sensation.

'Ah stop, please . . .' Amy moaned as more of the intense pulsings rioted through her. 'No more Jay . . . wait . . .'

'As you wish,' Jay said, surfacing from between her thighs and lying beside her. 'You taste wonderful, see?'

Covering her mouth he pushed his tongue between her lips and she tasted herself. There was musk there and something faint and new, like the sea.

Gradually her body returned to a plateau where the pleasure was contained and possible to gauge. This amount of feeling was frightening. She had never climaxed so easily, so completely, before now. It felt as if her body was out of control. She delighted in her responses to Jay and would be ready for more soon, but she needed to catch her breath for a moment.

Jay stroked her gently, his fingertips light as a moth's wings on her belly. He circled the soft flesh and then moved upwards to cup a breast, all the while kissing her, his tongue gentle, tender inside her mouth.

Her nipples awoke under his touch, tightening into hard little peaks. Amy moved against him, pressing upwards towards his hand, her desire for him building again suddenly and becoming a pressing need.

She felt a violence within herself and didn't want his gentleness now. She wanted him hot and hard inside her. She wanted to writhe on his rigid stem, to feel her own slick folds closing around the base of him, collaring his hard and thrusting member with a soft-as-silk female caress.

Jay seemed to sense what she wanted. He moved over her until he was lying between her legs. His hands slipped under her bottom and lifted her in readiness. Amy lifted her knees and opened her thighs, turning the purse shape of her sex up more prominently towards him. Jay gave a strangled groan and pushed his cock down into her, sliding the whole of his length into her tight passage in one slick, controlled movement.

'Oooh Jay. That feels so good,' Amy murmured against his mouth, as he filled her completely. 'Do it to me. Service me. Take me hot and hard.'

'Christ but you're a rampant little piece,' Jay groaned as he thrust against her.

She wrapped her arms around his back, urging him on with the gentle pressure of her fingers. The tips of her nails raked his back and then moved down to his thrusting buttocks. Jay kissed her deeply, his tongue plunging into her mouth as his cock plunged into the dark wet centre of her.

Amy rose to meet him, matching him stroke for stroke. His swollen cock-head nudged against her womb and she welcomed the pleasure-pain of it. Her clitoris felt hot and bruised, but it pulsed as strongly as before. She rubbed it against the base of his cock, where it joined his belly, delighting in the friction.

Oh God, how she loved the strength and wildness of the feelings that a man's member brought forth within her. It seemed like one version of heaven to be lying on the ground in the tumble of garments while Jay thrust into her. The cries of exotic birds were in her ears and the smell of India was all around them.

As her senses climbed to another peak, she tightened her whole body, letting the tension build and build. When it crested finally and broke, she had to choke back a scream. The pleasure was so intense that she thought she would faint.

With a strangled groan Jay drew out of her, his cock pumping out his seed onto her belly.

They lay entwined, Jay's heart beating hard against her own. It was some time before Amy's breathing returned to normal. Jay stroked her hair, which had come loose from its pins and had spilled onto her

111

shoulders. She ran her fingers lightly across his broad back.

'This seems so perfect,' she said. 'It's a shame that we won't be able to do this much longer. Father says that we are all to travel upcountry soon to avoid the hot season.' She brightened. 'There are rest houses on the way to break up the journey, aren't there? Perhaps we could slip away together under cover of darkness.'

Jay leaned on his elbow and looked down at her. 'Rest houses? Oh you mean the dak bungalows? Yes, you'll have the use of those. Being a civilian you'll travel overland by horse or *palki-garee* – that's like a coffin on springs!' They both laughed, then Jay went on. 'I'm afraid though, that soldiers travel by river. I don't suppose we'll see much of each other until we arrive at the hill station in the north. And then my duties will keep me busy.'

'Oh, I see. So this might be the last chance we get to be alone for some time?'

Jay nodded. 'Preparations are already underway for our leaving. It's a deuced awkward business to 'lay a dak' – sorry that's army slang, it means organise a journey. Postal officials have to arrange for a supply of bearers en-route and there's the *palki-garees* to fit out. They can be made quite comfortable . . .'

Amy listened absently as he spoke about the various difficulties of packing up and moving the whole regiment and their families up to the hill station. She hadn't realised that their time together was so short and felt sad that she and Jay would not be able to see each other so often.

She told herself that there would be compensations. The cooler northern weather and relaxation of protocol meant that she could spend more time out of doors exploring and there would be riding, tiger hunts and, according to Maud Harris, visits by the local rajah.

'What are you thinking about?' Jay asked, stroking her cheek.

'Oh I was wondering what it would be like living at the hill station,' Amy said. 'I expect there'll be plenty of ways to enjoy myself.'

'And will you miss me?' Jay asked seriously.

The way he said it, made Amy look sharply at him. His fair brows were drawn together in a frown. She tapped him playfully on the cheek.

'Of course I'll miss you,' she grinned. 'We've been good for each other.'

She realised that she had, inadvertently, used the past tense. And Jay had noticed. His face darkened under his tan.

'Oh, I'm sorry Jay. I didn't mean . . . It's just that nothing lasts for ever. I'm trying to be practical about this.'

He didn't seem to have heard her.

'Amy . . . I . . . I've never felt like this about anyone before,' he began hesitantly. 'I've been wondering whether . . . Oh dammit. I'm no good at this. Amy would you consider being . . .'

Amy felt a stab of panic. Oh Lord. He was going to propose, she just knew it. The last thing she wanted was to become an army wife. She had seen the life such women were obliged to lead and she knew that she would be choked by their self-imposed restrictions and prejudices, their narrow and jaundiced view of life. And the moment that she agreed to get engaged to Jay, he'd think he owned her. She would have to behave herself and curtail her sexual experimenting.

Bending over, she pressed her lips gently to Jay's mouth, cutting him off in mid-sentence. He kissed her passionately and drew her against him. Gently she freed herself and put him at arm's length, then, smiling brightly at him, she began pulling on her clothes.

'It's high time I started back now,' she said in a conversational tone. 'Mother will notice something's amiss if I'm late for breakfast twice in one week. Come along, you must help me dress.'

She saw that Jay was staring up at her in hurt confusion. It was plain that he had taken their liaison to heart. She really did feel affectionate towards him, but she didn't love him, and she didn't want to give him false hopes.

'Oh, now don't look so serious,' she said gently. 'You've been wonderful to me and I won't forget that. We've had great pleasure in each other, haven't we? Don't let's spoil that by making promises which neither of us will keep.'

Jay smiled, although she saw that it cost him an effort.

'You're right of course,' he said brightly. 'How astute of you to remind me of all the young women I've been neglecting these past few days.'

The smile did not reach his eyes, and Amy knew that he was putting on a brave face. It was the one way he could salvage his pride. It was obvious that he hadn't been rebuffed before.

As soon as she was dressed, and had repinned her hair under her pith helmet, she strode towards her horse. Jay lifted her into the saddle, his hands lingering at her waist. When she was seated he stood looking up at her, one hand on the reins. His brown eyes were dark and troubled.

'Amy, please . . . I . . .'

'No Jay. Don't say it. I must go now. We'll see each other from time to time. I'll think of you. And there'll be occasions when we can be alone together – '

'Dammit woman! It's not enough!' he broke in.

Amy wheeled the horse about.

'It'll have to be enough, Jay. It's all we have,' she said calmly. 'I can't give you what you want. I'm sorry.'

She knew that he stood for a long time looking after her but she didn't turn around. As she rode back towards the cantonment she was surprised to find that tears were pricking her eyes.

Chapter Eight

During the days that followed, Amy and Madeline, along with the mass of other civilians attached to the army, had been travelling towards the hills. They moved mainly at night, crossing the dusty plains during the cooler hours. The hottest part of each day was spent resting in the dak bungalows which were placed at regular intervals in the journey.

Amy lay on one of the narrow, string-framed cots which were provided for the women. Overhead a flounced punkah swayed back and forth, wafting a warm breeze around the sparsely furnished bungalow and providing some relief from the burning heat.

Most of the other women were asleep and the darkened room was full of the sounds of rustling and murmurs. Now and then there was a soft snore. Amy twisted and turned, marvelling that anyone could sleep in the stuffy cramped room.

She had been thinking about Jay Landers and wondering if they would be able to spend any time alone together once they were settled in the hills. It would be a pity if she was never able to lie with him again.

How good it had been to indulge herself with fleshly pleasures. And how soon she had come to rely on that outlet for her passions. It was only days since she last saw Jay but already she felt physically bereft.

Irritably she turned onto her stomach aware of the tingling fullness of her breasts and the way the thin fabric of her dress clung damply to her curves. If she had been alone, she would have eased her sexual tension with a practised touch.

'Madeline? Are you awake?' she whispered into the gloom.

'Yes. I'm too restless to sleep,' Madeline replied.

Rising from her cot, she crossed the room and paused next to a small table which held a covered jug and cups.

'Do you want some more soda water?' Madeline said, filling a cup for herself.

Amy wrinkled her nose. 'No thank you. It tastes horrible warm.'

'I have to agree but I'm too thirsty to care about the taste.' She drained the cup quickly and put the jug aside. 'It won't be long now before we reach the station at Mahableshwar, then there'll be ice to cool our drinks –'

'And strawberries instead of endless stringy chicken and rice with chutney,' Amy cut in.

'And streams to dip our feet in and curtains of damp grass in the doorways so that the breeze blowing through them is cooled.'

They both laughed. It was a game they played to lessen the boredom of the hours spent in inactivity. Madeline dragged her light cot across the bare wooden boards and placed it near to Amy. She lay on her side, facing her friend, her body shielding Amy from the other occupants of the room.

Madeline managed somehow to look cool and perfectly groomed, with her hair pinned up and a loose silk tunic worn over baggy trousers.

Like the other women, Amy wore only her chemise

and a light cotton wrap. Her face felt flushed and her hair was dark with sweat. It stuck to her forehead in wet strands.

'You should try to get some sleep, instead of day-dreaming about Captain Landers,' Madeline said softly, her long blue eyes shining in the gloom. 'It isn't good to get all heated up with thinking about bodily pleasures when you cannot bring yourself relief. In a few hours we'll be pushing on to the next village and there'll be no time for rest while we're moving.'

'I know you're right,' Amy said sighing heavily. 'But I just can't stop thinking of the way Jay kissed and caressed me. My body's on fire and my senses are crying out for easement. Do you think I am terrible? It just seems that the more I find out about pleasure, the more of it I want.'

Madeline shook her head. 'That is the way of it, pleasure is addictive. It is natural for you to feel like this.' She paused for a moment as if she was thinking of something that would help Amy in some way. She said softly, 'I could tell you one of my stories if it would relax you.'

Amy smiled and her face brightened.

'I'd like to hear one, but your stories usually have the opposite effect on me. They're scandalous!'

Madeline laughed. 'That is why you like them! I like the way they make me feel too. What would you like to hear? Have you a favourite?'

'Tell me the one about the young man and the temple.'

'Ah, that's one of my favourites too. Very well . . .'

'You'd best keep your voice down,' Amy said with a gleam in her eye. 'It wouldn't do for the others to hear your story. Why even that horse-faced Edith Taverner might feel an unaccustomed itch between her skinny thighs. That is, if she brushes away the cobwebs first!'

They exchanged conspiratorial giggles, holding their

hands over their mouths like naughty children. After a while they grew serious. Amy forgot about the heat and the cramped bungalow as she gave her whole attention to Madeline, aware as was her friend, that she had deliberately chosen a story that would feed her solitary lust.

As Madeline began telling her story, her voice grew soft and low and her blue eyes turned dark and penetrating . . .

The young Indian man's name was Jarishan.

He was poor and of low caste but he was handsome; his body finely made and he was intelligent. He knew that he was bound to his place in society but he was determined to better himself as best he could.

It seemed to him that, if he worked hard and saved a small amount of money, he could build a small mud-brick house and take a wife. Many knew of his ambitions and he was teased by the other young men.

'Why are you so special?' they would say. 'It is the custom to share a wife and house with your brothers. You are a tiller of the land. A peasant. Such men ought not to reach for the moon.'

But Jarishan did not listen. Every day, when he had finished working in the fields, he made an offering at the Lakshmana temple, asking the gods to send him a beautiful young woman who would fall in love with him and agree to live in the house he would build.

Jarishan loved the ancient stone temple with its beautiful carvings and rose-coloured stonework. Inside the temple there were many sculptures and he would study them for hours. His favourite was the one of a man and woman making love.

Although they were made of stone Jarishan felt a strong affinity with the couple. They seemed to be the embodiment of all his dreams.

The man was strong and handsome and the woman

was lovely, with high round breasts and flaring hips. The man was mounting the woman from behind, his erect stone lingam pushing into the subtly crafted, oval, peach shape of her yoni.

Jarishan ached to make love to a woman like that, a woman of his own. His only experience had been with a girl from the next village who had allowed him to put his hand under her skirt and close his fingers around her yoni. The feel of that hot wet place had made him so excited that he grew hard at once. The girl had opened her legs and he had pushed a finger into her, his breath coming fast and the blood pounding in his head.

'You can put your lingam inside me,' she whispered into his ear. 'If you promise to buy me a bracelet when you go to the market.'

He promised at once, bewitched by the feel of her silky juices which clung to his fingers. His tumescent member twitched and pulsed and there was an unbearable tension in his loins. It seemed to him that the village girl was the embodiment of the goddess Parvati, favourite of Shiva, as beautiful as the full moon.

He wanted the experience to last, to be memorable. He slid his other hand into the girl's sari and closed it around one fat breast. Then the girl stuck her tongue into his mouth and he became so excited that he lost control.

Jarishan's cheeks grew red with shame as he remembered how the girl had laughed and called him names when he spilt his seed into his loincloth.

'You are good-looking, but you are useless to a woman,' she said. 'Go back and work in the fields. There are many other young men who seek my favours.'

After that he did not dare approach her again. He knew that she would spread the word to the other girls and they would all laugh at him. The other boys told him how they persuaded young women to pleasure them in return for gifts and the envy burned within him.

He threw all his energies into working and put thoughts of women aside. His efforts were rewarded and the harvest was good. After selling the surplus at the market he was able to save a little money. Soon he would have enough to build a house and he began to think about looking for a wife, but he did not have the courage to approach any of the girls from the village nearby.

One of them in particular had caught his eye. She was called Menaka and she seemed to him to be perfect. She was small and slim and very pretty. At night he would dream of her, imagining stroking her cool dark skin. He could almost feel the sensation of her long hair brushing against his skin as she lay naked, pressed closely to him.

Time passed and one night Jarishan went to the temple by moonlight. He would ask the goddess to give him courage to approach Menaka. Lamps glowed in the temple's dim interior. The statues looked pale and magical. He went to stand next to his favourite, the one of the man and woman making love.

The beauty of the couple affected him strangely. Instead of feeling hopeful, he felt sad. Menaka did not know that he existed. He would never find a woman to love and take pleasure with. The need and desire rose up within him until they became a joint ache and he was moved to do something unthinkable.

While he kept his eyes on the calm, beautiful, stone face of the women, he put his hand into his loincloth and took out his lingam. Closing his fingers around his erect shaft, he moved his hand back and forth slowly.

He did not know if it was the forbidden nature of the act, or his yearning for Menaka, but the pleasure he felt in touching himself in the presence of the statues was deep and satisfying. He leaned forward and rested his upper body against the cool stone, while stroking himself. His nipples rubbed against the stone and the slight abrasive motion felt wonderful.

He imagined that it was Menaka's lips which were sucking at his hard male teats; her hand which stroked over the flat planes of his belly; her fingers which were curled around his member.

Squeezing gently, he smoothed his hand back and forth along the stem of his flesh. Soft moans crept out from between his teeth and a drop of clear liquid gathered at the slitted mouth of his lingam. Scooping up the wetness with his palm, he smeared it over his moist swollen glans, rolling his cupped palm over and around the bulbous plum.

His muscled belly was taut with the pleasure of the act. He had never felt so good, so powerful. The stone woman seemed to smile benevolently at him as he moved his hand faster and his hips began thrusting backwards and forwards.

He rubbed his nipples more firmly against the stone and sharp little shocks ran down his belly and found an echo in the pulsing sweetness of his loins. Rubbing vigorously at himself, he clenched his buttocks, feeling the pressure in his scrotum boiling upwards until it erupted in jets of creamy fluid.

He watched the drops spatter onto the stone figures and was overcome with dismay, but he was helpless to stop the flow of pleasure which left him weak and trembling. Leaning against the statue he regained his breath and said a little prayer of humility and thanksgiving. He felt in his heart that the stone figures approved of his actions.

After wiping the stone clean, he adjusted his clothing and began moving away from the statue. He had taken only a few steps when he saw the movement in the shadows beyond the stone sculpture.

Jarishan froze, his mouth drying with fright. The hairs on the back of his neck rose. Ah Parvati, save him. The statues were moving, coming to life to wreak their revenge on him for his profanity. He fell to his knees, his eyes squeezed shut.

A soft chuckle made him open his eyes. No stone woman stood before him but a living woman. She was small and slender and exquisitely beautiful. Her face was a dusky oval and her eyes were like dark stars. Unbound black hair hung over her shoulders.

Menaka.

Jarishan gaped at her.

'Have you nothing to say?' she asked gently.

He could not speak. His mind was whirling. She had seen; she must have. But she did not berate him. Her mouth was curved in a sensual smile and her eyes looked soft and luminous. She looked . . . aroused. A great hope rose within him.

'You did not seek me out or speak to me,' Menaka said. 'Yet I knew that you wished to. I watched you come to this place, night after night. And I have been waiting for you to notice me in the shadows, but you have only had eyes for the stone woman. Is it her then that you love?'

Jarishan's eyes opened wide for, as she had been speaking, Menaka had been loosening her sari. The fabric fell in a pool around her. Underneath she was naked except for bracelets and anklets of silver. His breath left him in a long sigh as he gazed on her high round breasts. Her nipples were wine-red and gathered into crests like ripe berries.

Menaka's waist was narrow and her hips curved. His eyes were drawn to the place between her rounded thighs, where there was a lot of dark hair – more than the village girl had had clustered around her yoni.

He took one step towards Menaka and then another, sure that she would melt away before his eyes – this

123

was so much like a dream – but she did not melt away. He put out his hand and placed it on her shoulder. She smiled at him seductively and moved backwards until her back was resting on the curved back of the stone woman.

'I am a real woman,' Menaka said. 'Within me is the power of the goddess. I am all women, virgin and whore. For you I am Shakti – the power principle of initiation. My lips are not made of stone. My caresses are not cold. Come to me.'

Spellbound, Jarishan watched as Menaka lifted her chin and spread her thighs wide.

Jarishan caught the odour of her yoni. It was rich and musky and the smell of it seemed to course through his blood. His lingam rose and became harder than before, thrusting potently against his loincloth, eager for escape.

'Come to me. Be inside me,' Menaka said softly.

Jarishan moved forward. He positioned himself between her parted thighs. For a moment he savoured her; the glossy dark skin; her finely rounded limbs; her belly which was a soft cushion, dimpled by her navel.

He buried his face in her neck and breathed deeply. Menaka's hair smelt of saffron and her skin of amber.

With a hoarse cry he thrust upwards into her. With one smooth movement he embedded his lingam to the hilt. As Menaka's hot silken flesh enclosed him, he began to weep. Cupping his face in her palms, Menaka put out her tongue and drank his tears.

'Weep no more, for you have found me,' she said. Then as he drew almost all the way out of her and surged forward again, she began to moan and push herself towards him.

Jarishan felt the thick bush of her pubic hair brushing against the base of his belly. At this evidence of her pleasure, he felt a thrill run straight to his heart. His lingam was stout and leaping with vigour. He swelled with pride.

Lifting Menaka's thighs, so that they settled around his narrow hips, he pushed strongly into her. She gripped him with her ridged inner flesh and the soft scraping of it was delicious on his sensitive glans.

Because he had enjoyed the solitary pleasure earlier, he was able to hold back his own release and concentrate on urging Menaka to her climax. She began to shudder and her eyes turned up, so that he could see the whites. Sharp little cries came from her and then Jarishan felt her internal pulsings and lost control.

He gasped as his seed left him and flooded into her, the sweet tearing pleasure of the emission making his thighs tremble. Menaka held him close, murmuring words of love as he lay his cheek on the firm pillow of her breasts.

Later, he helped her to dress and they stood looking at the entwined stone figures. Although Jarishan's heart was almost too full for words, he found that he was able to utter his thanks to the stone woman who had brought Menaka and himself together.

He knew that he would never be alone again. And his potency would never be a problem with the witch-woman, Menaka, who had seduced him and stolen his heart . . .

Madeline's voiced tailed off as the story ended. Her face was alight with triumph as she watched Amy and there was a calculated glint in her slanted blue eyes.

The tale of Jarishan and Menaka, like all Madeline's stories, possessed a poignancy and a dark eroticism that seemed to vibrate with the very soul of India. Amy felt the magic of the story settle over her, the sexual heat it brought creeping through her veins.

Her hands were crossed on her breasts. Slowly she moved them apart, her fingers dragging softly over the firm mounds and the nipples which were erect and tingling.

'That's it Amy,' Madeline whispered. 'Touch yourself. No one can see you, except me. Jay Landers awoke a fire in you and you need to let some of it fly free.'

Amy realised that Madline wanted her to solace herself. Surely she couldn't do *that* with Madeline watching her. It was too private an act to share with anyone. Oh, but she ached with desire. The story had made her feel even more aroused. A feverish heat seemed to have suffused her quim. Trickles of sweat ran down her belly and pooled in the curling red hair of her mons.

She was burning up with need, but she couldn't caress herself just now. Could she?

'Do it, Amy,' Madeline whispered. 'Stroke yourself through your gown. No one will see. And I will take pleasure in watching you spend.' She sounded breathless, her voice soft and encouraging.

Amy hesitated, then began to move her hand down slowly until her fingers came to rest on her fabric-covered pubis. She wanted to touch her sex but it was quite impossible to abandon herself to the pleasure of the act with Madeline watching.

Madeline sensed her reticence.

'Don't we share everything? I told you about Father Starr and I'll tell you of other secrets. Now – close your eyes. Forget I'm here.'

Amy had a better idea. She turned onto her stomach and pressed her face into the thin pillow. Now she could pretend that she was alone; forget everything except the feelings which were centred in the moist crevice between her thighs. She moved her hand, rubbing in firm circular movements on the outside of her cotton gown.

Though she longed to stroked her naked sex, to open the puffy sex-lips and plunge her fingers inside her lubricated quim, she did not dare to raise her skirts in case one of the other women was alerted by her movements. The possibility that she might be discovered added an edge of danger to her arousal. Furtively at first, she pressed and rolled her hand against her pubis.

Nothing moved in the room and she gained confidence, beginning to arch her back and thrust her hips back and forth. The sensations were growing and Amy muffled her sighs against the pillow.

Catching her bottom lip in her teeth, she began reaching for the ultimate satisfaction. Her plump folds were squeezed together by the pressure of her fingers and her swollen bud throbbed and pulsed inside the closed groove of flesh. She forgot that Madeline was watching. There was only the rapidly climbing curve of pleasure.

It didn't take long. She had been in a state of sexual excitement for hours and her flesh responded swiftly to her expert touch. As she climaxed, she turned her head and pressed her mouth against her dress sleeve, muffling her sighs as wave after wave of pleasure spread through her. She felt a gentle hand on her head and heard Madeline's soft laugh of delight.

After a moment she turned over onto her back. Only now did she feel embarrassed and loath to meet Madeline's eyes. But Madeline had no such inhibitions.

'Was that satisfactory?' she asked, bending close and kissing Amy's cheek, her mouth curving in an impish grin. 'Or do I really need to ask?'

Amy stretched languorously and removed the hand which had just been clamped between her thighs. She smiled tremulously.

'I can hardly believe that I just did that. With you watching me. I've never let anyone see me do that before.'

'I thought not. And I enjoyed watching you. Do you know that you squeeze your eyes shut tightly, just before you reach your peak? What a flower of passion you have become. I think that your English blood is being thinned by the heat of India.'

Madeline was so matter of act, that Amy felt only a mild embarrassment. Her heart was still thudding in her chest and the afterglow of her climax had brought the colour to her cheeks. She felt wide awake now and revitalised.

It was a good thing that the window blinds were drawn and the ancient punkah made a squeaky rattling noise as it swung to and fro. Otherwise her rhythmic movements and breathy little moans would have alerted the other women to what she had been doing.

Just the thought of their shocked faces made her smile. She was certain that none of them even dreamed of the beguiling pleasures of self-abuse. Only a short time ago it would have seemed incredible that she would risk touching herself like that. Yet the crowded room, the stifling heat, and Madeline's softly-accented voice urging her on had prompted her to an unaccustomed boldness.

She almost wished that she had been discovered, just to see the look of righteous outrage on Maud Harris's pinched little face. She looked up at Madeline, her eyes glinting with laughter and frowned.

There was a look on her friend's face which she had never seen before. Madeline was staring down at her with undisguised absorption. There was something measuring in her light blue gaze. Something which spoke of unexpressed need. A little shiver of apprehension ran up Amy's back.

What was Madeline planning now? She had a look of purpose about her; even something predatory.

Amy knew her friend well enough by now to suspect that it would be something challenging. It seemed that she was being urged forward, encouraged gently to

128

express herself in the fullest physical terms. There was a tight knot of excitement in her stomach.

In a day or so they would reach the hill station of Mahableshwar and she just knew that her education would continue there.

Chapter Nine

*A*fter the long hot journey up from the plains, it was a delight to reach the cooler climate of the hills. A shower of rain seemed to have brought out the best in the surroundings; trees and plants revived and creepers burst into blossom and hung from branches in graceful festoons.

As they approached the hill station the entourage broke up into little groups, each household with its retinue of servants and pack animals going off in different directions to their respective quarters. The straight street, neat bungalows and steepled church surprised Amy. The place looked something like a Swiss village. If it had not been for the lush vegetation and the fact that the outside walls of Government House were completely covered by screens of damp grass, she might have fancied herself anywhere but in India.

The house she was led to was a white-painted bungalow, with a thatched roof and spreading eaves. In front was a broad verandah which was furnished like an outside room. She looked forward to sitting out there and taking advantage of the cool evening breeze.

Cane furniture, blinds, potted plants and hunt trophies adorned the verandah. Amy averted her eyes from the bleached skulls of antelopes and the mounted tiger skin. She took no pleasure in these things. She had enjoyed riding with the hunt in Sussex but it was the excitement of the chase she loved best; the challenge of urging her mount over hedgerows and splashing through muddy ditches.

It had always seemed to her that it ought to be possible to have a hunt without a kill, although she knew that it was not a popular view amongst her peers.

She tore her thoughts away from such unpleasant things and examined her surroundings. Madeline had told her of the balls, the outdoor picnics, the scenic views, and the sport to be had in Mahableshwar. Protocol was more relaxed apparently and the festivities were entered into with something approaching abandon.

It was certainly going to be fun staying there for the next few months. She only wished that Captain Landers was stationed nearby but she had learned that he, along with a large part of the regiment, had gone to a different hill station. Jay was now part of the governor of Bombay's personal retinue and would be obliged to stay at the official residence, eight miles from Poona at Dapoorie.

Poor Jay. His amorous adventures would be curtailed somewhat. Although he had seemed to care for her, she knew that he would soon be pursuing other young women. He was too hot-blooded to deny himself physical pleasure. His loss was a blow to her, but she would just have to devise new entertainments for herself.

The cavalcade of carts, camels and *palkees* stopped in front of the white bungalow. A servant helped Amy to her feet and she stretched her cramped limbs. She turned to wave at Madeline whose family were staying in a fine, two-storey house at the end of the street.

As the *palkee* carrying her friend moved on down the

street, Madeline called out, 'It's the custom here for ladies to go riding in the early morning, just like in Bombay. I'll call for you the day after tomorrow.'

Amy could hardly wait. She half-turned away, ignoring the venomous look which Maud Harris shot her as she passed by on her way to her bungalow. Maud took every opportunity to enforce her disapproval of Amy's friendship with Madeline. Luckily her mother was of a more enlightened frame of mind. She had met Madeline and her family on many military occasions and had expressed a liking for her.

The following day Amy's mother was kept busy organising the house and giving the servants orders. Amy found herself left to her own devices. The situation suited her perfectly. She had slept well and was now filled with a new energy and vigour. It was as if the scenery, the wonderful fresh food and the clean air reached into some place inside her.

On the journey across the hot dusty plains she had felt drained and lethargic. Now it seemed as if she responded to everything around her with almost animal exhilaration. She went exploring by herself and discovered that there were turf banks to lie on and fruit to pick straight from the tree. Mahableshwar was famous for its strawberries, raspberries and peaches, and she ate the warm perfumed fruit with relish.

When Madeline arrived to go riding early the next morning, Amy perceived that her friend seemed to be infected with a similar lightness of mood. They cantered away from the station, finding that they could ride harder and farther than on the parched plains. The cool breeze and fresher air did not sap their strength.

The wealth of greens, the slashes of vibrant colour and the scents of rose and jasmine drew them on and away from the bridle paths which wove amongst the hills.

Finally they drew to a halt beside a muddy green pool

and tethered the horses to a tree. Jungle undergrowth pressed all around them and it occurred to Amy that they might be lost. When she said so to Madeline, her friend laughed.

'I have a sense of where we are, never fear.'

In fact Amy had not been alarmed. She felt strangely at ease amongst the green shadows and the shimmering bars of sunlight which threw lights onto the mossy ground. The sounds of monkeys and birds reached her ears and there was a rich exciting smell in the small clearing, like vanilla or spice, or some sweet alcoholic dessert.

She felt too restless to linger and jumped up from her seat on a fallen tree.

'Let's explore, shall we? What's that over there? It looks like the spire of a building.'

Madeline looked where Amy pointed.

'It could be the towers of a temple, but it seems a strange place to find one. There's no village nearby and we've seen no fields sown with crops.'

They struck out through the undergrowth, which grew so thickly in places that twigs and leaves seemed to pluck at their skirts. After a while they came upon a track, overgrown and ill-kept, but the stones which metalled it could still be discerned beneath a thick carpet of springy moss.

They couldn't see the tower now, as a veil of trees had obscured the view and they seemed to be moving downwards into a valley. Amy moved forward slowly, pushing aside a tangle of ferny branches. The temple appeared before her suddenly and she stopped in awe and delight.

'Oh my, Madeline. Just *look* at this place.' She had spoken in a whisper without realising the fact.

Madeline stepped clear of the undergrowth and they advanced towards the building together. Madeline said nothing, her light blue eyes wide with surprise.

The ochre-coloured stone of the small temple was fretted with patches of moss and lushly flowering creepers had clambered over the roofs and entwined themselves around the towers. Still visible beneath the living covering were the erotic carvings which covered every inch of the building.

Amy ran her eyes over the silky stone breasts, the hands outstretched in supplication. Here there was a head thrown back in joy, there a sculptured lingam pressing into the hungry stone plum of a yoni. The sculptures seemed to move and writhe as the greenish jungle shadows moved over them.

On some of them, gems winked and blazed, but in other places there were gaps where rubies or pearls had been prised from their settings.

A huge stone lingam stood alone to one side of the door, still dyed from ancient offerings and encircled with the withered brown relics of mummified marigolds.

'It looks as if no one has been to this place for twenty years or more,' Madeline said. 'How odd. Temples are revered in India and tended diligently. It's most unusual to see one neglected like this.'

She shuddered suddenly and reached for Amy's hand. 'There's something odd about this place, something wrong. Let's go back to the horses.'

Amy did not reply. She meshed her fingers with Madeline's and began to walk forward, urging Madeline to accompany her.

'There's nothing to fear. Come on. I want to see more.'

'You're not thinking of going inside?'

'Why not?' Amy said. 'There's no one to see us. I intend no disrespect. I just want to see the interior.'

In fact she was strongly affected by the decaying beauty of the building. It seemed sad that it was so neglected, so unloved. But as she moved closer, she realised that she was mistaken. Someone still came here. She caught the smell of fresh incense, smoky and jasmine scented.

Madeline pulled at her hand.

'Come away, Amy. Please.'

But something drew Amy on.

'You go if you like. I'm going inside. I have to see. Someone's in there.'

Madeline sighed resignedly. 'Then I'll come with you. But go carefully and don't make any noise.'

They bent under a great swag of creeper, their feet rustling through the leaf litter that clogged the entrance. Inside, the temple was dimly lit and cavelike.

Stalactites of carvings, tumbling with more erotic figures marched like soldiers into the interior. Amy and Madeline moved forward slowly into the vaulted room. Spears of sunlight poking through the lacework of windows, set high up in the walls, rained down on them. Dust motes danced in the smoky yellow light.

And now they could hear voices, soft murmurs, too low-pitched to be distinguishable words. Rounding a corner they were confronted by brighter golden slashes, which illuminated the painted ceiling and made the faces of stone sculptures resemble bronze. Amy saw that the extra light came from flickering torches, set into stone sconces, high up on either side of an enormous statue.

She drew in her breath as she looked at the sculpture. The image was of a man, thirteen feet high, four-armed and with the head of an elephant. It was fashioned of pinkish stone, gleaming as if it was veined with liquid honey. The four arms held a silver dish, an axe, a golden crescent and a flower. A belt of hooded cobras adorned his waist.

'Ganesha,' Madeline breathed, making a sign of respect. 'The embodiment of Tantric mysteries. Lord of beginnings. Gatekeeper and lord of the sex chakra.'

Amy was too intrigued by their discovery to ask Madeline to explain the meaning of her words, but she absorbed the name of the god. Ganesha. It was a beautiful name and seemed to find a resonance in some deep secret place within her. The strong male body of the god, topped by the beautifully carved elephant head, seemed at the same time ludicrous and enigmatic; it was also wholly sexual.

Into the dark silence then, came a sound; a sigh of pleasure. Unmistakable. Amy thought of Madeline's story. Was she about to discover her personal Jarishan and Menaka?

'Come on,' she whispered. 'I want to see who's in here and what they're doing.'

Madeline hung back a little at first, then she followed Amy with reluctance.

'You're too reckless for your own good sometimes. A little fear is no bad thing,' she hissed in a low voice.

Amy inched forward, taking care to move silently. Her feet made little sound on the cool stone floor, but she winced at each tiny noise. Then she saw the richly embroidered rug which was spread on the floor to one side of the statue, and she realised that the two people who lay there were too engrossed in each other to notice anything.

In the deep shadow cast by the bulk of Ganesha, Amy could not distinguish details clearly, but she could see that a man and woman were pleasuring each other. Both were naked, except for their ornate jewellery. Gold and silver bangles adorned their wrists and the woman wore heavy earrings and anklets.

As her eyes adjusted to the light, she saw that the woman was slender, finely-made and very dark-skinned. A thick plait of night-black hair hung over one shoulder. She was on her knees and the man who was mounting her was tall, lean and golden-skinned.

His hair was black also and streamed loosely down his back to his waist. Diamond studs glinted in his ears.

Amy and Madeline stood in the shadow of one of the carved pillars, watching the lovers through the open lacework of stone.

The woman threw back her head and moaned as the man thrust into her. He held her narrow waist in two hands and leaned back a little watching his lingam move in and out as he thrust between the rounded cheeks of the woman's bottom. For a while there was only the sound of the woman's bracelets ringing together, a percussive background to the subtler rhythm of skin sliding on skin.

Then the man said something in a low voice and drew out of his lover. His thick erect phallus gleamed wetly in the flame-lightened shadow.

Amy caught her breath as the man moved his head and, for the first time, his face was illuminated by yellow light from the flare. He was shockingly beautiful. With that fall of black silky hair he might have looked feminine, but he did not. Beautiful, superb. She could think of no other words to describe him. In that split second, she registered every detail of his face, consigning each of them to her memory.

She had never seen such looks on a man – indeed, he had no right to look that way. He had smooth golden skin, high cheekbones, a perfectly straight nose, deep-set black eyes and a full sculptured mouth. But it was not the sum of his features which so affected her, it was his bearing and the imprint of a fine intellect on his broad brow.

There was something intangible about this man, something else she had never seen before. He looked as wild and proud as a hawk. And like a hawk, she sensed that he could be dangerous.

Amy dragged her attention almost reluctantly to his lover. The woman had turned over and now lay on her back, a willing supplicant for the moment. The man stretched out his hands, moving his spread fingers up her narrow ribcage until they closed on her full round breasts. The prominent nipples, wine-red in colour, protruded from between his fingers. The woman sighed as her lover manipulated the hard little peaks.

Amy felt a dart of envy. The lovers were well-matched. The woman was also beautiful in a different, but no less unique, way.

In comparison to the man, the woman was tiny. A pocket Venus, she would have been called in England. Her limbs were softly rounded and she was very narrow at the waist, though lush and flaring at breast and hip. Her dark plait was like a thick twisted rope and would reach to her hips when she stood. But again, it was the woman's face which held Amy's attention.

Her dark skin was smooth and flawless, almost the colour of a ripe fig, and shone softly with brownish-purple lights in the dimness. Her face was a perfect oval, dominated by huge dark eyes, a small straight nose – perhaps a fraction over-long – and a garnet-coloured, rosebud mouth.

Amy pressed the back of her hand to her mouth as the woman sighed and arched her back, her fingers curling inwards, as her lover plucked at her nipples. She opened her thighs and raised them up to her chest and, with a groan, the man surged forward burying his rigid flesh inside her dark wet heat.

Their coupling became frantic as they rolled about on the embroidered rug. Inarticulate cries came from them both, the sounds caught and muffled by their seeking mouths. Amy felt only mild shame at being a spectator. She was enthralled by the beauty and savagery of the couple's lovemaking. Now and then they changed position, both of them were agile and able to bend their limbs into intricate postures.

They were the embodiment of the erotic carvings all

around and Amy hungered to be possessed by such a man. He was so adept, so considerate of his partner's pleasure. Watching the way he penetrated the woman, gauging his thrusts, now and then stopping completely and taking deep steadying breaths before surging into her again, she realised that she was an innocent still. What she had done with Jay Landers seemed tame and commonplace compared to this – feast; this jewelled banquet of sexual delights.

The woman gave a series of high little cries when she climaxed for the first time. Clasping her close until she subsided against him, the man drew out of her and sat up straight. His ankles were crossed and his thick phallus rose up in front of him like the stamen of some huge exotic lily. Kneeling in front of the man, the woman took the phallus into her mouth, stroking the shaft with her fingers while she sucked the bulbous plum of the uncovered glans.

The man threw his head back, exposing the column of his throat. Light flickered over his muscled torso and the taut, ridged plane of his belly. Amy imagined the taste of him, salty and animal-scented with an overlay of the woman's own musk. She had tasted herself on Jay Landers' mouth and knew it to be a potent spur to her senses.

Amy and Madeline watched the lovers for a long time, both lost in awe of their prowess.

The woman seemed insatiable, reaching her peak of pleasure time after time, and the man maintained his erection for an incredible amount of time, holding back until his lover was fully sated. At last, when Amy had pins and needles in one leg from remaining in the same position for over an hour, the lovers seemed satisfied.

With a great cry, the man climaxed, spilling his creamy semen onto the slight swell of the woman's belly. The drops looked pearly against her dark skin.

Smiling, showing the gleam of perfect white teeth, she massaged the fluid into her skin.

They lay together quietly for a while, stroking each other's bodies. Their low affectionate voices reached Amy and she heard the love in the words, even though she did not understand the language.

She was puzzled. Who were they? Perhaps each of them was married to someone else, or they were forbidden to marry because of caste differences; why else this clandestine meeting? But she sensed that this was not the case. The intimacy and rapport between them was too deep-seated, too instinctive, to be a transient thing. She would have said that they were long-term lovers, judging by their knowledge of each other's needs and the genuine affection between them.

Yet they had need of subterfuge. The mystery intrigued her, but she doubted that she would ever solve it.

'We can't go yet. They'll see us,' Madeline whispered. 'Stay hidden until they leave.'

Amy nodded. She didn't think she could move anyway. She had an actual pain in the base of her belly, where a curling knot of desire had been present for the entire time she had been watching the lovers. It had not been possible to ease herself and now the crotch of her drawers was sopping and the dull throbbing of her sex was maddening. At the first opportunity she was going to attend to her sexual needs.

'Ah, they're dressing,' she said at last with a soft groan of relief. 'We should be able to leave soon.'

The woman pulled a knee-length tunic over her head and then pulled on loose trousers. Her clothes were surprisingly plain; the yellow dye of the tunic patchy and of poor workmanship.

Amy was aware of a note of discord but was unable to discern the source of it.

She watched as the man's wonderful physique was

covered by an equally nondescript outfit. He knotted a rough cotton dhoti around his waist and pulled on a striped shirt to cover himself to the hips. Both of them wound strips of cloth around their heads, tucking their hair out of sight.

Hand in hand they passed barefoot past Amy and Madeline's hiding place. Amy turned her head to watch them leave. For a second they were silhouetted in the temple doorway. Then they separated and were gone.

'Well. What did you make of that?' Amy said as she emerged into the main body of the temple, flexing her fingers and toes to ease her cramp. 'Who do you think they were?'

Madeline was already hurrying towards the archway which led outside. Ducking to avoid the straggle of creepers, she called out without turning round, 'I don't know. I'll have to give it some thought. But I do know that we'd best hurry. This is our first outing together and we're going to be late for breakfast – again.'

Amy hurried after her friend. There would be time enough for discussion later. At the moment her main concern was getting back to the station. She must keep up the appearance of playing by the rules at all costs.

As Amy rode back towards the station, she was quiet and thoughtful. Madeline seemed disinclined to talk and let her be. Amy felt that she had just glimpsed something of India's soul in the temple. And she liked what she saw. It had surely been no accident that the lovers had chosen to pleasure each other in the presence of Ganesha. She would ask Madeline more about that mystical being later.

Something within her had come alive in the jungle. It was as if she had left part of herself down on the plains or had sloughed her skin and stepped out newly-clad. She felt light-headed and let her mind rove free; she thought back over key events in her life but her memories of Sussex, the house on the estate, and of Magnus, would not solidify in her mind. There was only room for India, with her sumptuous temples, her appalling poverty which existed side by side with splendour and her strange and powerful gods.

She was aware, at some subtle level of consciousness, that the ties of her British blood were loosening by the day – perhaps by the hour – the second – and she welcomed the change within her.

Now, more than ever before, she was going to guard her right to freedom jealously. Even it it meant keeping up a veneer of innocence and respectability and pandering to that silly goose, Maud Harris.

Maud Harris hurried towards Mrs Spencer's bungalow. She knew that the family would be taking breakfast on the verandah at this hour and felt assured of an appreciative audience.

She had just heard some disquieting news from her husband and wanted to be the first to pass it on. Of course that fast Amy Spencer would be there, looking down her far-too-pretty nose as usual, but Maud dismissed Amy as a minor irritation. What she had to tell her friend was extremely important.

She strode across the narrow street and approached the bungalow via the verandah.

'Maud, how nice to see you. Will you have some tea?' Mrs Spencer said at once.

'Thank you kindly. Yes please. Good morning to you, Amy.'

Maud seated herself and mouthed the expected niceties. She accepted a cup of tea and stirred it impatiently, eager to get to the real purpose of her visit. When there was a break in conversation, she seized on it at once.

'I came to tell you, my dear friend, that my husband has just received news from Meerut. I feel that I have to share it with you, but oh dear. It's . . . it's too dreadful for words.'

She paused and dabbed at her face with a handkerchief. Amy said nothing and her mother patted Maud's arm.

'There now, dear. Take your time. It can't be as bad as all that.'

'Oh but it is,' Maud said, catching her bottom lip in her teeth. She leaned forward slightly. 'There are rumours circulating that two British women have been martyred. One of them was . . . in a delicate condition, but it didn't save her. The other was ill in bed with smallpox. Both of them were murdered . . . by sepoys.'

Amy's mother blanched. 'Oh how dreadful. Surely this can't be true. Why would the native soldiers turn on defenceless women?'

'I don't know,' Maud admitted. 'The news has only just reached us. It's probably an isolated incident. But we must take care. Who knows what goes on in these darkies' minds.' She flashed a glance at Amy. 'This is what comes of making unsuitable friendships,' she said pointedly. 'It doesn't do, you know.'

Amy looked back, her amber eyes hard and a mulish expression on her pale face. She looked quite vicious for a moment. A nasty temper went with that unfortunate colouring, Maud thought. It was obvious that Amy thought she had come running, telling tales. Drawing herself up Maud pressed her lips together. It should be plain even to that unsound wretch that she was here doing her Christian duty.

Amy continued to lock gazes with her and Maud looked away first. She fancied that there had been a curl of hostility on that full little mouth. She felt her stomach curdle with dislike. If Amy was her daughter, she'd make sure that she knew how to behave. A few strokes with a cane across her palm and regular reading of certain bible passages would soon straighten her out.

Mrs Spencer looked at her daughter, her vague, pleasant face creased by worry. 'Perhaps Maud's right,

my dear. Madeline is a lovely girl I know, but well . . .
if this news is true . . .'

Amy stood up and slapped her table napkin down.

'Stuff and nonsense!' she said stoutly. 'What if it is
true? It has nothing to do with Madeline. She's a good
friend to me. And I shall go on seeing her whenever I
wish to. That is, mother, unless you expressly forbid it.'

'There's no need for that, dear. I just think that we
should all be careful. What if this unrest was to spread
south? There have been occasional stories of outbreaks
of fighting and there's all that business about the
bullets . . .' She tailed off and looked to Maud for
support.

Maud took a deep breath, pursing her lips with
exasperation. Really, Mrs Spencer was too good-
natured for her own good.

'You're quite right. We must be vigilant, my dear,'
she said. 'But let's not get things out of proportion.
After all, Meerut is a thousand miles away, and our
own sepoys are loyal and steadfast.'

'And we're receiving a visit from the local prince this
evening,' Amy said pertly. 'It would be a pity if we
couldn't enjoy all that excitement and pageantry, not to
mention his generous gifts. Do you mean that we
should shun him too?'

Maud coloured. 'Of course not. We must maintain
relations, be polite but distant. That's always been the
British way.' She looked across at her friend. 'It would
be extremely bad form to refuse any gifts. Besides it
ought to be amusing to meet the man. Of course you
will have heard that he's an absolute scandal. No? Then
let me enlighten you.' She lowered her voice, so that
the servants wouldn't hear.

'These native princes all indulge in wild . . . orgies,
you know. They have countless wives and paramours
who they entertain in rooms kept specially for all

144

manner of immoral purposes, decorated with the most racy pictures . . .'

Maud tailed off, smiling with malicious delight as Amy gave a snort of fury, spat a muttered, 'Balderdash!' and flounced into the house.

I would say that I won that round, she thought, and resumed her conversation with her friend.

Chapter Ten

*T*he extensive grounds of Government House had been decorated in honour of the prince's visit. Bunting hung from the main building and festooned the trees. Lanterns with red, white and blue candles were strung from wires set around the lawn.

Set out on the wide terrace were supper tables covered with spotless white linen and laid with the best monogrammed silver. Ropes of ivy entwined with flowers and ferns snaked artfully across the cloths. Silver bowls, filled with roses and towering confections of crystallised fruit, pralines and chocolates, formed centrepieces on all the tables.

Along with the other women, Amy dressed carefully in her most lavish ball gown. It was made of white Lyons silk, trimmed with white lace and green ribbon. She was corseted tightly to fit into the dress which had a twenty-inch waist. The ayah swept her hair up into a cascade of curls and then decorated her coiffure with combs decorated with dyed ostrich feathers.

Amy darkened her eyelashes with the cosmetics Madeline had given her, pinched her cheeks to give them some colour, and bit her lips to make them fuller.

At the appointed time the carriage arrived to transport the family.

Madeline was already there when Amy reached Government House. She hadn't seen her friend since the day they discovered the temple and she was eager to speak to her. They found a seat on the crowded terrace and were served with drinks. All around were women in evening dresses, as exotic as butterflies and hummingbirds.

Amy took a sip of the daring new cocktail, called Alexanders, and decided that she liked it very much indeed. She asked the English butler what was in it.

'Vermouth and creme de cacao over ice, all topped with whipped cream, madame,' he said stiffly. 'I'm glad you approve.'

Madeline pulled a face behind his back and Amy giggled.

For a while they flirted with the officers, resplendent in their best uniforms, and sipped their drinks. Amy thought of the last occasion when she'd been to a similar function in Bombay. That time Jay Landers had been there. She wished he was there now. There were some good-looking officers waiting to speak to her but none of them quickened her blood in the way that Jay had done. She was missing him more and more.

After a while she realised that she wasn't enjoying herself. She felt vaguely depressed and a little set apart from the celebrations. Maud's visit that morning played on her mind.

'Can I ask you something?' she asked Madeline and, when her friend nodded, proceeded to question her about the spreading unrest and the recent murders in the north.

'What you have heard is true,' Madeline said gravely. 'But I believe that the Indian people have cause for resentment. The British have stamped on many toes over the years and made little attempt to mollify the

147

local princes. Also there are rumours amongst the Bengali army sepoys. They fear that they will be forced to become Christians. Understandably the notion fills them with outrage.'

Amy felt woefully ignorant. Madeline was so much better informed than she was. Army politics were something that were never discussed in the family house. She would pay more attention to them from now on.

'I knew the situation couldn't be as simple as Maud implied,' she said. 'Too many of us are blind to everything except what happens on our front lawns. I can't help but believe that if we took the trouble to understand the people and customs, most problems could be averted.'

'Why Amy, I didn't know that you felt like that,' Madeline said warmly. She gave her a hug. 'You are extraordinary. I'm beginning to think that you're the braver of us. You say just what you think and never mind the consequences. It's a good thing you aren't in the army, you'd be hung for sedition!'

Amy laughed, about to answer, when the sound of the brass band striking up *God Save The Queen* announced the arrival of the prince and his retinue. Amy and Madeline stood up, craning their necks to see through the crowds of people.

In the excitement of seeing her first Indian prince, Amy forgot all about politics.

The royal party was met by the governor and escorted through the imposing stone gates. All Amy could see was the tops of turbans and long-handled, peacock-feather fans.

Then, as the prince and his followers moved towards the lawn, the crowd parted and Amy had her first view of the royal household. There were a great many of them and an army of servants all dressed in white with orange turbans. Here and there she saw the vivid silk drapery of a sari.

In a gold chair, borne on the shoulders of servants, sat the prince. A bearded elderly man, he wore a turban blazing with jewels. His buttoned, knee-length jacket was embroidered all over with gold thread. Tight white trousers tapered down to gold, tooled-leather shoes.

The ladies and men of his household were all as richly dressed. Amy watched them pass. In the centre of the group, surrounded by servants waving peacock fans, there was a tall figure, whose stillness caught her eye. Everyone else was smiling and exchanging greetings, but he held himself aloof.

The tall young man wore a fitted jacket and narrow trousers of smoke-coloured silk. His turban was white and blazing with emeralds and diamonds. There was the gleam of precious stones in his ears, around his neck and on his wrists.

Amy was struck by the arrogance and pride in the young man's bearing. She could see only his profile as he looked around slowly, a haughty contemptuous expression on his face. His skin was smooth and golden and his profile as pure as a cameo.

There seemed something familiar about the young man. Amy found herself holding her breath. A suspicion was forming in her mind. She saw that same young man with his long black hair loose over his shoulders, his golden skin imprinted by shadows.

It couldn't be him – could it?

Before she could think better of it, she began pushing her way through the crowd. Heedless of the mutters of disapproval, she shouldered people aside.

'Excuse me. Let me pass please . . .' Why wouldn't they move out of her way! Now she was almost near the front of the crowd. Only one row of people stood between her and the prince's retinue.

There was a drubbing in her ears and the sound of the brass band sounded loud and discordant.

'Turn around. Look at me,' she whispered under her breath, willing the tall young man to notice her.

She thought he was going to walk straight past, then, slowly he turned his head. As if they had been joined by a cord, he looked directly at her. Pinned by his deep-set black eyes, she couldn't look away.

Oh Lord, it was really him. But he looked so different. In the temple he had worn simple farmer's clothes. Now he was dressed as richly as the prince. He looked bored by everything and everyone. It was plain that he despised her countrymen. Amy's heart plummeted. He must hate me too, she thought. And was surprised by the knifelike pain of disappointment that twisted her belly.

Then she ceased to think as the young man's almond-shaped eyes bored into her. She saw his eyes narrow and his interest quicken. He looked her over almost insolently, his gaze lingering on her face and hair.

Lifting her chin, she let him look. I'll not have him think that I'm in awe of him, she thought. She sensed that his coldness was an act, a way of protecting himself from unwanted attentions. She knew that he was anything but cold. Remembering the scene inside the temple, she smiled.

And, in that moment, she saw a change come over his face. The line of his mouth softened and his eyes grew less fierce. His beauty made her weak at the knees. For a full two seconds he returned her smile, his full lips parted to reveal perfect white teeth, then, before heads began to turn in curiosity, he turned away and carried on walking after the prince.

Amy couldn't move. She felt seared by his smile. In the brightly-lit garden he had looked as vibrant and enigmatic as a god. She had to find out who he was.

150

'There you are,' Madeline said at her elbow. 'Where did you get to? I've been looking everywhere for you.'

'I've seen him,' Amy said faintly, grasping her friend's sleeve.

'Seen who?'

'The . . . man from the temple. He's here, with the prince.'

'No! Is he? You're sure. I can't believe it. Point him out to me.'

So Amy did, although all Madeline could see was the back view of the tall young man wearing grey. For a moment Madeline studied the man. She shook her head.

'I can't tell anything from this angle. I need to get a really close look.' She grabbed for Amy's hand. 'Come on, follow me. If we're quick we can get a place at the table near to where the prince and the highest officials are to sit.'

'But what about the place cards? The order of seating has all been worked out carefully. We'll have been placed a mile away from the top table.'

Madeline laughed. 'Amy Spencer! Do you mean to tell me that you're going to let a little thing like that stop us? Cards can be swopped, can't they?'

Amy threw her a scandalised grin. 'I didn't think of that. There'll be hell to pay afterwards, but let's do it!'

Ravinder sat at one end of the head table, drumming his long fingers on the spotless white cloth. Inwardly he was seething. He did not want to be here amongst the stuffy British men and their vapid wives. His favourite elephant was about to give birth and he ached to be beside her. He knew that the mahouts would ensure that nothing went wrong, but still he wished that he could be present.

He sighed inwardly and stifled a yawn. These events were so dreary. He was not fooled by the smiles and pleasant words, the British despised his people. No matter if his father was a prince, to the army officers they were all 'damned darkies'. It might be necessary for his father to maintain good relations with the foreigners who ruled his country but Ravinder would give them only token politeness.

He glanced idly down the avenue of tables, each gleaming with polished silver and crystal glasses, realising with surprise that he was looking for *her*.

The single high spot of this event had been the glimpse of the woman in the crowd; the woman with the sun in her hair. He had never seen such colouring; that milk-white skin, marigold hair and eyes like a she-tiger. But it had not been her looks alone which had so impressed him.

It was the openness of her expression, the frank approval. She found him attractive and didn't trouble to hide the fact. Even rarer in a woman of her class was the fact that she looked at him as if he was simply a man – not an Indian man.

There was something else too – recognition? Extraordinary, but there it was. Something within him responded to the woman. Indeed his blood leapt at the sight of her. Even in the few seconds they had gazed at each other he felt as if he had somehow absorbed the smell and feel of her. She was vanilla and almonds. Her pale skin would be as cool as marble under his palm, her wonderful hair would be silky and hay-scented.

He was used to taking women when he wanted them and his responses were fiery and finely honed but, this time, he fought down the ready desire. It was not likely that he would see the flame-haired woman again. That was good. A woman like that could be trouble.

She was probably married or betrothed to an officer in the army and the British guarded the virtue of their women well. In their own way the British women were prisoners, just as much as the Muslim women who were kept in purdah by their men.

Ravinder smiled inwardly. He was wealthy and powerful enough to make up his own rules; and frequently did. The women of his household were given a great deal of freedom and he found their independence and informed views stimulating.

There would even be room in the *zenana* for the striking British woman – if such a thing was possible. He thought of Shalini's face and almost laughed aloud. How his beloved half-sister would hate to have a new rival for his affections. She was as jealous as a cat, falling into sulky moods whenever he took a new lover.

The unlikely scenario of the British woman reclining amongst the dusky beauties of the *zenana* amused him and lightened his mood. He began to eat, finding the food surprisingly good. Even the fact that, as a minor son he was not given the honour of sitting next to his father, the prince, ceased to annoy him.

He would do his duty and pay his respects to the officers and their wives – those women with their washed-out looks and pinched expressions. Later he would slip away. It was still possible that he would be there when his elephant gave birth.

Amy ignored the expressions of outrage as she took her place at table. She smiled serenely at the officers sitting opposite and at their wives on either side of her.

It was difficult not to laugh as she imagined how much more furious would be the couple who had been relegated to the seats which Madeline and herself were meant to occupy. But none of them mattered. From here she could just see Ravinder, as she now knew he was called. The towering centrepiece on the table hid her from him, but she was able to watch him throughout the meal.

She hardly touched the procession of dishes which

were placed in front of her, too excited to do more than nibble at the almond soup, followed by fish, beef olives, quails, quenelles of partridge and other savouries. When the desserts arrived, she ate a meringue filled with mango cream. Ravinder, she saw, ate heartily of the dishes especially prepared by the Indian cook. Her eyes hardly left him, though she took care to be discreet and not attract too much attention to herself.

They had finished eating now at the top table. The governor stood and everyone else began getting up and moving off to the place where entertainments had been set up. Hurriedly, Amy swallowed the last of her meringue and dabbed at her lips with her napkin. Smiling politely at those sitting closest to her, she rose to her feet.

'Do excuse me, won't you. I'm in need of some air. I feel a little faint.'

'Well, really. Young people today . . .' someone said loudly.

Amy ignored the comment. She had left the table before the scandalised muttering broke out and she didn't look back. Lifting her chin and squaring her shoulders she followed the procession of dignitaries onto a cleared area of lawn.

The military band was playing a waltz and the lanterns danced like fireflies in the fresh breeze. The prince's retinue were seating themselves on chairs and cushions in an especially constructed, open-fronted marquee.

Amy hesitated in the shadow of an enormous banana tree. She wanted to get closer to the marquee, but knew that she couldn't strike out alone across the empty expanse of lawn. Fairly quivering with impatience she stood behind the tree, resigned to waiting until she could slip into the marquee unnoticed amongst the crowds of revellers. A deep, cultured voice at her side made her jump.

'Good evening,' Ravinder said, in barely accented English. 'Are you not joining in the festivities?'

Amy swallowed hard. Close up Ravinder was almost overpowering. He towered over her by at least a foot and his smooth golden skin looked luminous in the darkness. A cloud of perfume came from him. She smelt something citrus with woody undertones.

Her response to his nearness was immediate. She was aware of a pulse beating strongly in her neck, a prickle of heat under her corset. He smiled, a mere lifting of the corners of his sculpted mouth, and she thought, he's aware of the effect he has on me. It amuses him.

For some reason that angered her. He thought she was a plaything. No doubt someone like him was used to getting everything he wanted.

'I . . . was just taking the air. It was hot on the terrace,' she said stiffly.

He nodded gravely. 'And you do not enjoy these occasions?'

'No. I do not,' she said, meeting his eyes boldly. 'Perhaps for the same reasons as you.'

She saw the surprise on his face. Then he laughed, the sound of it deep and husky. He bent closer.

'It would please me to find something that you would enjoy. Unfortunately I have to leave now or we could discuss your likes and dislikes at length. If I invited you to come with me on a tiger hunt, would you come?'

Before she could stop herself she said, 'I do not relish seeing animals being killed.'

His black eyebrows rose. 'An unpopular view in your country, I imagine. You prefer life to death? I too, like many of my people. Then, will you come riding with me? I can promise that you will not regret the experience. Bring one of your women friends or an ayah along as a chaperone if you wish.'

As Amy looked up into his face, she felt a tremor of

fear. This man was dangerous for her; not in a violent or bad way. He was much too attractive, too charming. Beneath that cool exterior burned an intelligent and passionate man. She found that she liked Ravinder and that made the attraction between them all the stronger.

His dark eyes flickered over her face, her neck, her hair. He seemed fascinated by everything about her. The feeling was mutual. She knew that it would be better to walk away, to make some excuse and refuse his invitation. But she knew that this was what she craved. Why else had she been pursuing him since the moment she set eyes on him?

'Thank you. I'd like to ride with you,' she said.

'You will come? Excellent. I will come to your house tomorrow. It will be early, before the sun is hot.'

For a moment she thought of asking him to meet her somewhere less public. Then she thought of Maud Harris's face when she saw her riding beside the prince. Oh it would be priceless.

Hiding a smile, she nodded.

'I'll be ready. I rise early and often ride in the early morning.'

Ravinder inclined his head. 'Very well. I shall anticipate our engagement. And now – I really do have to leave.'

Amy was disappointed, although she could not have said why. Ravinder's manners were perfect. Somehow she had expected more. She looked up at him through lowered eyelids and said, 'That's a great pity.'

'It is indeed,' Ravinder said softly, reaching for her hand.

Amy was wearing elbow-length white gloves. Ravinder lifted her hand, bringing it towards his lips. With his other hand he unfastened the three mother-of-pearl buttons at her wrist, and spread the opening so that the pale flesh beneath was exposed.

When he pressed his lips to her skin, Amy shuddered. The feel of his firm, hot mouth on her wrist sent shivers down her spine. He did not kiss her once, but three times, lingeringly as if he loved the feel of her pulse fluttering beneath his lips.

Raising his head he smiled down at her. She saw the desire in his eyes and knew that he could read the same expression on her face. She did not try to hide it.

'Until tomorrow, Amy,' he said.

She swayed towards him, but he was already gone, slipping out of the shadows and striding towards the retainers who waited for him. Ravinder knew her name. He must have asked someone to find out who she was, since she hadn't told him herself.

The realisation that he was seriously interested in her filled her with joy. For he was, quite simply, the most handsome, mysterious man she had ever met.

Amy's hands trembled as she dressed the next morning. She could hardly fasten the buttons on her high-necked white blouse. She managed it eventually and checked her appearance in the cheval glass.

She looked fresh and young in the pin-tucked blouse and khaki riding skirt, her waist defined by a broad leather belt. Her topi was covered with a white veil, which would protect her pale skin from the sun.

Her mother was dressed and waiting with freshly-brewed coffee when Amy emerged on the verandah. Amy knew that her mother had told all her friends that her daughter was going riding with the young prince. There would be many eyes watching when she rode down the street with him. Madeline arrived, bringing with her the two ayahs who were to accompany them.

'I must speak with you urgently,' she said to Amy, taking her to one side.

'What is it?' Amy asked.

'It's about Ravinder. I've seen how you look at him

157

and I thought you should know what is said about him.'

'Go on,' Amy said, knowing that whatever Madeline told her it wouldn't make any difference.

'One of the ayahs, a village girl, has told me about him. It appears that he is one of the prince's many sons, by a minor wife, and is not likely to inherit a position of power. Because of this the prince has let him run wild, giving him his own palace and an allowance. He is said to pursue any woman he wants and to enslave them utterly. No one is safe from his advances.' She paused, her lovely blue eyes troubled.

'There is something else,' Amy stated. 'I can see it in your face. Tell me all of it.'

'Ravinder is rumoured to dabble in black magic. Some say that he's a witch.'

Amy laughed. 'And you believe that? Isn't that what's always been said about those who are different? I'm not going to listen to the ravings of some village woman, who's probably jealous because Ravinder passed her by!'

Madeline grinned. 'My sentiments exactly! I do not sense anything evil about Ravinder, but he is fascinating and as handsome as a god. I can quite believe that it is possible to lose your mind over him. Are you sure that you know what you're doing? You could find that you have a tiger by the tail.'

Amy was about to answer, when she heard the hiss of her mother's indrawn breath. Suddenly Mrs Spencer clapped her hands to her face.

'Oh heavens! Just look at that.'

Into view came a parade of elephants, the cries of the mahouts clear on the still, morning air. Amy began to laugh and Madeline joined in.

'I thought we were to be riding horses,' she said. 'But this looks much more fun! Oh won't our neighbours be envious?'

As the elephants drew nearer Amy saw that the leader of them was an enormous tusked beast. Each of the elephants was decked with tooled-leather trappings and carrying a canopied howdah on its back. Ravinder sat on the foremost elephant, resplendent in the magnificent gilded howdah.

Halting outside the bungalow, the mahout gave a word of command, and the elephant knelt down. Ravinder descended nimbly. After greeting Amy's mother, he helped Amy to climb into the howdah and took his seat at her side. In no time at all Madeline and the two ayahs were in place and the little parade moved off.

Amy soon became used to the alarming swaying motion of the elephant and began to feel at ease. The bungalows and station church looked very small from her vantage point. In the distance shrouded by mist she could see the area that was Bombay.

She waved at Maud Harris and Edith Taverner who hadn't been able to resist stepping out into the street to watch them pass.

Soon they reached the edge of the station and the mahouts urged their mounts onto a path which led into the undergrowth.

'Where are we going?' Amy asked Ravinder, acutely aware of his nearness in the restricted space of the howdah.

'On a tour of the area my family owns – or used to own,' he said, trying unsuccessfully to hide the bitterness in his voice. 'And then on to my house. I have something I want to show you.'

Amy stole a glance at Ravinder when he wasn't looking. He looked startlingly handsome in a tightly-fitting jacket of dark blue silk over slim white trousers. Leather boots encased his legs to the knee and his white turban gleamed with sapphires and tufts of egret's feathers.

She hardly noticed the scenery or the heat of the sun,

Ravinder's presence commanded all of her attention. Now and then he would smile at her or offer her a drink of the fruit juice, packed in ice, which was stored inside a seat. Once he stretched out his hand to adjust the veil over her face. She felt the lightest brush of his fingers against her cheek, but it was enough to send a dart of lust straight to her groin.

She had to muffle the sigh which rose in her throat. Her reactions to him astonished and shamed her. She seemed unable to control the erotic tension which was building inside her. If he had told her to pleasure him, now, while the mahout had his back turned to them, she would have done so willingly.

Ravinder looked at her then and she crimsoned. He knew that she wanted him. But he couldn't know how much.

There was more than sexual attraction between Ravinder and herself. She was aware of everything about him, his strong, sensitive hands, the set of his head, the way his dark eyes would lighten when he laughed.

No one, not Magnus or Jay Landers had made her feel this way. She knew now about his reputation, but it made no difference to the way she felt about him. In fact the hint of danger only added an edge to her desire.

Inside her was something that felt like hunger. But it was more concentrated, gnawing away at her like a live coal. The desire was not just centred in the moist, pulsing place between her legs, it seemed to be all over her. The place on her wrist, where he had kissed her, seemed to tingle and burn.

She found herself longing fearfully for the moment when they would be alone together.

It was cool inside the elephant house after the brightness of the morning. Ravinder took Amy's hand to lead her inside.

He felt how her fingers trembled in his and he smiled

to himself. Soon they would enjoy each other. What a feast that would be. He had been longing to put his hands on her since the moment they met under the tree at Government House.

But first, he had promised to show her something.

'You remember that I had to leave the party early, last night? There is the reason why. Can you see her in the darkness? I have named her Ayesha.'

He was pleased to see the look of wonder and delight on Amy's face as she peered into the stall at the baby elephant.

'Oh Ravinder. She's beautiful. I've never seen anything so sweet. Do all new-born elephants have fuzzy heads like that and smooth skins?'

He smiled and slipped his arm around her waist. 'Yes, they do. I'm glad you like her. You must come and see her again, when she has grown a little. Come, we should go now. I do not want to alarm the mother.'

Amy leaned into him as they walked down the central aisle. He was conscious of the slight weight of her against his side and something inside him gave way. Pulling her into a cleaned empty stall he pushed her up against the wall and began kissing her.

She opened her mouth under his lips and he pushed his tongue inside, tasting and savouring her. His lingam was strongly erect and he pushed it against her, half-expecting her to pull away or exclaim in disgust.

She did neither. She made a little sound of eagerness in her throat and he wrapped his arms around her neck.

Ravinder wanted to show how much he could please her, teasing the responses from her body, while her sighs made music for his ears. But he was hot and ready for her now and he couldn't wait. He knew that she felt the same. So be it then. There would be time enough for gentleness later.

Moving his hands down her body, he began to lift her skirts.

Amy slid down into the clean straw with Ravinder's body half covering her own. Her topi came off and rolled into the corner, but she paid it no heed.

The tide of lust was rising within her. All she could think about was uncovering herself, so that he could push his hard cock into her body. She had thought of nothing else for hours and she knew that her quim was awash, the lips hugely swollen and her pleasure bud pushed out into an aching little knot.

She had not wanted to lie with him in a stable, but that didn't matter now. The only thing that did matter was that he did it to her.

'Yes. Oh yes . . .' she whispered, as he pushed aside the open crotch of her drawers and thrust his hand inside.

She opened her legs, shuddering as his long fingers slid up the furrow of her engorged sex. He grunted as he discovered how wet and ready she was and Amy pushed herself against his hand. His thumb was pressing on her bud, stroking and circling and she gave a little sob of wanting.

Never had she felt so desperate for easement. When he said to her, 'Uncover your breasts. Give them to me,' she tore at her blouse buttons, already anticipating the hot wet mouth that would suckle her.

She couldn't think, she could only feel, only obey him as he urged her to hold her breasts up to him. Oh God, he had pushed his fingers into her and was circling them and she was thrusting herself towards him, impaling herself on his hand. Tearing open her blouse and hearing a button pop free, she struggled to loosen the neckline of her chemise. The ribbon slackened and she lifted her breasts free.

'Hold them. Yes. Squeeze them,' Ravinder murmured as he used his free hand to loosen his trousers.

Amy held her breasts up for him, pushing them together so that the nipples were side by side, her

162

cleavage high and deep. Ravinder gave a groan and
bent his head to mouth her nipples, lipping them and
grazing them with his teeth. His fingers, buried inside
her, thrust and pressed on the sensitive pad behind her
pubic bone. The joint pleasure flowed together, became
one tingling, soaring ache. Amy arched her back and
climaxed, feeling her flesh convulse around his fingers.

Ravinder smiled down at her and removed his hand.
She felt the hot, blunt head of his cock. He did not
thrust at her, but pressed down a little so that he was
collared by her puffed-up sex-lips.

'Do you want my lingam inside you?' he said, his
voice harsh and breathless. 'Your yoni is tight and wet.
Very wet. She weeps for love of my lingam.'

Amy lifted her legs and let them fall open. She loved
the feeling of the big, ridged cock-head lodged just
inside her vagina. Reaching up she placed her hands on
Ravinder's smooth golden jaw and drew his mouth
down to her. How she loved his lips. She wanted to
have his tongue inside her mouth, to be doubly pierced
by him when he entered her quim – or her yoni. She
liked the way he said that.

She gave a muffled whimper when he slid smoothly
into her. Her womb fluttered as Ravinder butted against
it and she cried out at the visceral pleasure as he
churned against her. His heavy balls brushed against
her upturned buttocks and she rose to meet him, thrust
for thrust.

Her tongue duelled with his and she felt straw
prickling her legs and bare shoulders, but she ignored
the discomfort, wholly absorbed in the strong, rhythmic
plunges of his lingam. Ravinder's hands found her
breasts and he palmed them, rubbing them together as
he thrust hard and deep.

Amy let her head fall back and felt him mouthing her
neck. He was near now, she sensed it and she too was
on the brink of another orgasm.

163

'Tell me when you do it . . .' Ravinder groaned.

She realised that he was holding back, waiting for her to crest with him.

As he pushed into her slowly, with great control, the ripples of pleasure built to a peak.

'I'm . . . spending . . .' she gasped. 'Oh God. I'm doing it – now.'

With a groan Ravinder surged against her, his lingam buried inside her to the hilt. At the last moment he drew out of her and spilt himself on her petticoats. She felt the way he thrashed and grunted and was surprised by the strength of his reactions.

After a while, he propped himself on his elbow and looked at her. Stroking her cheek with one finger, he smiled.

'This was not how I imagined it for you. I apologise for the roughness of our couch.'

She laughed. 'I did not notice. My need for you was too great. All I could think of was having you inside me.'

'You're an unusual woman, Amy. Fascinating as well as beautiful. Come. Let me help you up. We'll go into my private pavilion and I'll have my women attend you. Then I'll show you that I'm not always such a brutish lover.'

'You mean . . . we can do this again?'

'Why not? Don't you want to.'

Amy linked her arms around his neck. She knew now that Ravinder was her nemesis and she could no more resist him than stop breathing. Perhaps she ought not to let him know this. But it was already too late to be anything but honest. For good or ill, she was under his spell.

'There's nothing I'd rather do,' she said against his mouth.

Chapter Eleven

The pavilion Ravinder spoke of was a domed building of white marble set in an expanse of lush
greenery. It was placed some way from the main
building of the palace and connected to it by a path
made of many small glittering tiles.

Ravinder led Amy through an archway and into a
spacious domed room, where women lay around on
low couches, talking excitedly. Carved ivory tables held
dishes of sweetmeats and hookah pipes. Amy had the
feeling that she was the main topic of conversation and
her fears were confirmed when all eyes turned towards
her and the women fell silent.

'It is your beauty which dazzles them,' Ravinder
whispered in her ear. 'The news of my interest in you
has travelled fast. Do not be alarmed. They might view
you as a rival for my affections, but no one will dare to
risk offending you.'

Amy braved a smile, although she felt under dressed
and horribly conspicuous in her skirt and blouse. The
scene before her was like something out of the *Arabian
Nights*, a picture book which she had loved as a child.

All the women were beautifully groomed, their hair

gleaming and gold jewellery flashing from necks and wrists. They wore saris of red and orange silk or loose tunics and trousers in vivid blues and greens. Their garments were sewn with beads which shimmered as they moved.

Amy saw Madeline and tried to catch her friend's eye. Madeline was reclining on a bed which was swaying gently, little bells tinkling on its chains. She looked completely at ease and was deep in conversation with a slightly-built woman wearing red, who had her back turned to Amy.

'Come,' Ravinder said, 'I want you to meet my sister, Shalini.'

As Ravinder led Amy across the room, the soft buzz of conversation was resumed. Madeline looked up as Amy approached and smiled, but there was something odd in her expression. Then, as the slender woman in red turned, Amy saw the reason for Madeline's consternation.

She hardly heard Ravinder introducing her. Her eyes were riveted on the strikingly lovely woman who was regarding her with huge dark eyes.

Shalini was the woman she had seen Ravinder making love to in the temple.

'Will you come this way,' Shalini said to Amy when Ravinder had left the room, having promised to come to her when she had bathed and rested. 'I will entertain you and your friend in my private apartments.'

Amy flashed a quizzical look at Madeline. She was horrified by her new knowledge. It seemed that the stories about Ravinder were true. He obeyed no laws but his own. To be having sexual relations with his own sister – it was too awful. Part of her wanted to run away and never return. But she was aware that her desire for him was not diminished and her fascination was, if anything, even stronger.

When Madeline stood up and linked arms with her, Amy allowed her friend to lead her through an archway after Shalini. Shalini's ankle bracelets clashed together as she moved across the smooth marble floor. She walked with a gliding motion which was both graceful and languid.

'Madeline, wait,' Amy whispered. 'You know who this woman is?'

Madeline patted her arm. 'It is not quite what you think. Shalini is Ravinder's half-sister. They had different mothers – something which is common amongst princes. They were educated separately and lived in different areas of the palace. They never met until they were adults.'

'Even so . . . It's not right, is it?'

'Who can say? Their lives are their own. What harm are they doing? Are you revolted by the thought of Ravinder and Shalini being lovers?'

'Yes. No. I'm not sure . . .'

Madeline laughed softly. 'Look into your heart, Amy. Your British blood is colouring your judgement. Why do you care what Ravinder and Shalini do together? Is it possible that your emotions are clouded by something other than moral indignation?'

As they travelled down cool marble-lined corridors, Amy mulled over Madeline's words. Her friend was very astute. She realised that she was less censorious than jealous. Yes, that was it. She could not rid her mind of the images of Ravinder and Shalini in the temple.

A male servant pulled aside the dampened vetiver screens which hung across the doorway to Shalini's rooms. A waft of jasmine met them as they stepped inside. Amy's first impression was of fabulous colours. The walls were covered with tiles depicting extracts from Hindu myths. Huge metal containers held palms and flowering shrubs. Every surface seemed to be gilded and glowing with precious gems. More male servants moved silently through the room, passing by on some task or other.

Amy was captivated by the opulence all around. Through another archway, she glimpsed the still, greenish surface of an indoor pool. From this room, four handsome young men, dressed only in loose, white silk trousers and broad leather belts, appeared. They pressed their palms together and bowed to Shalini.

'Bring food and drink for my guests,' Shalini said imperiously. 'We will eat in my chamber. After we have taken our ease you will attend us. My guests shall benefit from your . . . singular expertise.'

Amy realised that they hadn't seen a single woman since they stepped into Shalini's private rooms. It seemed that Shalini chose to be waited on by male servants entirely. She hid her shock. But surely Shalini must have women to attend to her clothes, dress her hair, and perform the many intimate tasks which an ayah would do for a lady. It was unthinkable that men should help Shalini disrobe or worse – bathe.

Shalini seemed aware of Amy's curiosity. Her dark eyes sparkled with amusement. She turned to Amy and Madeline, flashing them a brilliant smile.

'This way, if you please.'

The octagonal chamber they stepped into, was filled with a diffuse, golden-green light. The afternoon sun blazed through pierced window screens, fracturing in geometric shadows onto the green malchite floor. Brass bowls were filled with smoking incense; pungent and scented with otto of roses. There was the sound of running water. Amy saw that silver peacocks spouted jets of water into marble basins.

As she took her place on a cushioned dais, Amy felt her stomach tighten with excitement. This place was so opulent, so arousing to all her senses. The heavy perfume, the veil of blue-tinged smoke that hung low

over the carved wooden tables, the exquisite gold statues of various gods and goddesses, these things were
so pleasing to her.

This was the real India, mysterious and fabulous, not
the watered-down anglicised version of the army
cantonment.

She was aware too that it was the peerless beauty of
Ravinder's half-sister which drew her fascinated gaze.
Everything about Shalini; her dense dusky skin with
the bloom of ripe figs; her small features; the graceful
movements of her hands; the hint of promise in her
words, all these things and more spoke of a deep and
earthy sensuality.

Amy was finding it less incredible by the minute that
Ravinder had fallen under his half-sister's spell.

'It seems that you have caught my brother's eye,'
Shalini said, breaking into her thoughts. 'It is most
unusual for Ravinder to invite a British woman to this
house or to take her to the elephant house. Those
animals are his prized possessions.'

Amy looked for any trace of malice on Shalini's face
and found none. She smiled.

'Ravinder is handsome and cultured. What woman
would not be charmed by him?

Shalini seemed pleased by her answer.

'Ravinder does not give his favour lightly. Take care
that you value what he offers you,' she said.

And Amy had the feeling that she was being warned
not to offend Ravinder. How extraordinary. Did Shalini
know what they had done in the elephant house? She
seemed quite amiable about sharing her brother-lover
with another woman.

They conversed amiably while they ate, Madeline
adding a comment now and then. Madeline and Shalini
were perfectly at ease with each other. It seemed that,
while she and Ravinder had been making love in the

stable, Madeline and Shalini had been forming a friend-ship of their own.

Shalini's almond-shaped eyes often alighted on Madeline's face and her slender fingers brushed against Madeline's arm at every opportunity. Madeline seemed to be enjoying the attention. It was not surprising that Shalini found Madeline beautiful. The Indian woman and her brother were obviously connoisseurs of lovely things.

The handsome young men moved back and forth between the women, serving them with small dishes of spicy snacks and pouring cups of thick, sweet *lassi*, flavoured with ground almonds and cardamom and topped with squares of yoghurt cream.

Amy tried not to stare at the half-naked young men; all of whom were regular-featured and well-formed. She ate with relish, hungry after the elephant ride and the energetic coupling with Ravinder.

The bold glances of the handsome servants made her feel strange. One in particular seemed unable to keep his eyes off her. It was pleasant to be admired, but the frank sexuality in his eyes made her feel uneasy and self conscious.

After the meal they relaxed against silken cushions. Shalini passed a hookah pipe around. Amy declined, but Madeline and Shalini smoked with relish. Dipping her hand into a basket, Shalini extracted something and laid it on her lap. At first Amy thought it was a piece of jewellery, then she saw that it was a green chameleon, with a tiny gold chain around its neck.

She watched fascinated as the tiny creature seemed to bleed colour as Shalini held it. Soon the chameleon was the rich, purple-brown colour of Shalini's skin. Tiring of playing with the creature, Shalini put it back in its basket. She stretched and stood up.

'It is so hot today. I'm sure that you must be

uncomfortable in all those petticoats. Take off your clothes and we will swim. My servants will attend us.'

Madeline needed no urging and began stepping out of her clothes. The bodice of her khaki riding costume fell to the floor, followed by her frilled corset cover. Two of the young men appeared silently beside her and began to gather up the garments.

Amy's hands felt stiff and cold. She did not think that she could manage to undo the many small mother-of-pearl buttons on her blouse. But she found that she didn't have to. She felt hands on her as the attentive young men began loosening her belt and removing her blouse and skirt.

She felt panicky. It seemed impossible to strip in front of all these people, but she did not know how to refuse.

The other women were already half-undressed. Shalini stood in a pool of bright silk fabric. As Amy watched, a servant unfastened the back of her short bodice and drew it down her arms. Shalini's high round breasts, peaked by large wine-red nipples, bobbed into view. An underskirt of red silk was slung low on Shalini's hips, serving to emphasise the narrowness of her waist. Her naval was deep and shadowed. A dark red jewel gleamed there, suspended from a tiny ring which pierced the tender skin.

Amy coloured and lowered her eyes, shocked by the enjoyment she gained from just looking at Shalini. She felt this way about Madeline, but to a lesser degree. It was surely natural to enjoy looking at beautiful things, but Shalini affected her strangely. Shalini was so – exotic, so sexual, unlike any woman she had ever seen before.

Perhaps part of Shalini's charm was her blood-tie with Ravinder. Amy desired Ravinder in a way that was visceral and bone-deep. She could not help but be aware that there was a reflection of that emotion in her reactions to his sister.

171

Tearing her eyes away from Shalini, Amy tried to calm herself. She dreaded the moment when she would stand naked beside the others, but the moment was imminent. Efficient but gentle hands drew her white blouse down over her shoulders and urged her to step out of the crumpled folds of her skirt.

She tried not to think of the way her breasts jutted over the top of her corset, the nipples barely covered by the lace on the low neckline of her chemise. Soon she was unlaced, her corset drawn free, and her chemise was lifted over her head. Stepping free of the froth of petticoats, she felt the sweetly-perfumed air caressing her bare skin.

'Take those garments to the women for repair,' Shalini said to a servant, glancing in Amy's direction.

Amy felt her face grow hot as she realised that Shalini had seen that there were buttons missing from her blouse and a slight tear on the front. Remembering how she had torn it, she felt a tingle of latent desire. Now she was sure that Shalini *did* know that Ravinder and herself had made love.

Amy caught sight of her reflection in a panel of tooled bronze. Beside the dusky darkness of Shalini and Madeline's light brown skin, her own milk-white colour seemed startling and insipid.

She felt horribly exposed. It was impossible to ignore the presence of the hovering servants. One of them in particular was raking her body with hot eyes. Shalini too was staring at her with undisguised fascination and Amy could not stop herself blushing from her toes upwards.

Shalini laughed delightedly.

'How prettily your skin changes colour. You are like my tiny chameleon. But you have no cause to feel ashamed. You are as slender as a lotus stalk, except for the rich fruits of your breasts. And the hair on your yoni is so bright. Do you dye it with saffron?'

172

Hardly able to believe the intimate nature of the conversation, Amy attempted to answer without stammering.

'My colouring is natural,' she said.

'How extraordinary. I can see why Ravinder is captivated by you. My brother has an eye for beauty. He could not resist this white goddess, a pillar of marble touched by the sun.'

Shalini reached out and touched Amy's shoulder, trailing her fingertips down over the length of one arm. Then she smiled and padded into the adjoining room. Her unbound hair hung down to her hips, screening her body with silky night-black tresses.

Madeline reached for Amy's hand.

'You can swim I suppose? I never asked you.'

'I used to swim in the river on our estate in Sussex.'

'Good. Follow me. I'll race you!'

She let go of Amy's hand and ran after Shalini, her full breasts bouncing up and down. Infected by Madeline's mood Amy followed. All three women dived into the pool. Surfacing first, Amy wiped water from her eyes and laughed with delight. Shalini bobbed up next to her, her hair swept back as shiny and sleek as a seal. Silver drops ran down her flawless skin.

The water felt wonderful and Amy lost all sense of self as she swam and splashed with total abandon. Even the presence of the male servants did not deter her from floating on her back, her hair streaming out behind her and the white mounds of her breasts and her pubis pushing up through the water.

After some time, Shalini swam to the side of the pool and climbed out. She walked over to one of the low wooden couches, which were set in shallow alcoves all down one wall. Immediately one of the servants stepped forward to attend her, washing her hair and pouring hot, perfumed water over her skin.

Shalini sighed and lay face down as the young man

scooped a paste made of almonds and cream from a glass jar and began to massage it into her skin.

'Lie on the couch and one of my young men will see to your needs,' Shalini said to Amy as she emerged from the pool.

Madeline was having her hair washed now and there seemed to be nothing for Amy to do but follow suit. It felt strange to have a man's strong young hands on her body. But she had to admit that it felt good. The servant rubbed her hair with perfumed soap and began massaging her scalp with his fingertips. Amy relaxed under his touch.

The servant attending her was the young man who had been eyeing her with interest from the moment she set foot in Shalini's rooms. He had smooth dark hair, light brown skin, and wonderful liquid brown eyes. His lashes were as long and dark as a girl's.

'What is your name?' she asked him.

She sensed his surprise in the altered pressure against her scalp. Was she not supposed to pay any attention to servants? He hesitated before replying, then said quietly.

'Jalsa, memsahib.'

'You have a light touch, Jalsa,' she said.

'I am happy to serve you,' he said, his voice pleasant and with only a trace of an accent. 'I give you much more pleasure. You will see.'

Amy closed her eyes as Jalsa rinsed her hair and body, then bade her lie on her stomach. He began massaging her skin with a creamy paste, followed by a jasmine scented cream. Lulled into a trance by the rhythmic movements, Amy gave herself up to the pleasant sensations.

Jalsa moved his palms across her shoulders and down the sides of her waist. He stroked downwards over the small of her back and kneaded her buttocks. As he lifted the firm flesh and rolled it under his palms, she felt him drawing her sex upwards. As he exerted pressure downwards her buttocks parted, giving him a clear view of the shadowed valley between them.

She tried not to think of what he must be able to see, but was horribly aware that the tight pink rose of her anus was exposed and forced to gape a little each time he rolled her buttocks apart. If he squeezed and pressed lower down, at the underswell of her bottom, he would be able to glimpse her vagina as her sex-lips were pulled open by the rolling motion of his thumbs.

She sensed that each of his movements were deliberate and calculated to build the sexual tension within her. And indeed, she found herself longing for him to handle her ever more intimately.

It was possible to lie still and pretend that this was just a relaxing massage and allow the sensations to creep up on her. Jalsa was patient and did not seek to hurry her, rather he seemed set on prolonging her enjoyment.

'Does the memsahib wish me to proceeed?' Jalsa said, his voice soft and deferential.

'Mmmm,' she murmured, turning her cheek and resting it on the back of her hand. 'Do whatever you think necessary.'

'As you wish.'

Spreading his fingers he stroked the firm swell of her flesh, somehow palpating the skin so that tiny tremors spread right through to her belly. Amy sighed with pleasure. The almost casual, expert handling of her buttocks was very arousing. And now the subtle, referred pressure began to awaken her sex.

Each time he leaned into her, pressing gently downwards, her pubis was pushed against the wood of the bench. Her sex was tightly closed, but inside its fleshy prison her bud began to swell and throb. The familiar heat and tension gathered strength and she felt herself growing moist and receptive.

At first she tried to hide the signs of her arousal, but Shalini's soft groans and Madeline's sighs told her that the other women were receiving the same treatment. Shalini seemed to have no such inhibitions at all.

Amy chanced a quick look sideways and saw that the Indian woman was arching her back and thrusting her buttocks wantonly towards her servant. The young man attending her had one hand buried between Shalini's parted thighs and was moving it back and forth.

'You like to watch while my mistress and your friend are pleasured?' Jalsa said obligingly.

Amy jumped guiltily. The denial rose to her lips, but Jalsa sounded so matter of fact, that she found herself nodding. Jalsa moved the wooden bench so that she had a clear view of the other women, both of whom seemed oblivious to anything but their own pleasure.

Shalini had turned onto her back and one of the handsome young man was pressing her knees in towards her chest. Her upturned sex looked shockingly red and swollen. She emitted a series of hoarse little grunts as a second servant dipped his fingers into a jar of sticky paste and rubbed it all over her pouting sex-lips.

Amy could see how the stickiness caused the delicate skin to drag a little as if it clung to the servants' fingers. Shalini closed her eyes in ecstasy as the servant tapped her stiffly protruding bud with the pad of one finger.

'Both of you – now,' Shalini breathed and moaned softly when one of the servants slipped two fingers inside her.

The other pinched and rolled her erect pleasure bud between finger and thumb, while slapping her upturned buttocks in a measured rhythm.

The sound of a palm hitting flesh was loud and shocking. Amy pressed her hand to her mouth to hold back a little moan of her own, as Jalsa parted her thighs and slipped his hand between her legs. Although per-

176

turbed by this new intimacy, she did not resist him. It was a relief to have his clever fingers parting her moist folds and seeking out the throbbing little pad in its hood of flesh.

Shalini's sharp cries of pleasure were a spur to Amy's aroused senses and she no longer tried to hold back. She began panting and arching her back, rubbing her pubis against the wooden couch as Jalsa slid his fingers up and down the slippery groove of her sex.

As he continued to move his hand, Jalsa knelt on the couch between her parted thighs, nudging her legs more widely apart. Amy didn't care now that the whole of her sex and parted flesh-valley were on show to him. Her one thought was her quest for release. She loved the feeling of being opened, her buttocks spread apart and the split pink plum of her sex hanging down moistly between them.

She felt the pad of Jalsa's thumb stroking across her anus and her quim trembled and pulsed. She tensed, thinking that he would penetrate that secret place, but he did not. His fingers slid inside her vagina and she gave an uncontrolled groan of pleasure. Her breasts were squashed almost flat against the wooden couch and her nipples yearned to be stimulated. She moved from side to side, rubbing the aching peaks against the smooth wood as Jalsa turned his fingers stroking her inner flesh walls and exerting a gentle pressure on her womb.

Shalini's buttocks glowed a dull dark red now. The sticky paste on her sex had liquefied and it ran down her buttocks in dark oily streaks.

'Hit me harder,' she screamed. 'That's it. I want to sting and burn. Ah . . . penetrate me more deeply . . .'

Madeline gave a little sob as the servant attending her began to slap her bottom gently. She writhed as the fingers which penetrated her were worked slickly in and out.

Amy was fast approaching a climax. Jalsa moved his fingers in and out of her and just at the moment when her pleasure crested and broke, he slapped her buttocks with his free hand. One, two, three blows crashed onto her bottom. Following on swiftly from the sharpness of pain came a tingling heat.

'Oh . . . oh . . . stop . . .' Amy whimpered, tipped over into a realm of sensation as yet unexplored.

Jalsa obeyed, running gentle fingers over the swell of her reddening bottom, his other hand still at work inside her. Amy sobbed as she came, her whole body shuddering and trembling.

After she had recovered somewhat, Jalsa completed her body massage. He was deft and efficient and there was once again the invisible barrier of mistress and servant between them. At length he said, 'Would you rise please, memsahib? There is refreshment in the adjoining room.'

Amy sat upright, her damp red hair cascading around her shoulders and down her back. Her skin glowed softly like a pearl. She stretched feeling completely relaxed and sated.

'Thank you Jalsa,' she said and he flashed her a surprised grin.

'It was a pleasure to serve you, memsahib. I hope that I have the honour of doing so again.' With a small bow, he backed away.

Amy followed Shalini and Madeline, who were making their way back to the adjoining room. The marble floor felt cool under her bare feet. She was aware that she was swinging her hips as she walked. The massage and sexual pleasure had made her aware of every inch of her skin. She felt vital and very much a woman.

She saw that Madeline and Shalini felt the same. The two women walked side by side and, as Amy watched, Shalini slipped her arm around Madeline's waist.

The prickle of jealousy surprised Amy. Madeline was her best friend. She did not like the thought of Shalini trying to usurp Madeline's affections. Then she realised that Madeline was leaning in towards Shalini, her hand coming up to rest lightly on the curve of the other woman's hip.

The gesture was no longer simply one of friendship, it was heavy with erotic possibilities.

Chapter Twelve

*A*my followed the two women into the chamber, unsure what to do next.

It was obvious that Madeline and Shalini only had eyes for each other. She felt troubled and excluded and did not know how to react. As she watched, Shalini drew Madeline into a close embrace and kissed her passionately.

How selfish they were. She might not have existed anymore. She thought of leaving them to themselves and going into the small courtyard garden which was visible through a stone archway, but she didn't dare to go outside naked. She looked around for a robe or veil to cover herself with, but the servants had removed all of their garments.

Then she saw Ravinder.

He was lying on a low couch, wearing a black silk, open-necked tunic and loose white silk trousers. She realised that he had been watching her for some time and the colour rose into her face. Had he also watched Jalsa pleasure her in the bath house?

Ravinder rose and moved towards her, his black brows dipping in a frown.

'Why do you wear this look of dismay?' he said. 'Do you not find pleasure in the company of Shalini? My sister offers potent pleasures for her guests. If she has been remiss or offended you in some way, she will be deeply concerned.'

He wore no turban and his black hair streamed over his shoulders. His beauty struck her anew. How striking he was, with his hawk-like looks. She thought that she would need a lifetime to tire of looking at him. They had been apart for little over an hour. Suddenly she could recall the taste of his mouth, the way he had grasped at her breasts. She felt a surge of desire for him and her already aroused sex tingled and fluttered.

'I . . . I was feeling left out, but I don't anymore,' she faltered.

Ravinder smiled, his dark eyes sweeping appreciatively over every detail of her nakedness. She was aware of the intensity of his eyes, the straight line of his dark brows and that particular set to his mouth which she was coming to recognise.

'Ah,' he murmured, glancing towards Shalini and Madeline. 'You envy your friend. Do you wish to join with her and Shalini?'

'No! That's not what I meant . . .' Amy stopped, unsure as to exactly what she *did* mean.

Her emotions were confused. She did not want to examine them too closely. Ravinder had put something into words which she had hardly begun to acknowledge. The jealousy she felt and the secret fascination was too new, too raw, to bring out into the open just yet.

Ravinder seemed aware of her inner turmoil. He smiled equably and stretched out his hand.

'No matter. Will you come and lie beside me? We have some hours before you must return home and there are many things I would show you. But first . . .'

He handed her a box made of sandalwood inlaid with

181

mother-of-pearl. She sat on the edge of the couch to open it. Inside, on a bed of embroidered black velvet, was a pair of tooled-gold earrings. The intricate gold lacework was hung with pearls, each one a perfect milky sphere.

Amy gave a cry of delight. 'They're beautiful. I've never seen anything like them.'

'Allow me,' Ravinder said, unhooking her neat silver earrings.

His fingers were cool on her skin as he slipped the gold wires into her ear lobes. The weight of the new earrings was unfamiliar. The pearls brushed against her neck as she moved. She stroked them, feeling how they absorbed the warmth of her skin.

'A perfect match for your colouring. The pearls will take on the lustre of your skin and grow more beautiful the more you wear them,' Ravinder said, bending his head to claim her mouth.

His mouth was firm on hers and his tongue pushed strongly and insistently into her mouth. Was he expecting to exact a price for his gift? No doubt that would have been the case in the circles she moved in normally, but Ravinder had no need to bribe her for her favours.

Besides, she thought with a smile, she was already naked – her body expertly groomed and prepared by Jalsa – and she was longing for Ravinder to make love to her again. With him she was utterly wanton. Just what would that busybody Maud Harris make of that?

Amy clung to Ravinder, her head reeling with the power of his kiss. When he moved away, she whispered against his lips, 'Thank you for the gift. I will treasure it.'

Ravinder didn't answer. His hand found her breast and he ran his thumb across the hardening nipple. She could feel the warmth of his chest through the thin silk. Pressing her palm to his tunic she rubbed it against his hard muscles, aware of his heartbeat. He seemed at the same time both vigorous and wholly male and possessed of ordinary human frailty.

Ravinder put her from him gently, turning her so that she was resting her back against his chest. Her head fitted into the hollow of his shoulder and she felt his lips moving through the tangle of her damp hair.

'Look there. Tell me what you see?' Ravinder said, pointing across the room to the shadowed alcove, where Shalini and Madeline lay in an intimate embrace.

'I don't know . . . I can't see properly. It's too dark.'

'Tell me, Amy,' he said sternly.

It cost her an effort to overcome her reluctance. Why was he doing this? Did he enjoy her embarrassment. She felt her cheeks grow warm.

'I . . . I see Madeline kissing Shalini,' she said slowly.

'And?'

'Oh, and now Madeline is sliding down Shalini's body and licking her breasts . . . Shalini is stroking Madeline's bottom. Oh they are shameless. I can't watch . . . I won't watch.'

She tried to turn her head away and Ravinder cupped her chin in one slim golden hand. His touch was gentle, but he held her in an implacable grip. She sensed that if she tried to turn away completely he would insist that she remained in position.

'Now my pearl, overcome your reluctance. Let us watch my sister and your friend as they pleasure each other. Trust me. Observing the sharing of the female power principle will make the fires of our passion all the stronger.'

Amy averted her eyes from Madeline and Shalini, trying to shut out their sighs and moans. She did not want to admit to a little shiver of guilty pleasure. She was sure that Ravinder saw through her façade of outrage. Gently but firmly, he was insisting that she faced up to her own negative reactions.

'But surely such a union is unnatural,' she said stubbornly.

Ravinder laughed huskily. 'You sound so . . . British! Unnatural. Why so? Ah I see that I must explain. In your culture the pleasures of the body are not celebrated. That is so?'

Amy nodded. 'People don't even talk about such things. I don't think many women like doing it, even with men. I've never heard of women doing those things together.'

'How very odd,' Ravinder said. 'In wealthy households like my father's, a girl is brought up with female companions called *Sakhis* who share her bath and her bed. A *Sakhi* adds her own qualities and experiences to those of her 'sister'. Often when a noblewoman marries she will take her *Sakhi* to live with her.'

'So many women indulge in shared pleasures?' Amy could not quite believe that something so astounding could be commonly practised amongst highborn Indian women.

'Certainly. Mutual caressing between women is encouraged in my culture. It is an expression of real caring. We consider it to be vitalising and auspicious. Now – no more explanations. See for yourself. Watch Shalini and your friend and you will see how pleasurable it can be. Does what they are doing seem wrong? You decide. Open your mind. Concentrate on the feelings in your yoni. You will find the experience arousing, I promise you.'

Hesitantly Amy raised her eyes.

Madeline now lay back on the couch her legs spread wide. Her lovely face was softened by desire and her light blue eyes glowed like aquamarines. Shalini lay to one side of Madeline, her hand stroking gently up the parted lips of Madeline's yoni. Inside the dark curling hair, Amy could see the moist red flesh of her aroused sex. It glistened wetly as Shalini moved her fingers, spreading open the fleshy lips so that she could circle the erect bud of pleasure.

Madeline clutched at her lover's shoulders, her moans muffled against Shalini's mouth. Her hips began to work as Shalini stroked her sensitive flesh and then pressed against the erect bud. While Madeline writhed and pushed against Shalini's hand, Shalini laughed softly, mouthing words of love and trailed her hand up over the thickly furred mound to the softly pouting belly.

After circling her navel with gentle fingers, she bent her head and began lapping at it with her tongue. Her hand now moved upwards again and she stroked the area between Madeline's breasts. Madeline uttered little groans of pleasure, her hands roving over Shalini's shoulders and tangling in the silken strands of her black hair.

'See how expert my sister is. She is stroking the whole of your friend's body. Soon her yoni will begin to secrete the nectar of the goddess. We consider these fluids to be highly beneficial.'

Despite her reluctance to watch, Amy began to find the spectacle arousing. It was just as Ravinder said. Her own yoni seemed to feel the echo of the pleasure which Shalini was giving to Madeline. Now Shalini moved, so that she was kneeling between Madeline's spread thighs.

'Yes. Oh yes . . .' Madeline murmured, moving her hands down her body as Shalini began kissing and licking her way down her inner thigh to the soft hollow behind her knee.

She repeated the caress with Madeline's other leg and then dipped her head and planted a firm, wet kiss directly on the red mouth of the spread yoni. Madeline gave an inarticulate cry and Amy felt a firm, hot throbbing response between her own thighs.

Ravinder slid his hands around Amy's waist and

185

moved them upward to cup her breasts. She sensed that he smiled when he discovered that her nipples had gathered into stiff little cones. He stroked her firm flesh gently, his fingertips brushing up and down the hollow of her cleavage. As he began rolling her nipples, he whispered in her ear.

'Do you not find the sight of two women sharing pleasure erotic, my pearl? Is not your yoni swelling and becoming dewy with your juices? Be honest now.'

Her mouth seemed to have dried. She managed to whisper, 'Yes. I have to confess that I do like watching . . .'

Little prickles of pleasure spread out from her nipples as Ravinder plucked at them. His words were arousing too and it was true that she was getting very hot and excited from watching Shalini pleasuring Madeline. Wicked images filled her mind of Shalini tonguing *her* sex, kissing *her* mouth, while Ravinder looked on approvingly.

When Ravinder slid one hand over her belly and cupped her sex, she rose up against him, turning her head so that she rubbed her cheek against his chest. The clean male smell of him was intoxicating. She felt the softness of his chest hair against her mouth and opened her lips, questing for his tight copper nipples. Finding one she took it between her lips, sucking and tasting, then she bit down on it gently.

She felt Ravinder's indrawn breath. 'Little cat,' he hissed delightedly.

Ravinder caressed her slowly, his movements mirroring the caresses which Shalini had used on Madeline. His fingers moved down to her belly and tugged gently at the indentation of her navel. When he stroked the red-gold curls on her pubis Amy parted her legs, wishing that he would move lower, but loving the way he teased her with light touches, allowing the tension to build and build within her body.

All the time he caressed her, she watched Shalini and Madeline, no longer even pretending to be uninterested. The soft sighs of pleasure, the sounds of lips sliding on skin, the moist sucking sounds of mouths on yonis, added an extra intensity to her own responses.

Ravinder's hand closed over her venus mound. Amy could not hold back a little groan as he slid his finger down to the hood which covered her bud. Gently he exerted pressure and smoothed the tiny hood back, lifting the erect bud and exposing it. The movement sent a throbbing heat straight to her womb. Amy arched her back and felt his lips on her neck, his breath hot in her ear.

When he told her to part her legs, she did so tensing her belly as he used two fingers to stroke either side of her straining bud. With subtle movements of his wrist he stroked and vibrated her folds, rocking the pad of one finger against the little cushion of flesh between her vagina and anus. Now and then he dipped into her vagina, moving around the inner flesh walls.

'Your yoni is lush and melting, my pearl. Taste the honey for yourself.'

Raising his hand, Ravinder stroked his wet fingers across Amy's lips. She slid her tongue over her mouth, absorbing the taste of her creamy juices and smelling the jasmine-perfumed musk of her vagina.

Twisting around from the waist, she linked her arms around Ravinder's neck.

'I want you,' she whispered. 'Do it now. How do you say it . . . Put your lingam in my yoni, please.'

He kissed the tip of her nose.

'Don't you know that a feast is to be savoured? I wish to partake of your yoni essence first.'

Ravinder pulled her down gently, so that her upper body rested against a pile of pillows. Quickly disrobing, he moved around and crouched between her thighs. He stroked the red-gold fleece around her sex, smoothing it back from the parting of her flesh-lips.

'You have a beautiful yoni. So pink and neat,' he said huskily. 'And now I'm going to taste you. Give me your essence, my pearl, that I may honour the gateway to life.'

He held her sex open with two fingers and she felt his warm breath on her bud. Then she almost cried out as he closed his mouth over the pulsing morsel and began to suck gently.

Magnus had used his mouth to give her pleasure but she had never felt anything like this. God, what was Ravinder doing to her? The most incredible sensations were spreading outwards from her groin in warm, tingling waves. His lips stroked her sensitive flesh and his tongue lolled against the hard bead of her bud. She was going to climax soon – very soon.

The feelings were wonderful, so subtle but somehow more intense than anything she had ever experienced. Ravinder's tongue felt smooth and hot. Sometimes he pushed it into her vagina, using it like a tiny lingam, and at other times he smoothed the whole oval area of her sex, bathing it with long slow licks.

Madeline moaned loudly and the sound of her friend's pleasure, the images which were imprinted on her sense, drove Amy into the throes of a deep and satisfying orgasm.

Ravinder sucked and lapped at her juices as she bucked against his mouth. She heard herself sighing and grunting and did not care. She had always been embarrassed about making noises when climaxing, but now she let herself go.

Amy let out her breath in a long sigh as Ravinder removed his mouth. She clutched at his shoulders and he smiled down at her. Did he know that she ached to be penetrated? It seemed that he did but he was not ready to give her that ultimate pleasure.

'Soon, my pearl. Soon,' he murmured.

Moving around so that his body covered hers, Ravinder placed one heavily muscled thigh on either side of her head. Amy did not need to be told what he wanted. His lingam, strongly erect and smelling of fresh male arousal was pointing down towards her. The stem of it was dark gold and the moist purplish glans was visible through the pouting cock-skin.

Opening her lips eagerly she took the covered glans into her mouth. He tasted warm and salty. She smoothed back the skin with her relaxed open mouth and suckled on his uncovered bulb. Pressing her tongue to the underside of his cock-shaft, she made tiny flicking movements across the tiny ridge where the skin joined the stem.

'Oh yes. My pale love. Honour my lingam as the Shiva lingam. Yes, yes. Suck me as if your mouth was a second yoni,' Ravinder whispered hoarsely.

Although Amy didn't understand everything he said, she found his words and the tone powerfully erotic. When he stretched his body out to cover her and began licking and kissing her sex again, she opened her mouth wide around his cock and took him deeply into her mouth.

The sensations in her mouth and sex seemed to merge, becoming one long moment of pleasure. The ripples of another orgasm swept over her, more gentle and unfocused this time. She closed her eyes as the inner pulsings subsided, and began sucking more strongly on the firm shaft.

Ravinder gave a hoarse sigh and lifted his head away from her sex. Encircling the base of his lingam with her curled fingers, she moved them up and down in time with the strokes of her mouth. His balls tightened and she knew that he would come soon. Gently he disengaged himself.

'Stop now, my pearl,' Ravinder said. 'What you are

189

doing is delightful but I must conserve my water of life if I am to take pleasure inside your yoni.'

Gathering her up in his arms, he lifted her so that she was sitting astride him with her legs on top of his. Supporting her buttocks with both hands, he eased her down onto his lingam.

Amy let her head fall back under its own weight as she sank onto the swollen cock-head. In this position, she was very aware of the swollen ridge just under the glans. As Ravinder lifted her up and down, working her on the shaft of his lingam, she felt the big glans stretching her entrance as it slid partway out.

She put her arms around Ravinder's neck and drew his mouth onto hers as her sex slid up and down on his quivering erection. Now and then he paused and stroked her body, while she sat completely still, aware of his length buried inside her to the hilt. If she rocked gently she could feel the big swollen head knocking against her womb.

Soon she sensed that Ravinder was near to spending. She wanted him to spill over now, to watch his face as he climaxed. Stroking his long black hair, she kissed him tenderly, almost reverently, because he had shown her so many different pathways to pleasure in a single day. And also simply, because he was beautiful.

When Ravinder came he cried out and she felt the echo of it somewhere within her. He lifted her high up, so that his lingam gave up its jism in creamy jets which spattered her stomach and mons. She did something then, which she had never done before. Slipping down his body, she sucked him clean, lapping up the creamy drops which ran down his shaft. She licked the tiny drops from his belly and then kissed the taut muscles, pulling gently with her teeth at the silky dark hair which grew up to a point at his navel.

Afterwards, she lay cradled in his arms, her cheek

resting on his chest. Ravinder's hands were gentle on her hair, stroking and teasing the rich red strands.

Glancing towards the alcove, Amy saw that Madeline and Shalini lay together, also entwined. They looked like a sculpture of ebony and ivory, Madeline's light brown skin seemed so pale beside Shalini's darkness.

The army cantonment seemed like a dream. This is reality, Amy thought. She had no desire to leave but knew that she must. Already the sun cast long shadows on the malachite floor tiles and a cool breeze caused the mother-of-pearl wind chimes to tinkle musically. Somewhere in the distance she heard the chatter of women as they went to collect water from the well.

She lifted her head with reluctance and kissed Ravinder's cool shaved cheek. Under the smoothness, she could just detect the beginnings of a beard growth.

'We have to leave,' she whispered. 'Although I would rather stay.'

He encircled her wrist with lean golden fingers. She was surprised at his strength. He had been so gentle in his lovemaking.

'Then stay. Never return,' he said passionately. 'You would be welcome in my house.'

She smiled, thinking of something light to counter with. Then she grew serious. He meant it. His beautiful hawk-like face looked hard and implacable and for a second she was afraid. Once, she had sensed that Ravinder could be dangerous and now she was reminded of that fact.

'I cannot,' she said gently, stroking his strong jaw and gazing into his fierce black eyes. 'Surely you wouldn't seek to keep me here against my will?'

He smiled and his expression softened, his deep eyelids sweeping down to mask the expression in his eyes.

'It is true. I would not. I have no wish to listen to a caged bird sing. I want you to be free to choose.'

'Then you will invite me to come here again. And I will come. How could I resist? And I have these,' she put her hand up to the earrings, 'to remember you by, should I forget.'

He smiled again, knowing that she spoke lightly, and she was dazzled by the light in his face.

'You will come back to me often,' he stated with conviction. 'Together we shall explore the many arts of love. And, eventually, you will stay.' Reaching for her hand, he pressed it to his chest. 'I feel it – here.'

Looking up at him, half fearfully and half in astonished delight, Amy almost believed him.

Chapter Thirteen

Water lay like glass over the paddy fields, tinged pink by the morning sun. A group of cranes stood awkwardly on single legs, the rice shoots sticking up around them like the tips of tiny green spears.

Amy glanced away from the birds and urged her horse into a gallop. She had promised her mother that she wouldn't go beyond the boundary of the station and, for once, she intended to keep that promise.

Standing up in the stirrups she bent over the muscular brown neck, moving her body in time with her mount's long strides. She needed to tire herself, so that her mind and body would not ache to be with Ravinder. Her every waking thought centred on the experiences she had shared with him and Shalini.

It was three days since Madeline and herself had visited the marble pleasure pavilion and likely to be twice as many more before she could accept Ravinder's invitation to visit him again. Her mother, usually so vague and affable, had suddenly demonstrated a more forceful side to her character.

'I know that Maud Harris is a dreadful gossip, dear, but her instincts are sound on this occasion,' she had said on the evening that Amy returned from Ravinder's palace. 'There has been more unrest, this time in Oudh. More British people have been killed and a full scale revolt is feared. Your father and I won't have you going off anymore with just Madeline and an ayah for company. You know that I like Madeline but in the circumstances I think you should put less emphasis on your friendship.'

Amy looked at her mother in dismay. This is partly due to Maud Harris, she thought. Maud had never approved of Amy's friendship with Madeline and she had no doubt seized the opportunity to pour more of her poison into her mother's ears.

'Goodness knows if the violence will spread southwards, but we must be prepared for that,' her mother went on. 'Now Amy, you will stay close at hand for a time. Promise me now.'

'But mother, I haven't been out tramping the countryside. Madeline and I were with the prince and his sister all day. Ravinder has countless guards and retainers. We were quite safe.'

'Nevertheless. I want your promise.'

Nothing Amy had to say would make her mother change her mind. She'd miss Madeline but she resolved to be obedient for a few days in the hope that her mother would be reassured by her compliance and relax into her old, easy-going self.

'I promise then,' she said reluctantly. 'But I think I might dry up with boredom.'

Amy's mother kissed her cheek. 'Nonsense! There's a wonderful round of social events to attend. Dances, races, dog shows, amateur theatricals, even a moonlight picnic. It will be pleasant to have you along. You'll enjoy yourself if you'll just put a curb on that restless spirit of yours. You do so take after your father.'

Smiling ruefully as she recalled that conversation with her mother, Amy turned her horse in the direction of

194

the station and began cantering back towards her house. She was hot and dusty and her muscles ached. The thought of a bath then breakfast was very pleasant.

She sighed. It was only now, when her freedom was curtailed, that she realised how privileged she had been. She missed being with Madeline, sharing her confidences and, most of all, she missed the feeling of excitement and danger that every outing with her friend brought. More than ever the daily routine of army life and the company of the British women drained her spirit.

Everything within her yearned to be back in the marble pavilion. There were so many things there to enchant her: the air heavy with smoky perfume, the rich, glowing colours of the walls and furniture, the potent pleasures of Shalini's handsome male servants. And first and last of all these enticements was Ravinder himself.

A wave of depression settled over her but it was not in her character to be sullen. Since she couldn't do as she wished, she decided to make the best of what was ahead.

For the next four days she accompanied her mother to tea dances, costume balls, and card parties. Everywhere the talk was of the erupting violence in the north. Women and children from small outposts were fleeing towards Lucknow.

'The mutineers and their allies have overrun most of the out-stations,' someone said.

'I've heard that our troops in Lucknow will be forced to withdraw to the residency soon,' offered another.

The accounts of killings and further uprisings were daily more numerous. Amy began to see that her mother was not just being over-protective. There was serious cause for alarm. She detected a sort of frenzied edge to the gaiety all around her. It was as if everyone felt that they must make the best of every moment, for the world they knew might come crashing down around them at any moment.

While Amy felt dreadfully sorry for the women and children who were trapped by the fighting in the north, her thoughts turned again and again to Ravinder. How was she going to be able to visit him as she had promised? He was Indian after all and it was Indians who were killing her countrymen. She knew that her sentiments were entirely selfish but she couldn't help it. She felt detached from her peers and her sadness at the killings was general, not centred on the British army. She did not voice these sentiments, knowing that they were seditious.

No longer was she the same young woman who had galloped across the Sussex Downs, the only thought in her head to meet Magnus. She was sure now of what she wanted, but was she brave enough to reach out for it?

The essence of India had seeped into her veins and seduced her, diluting her Western blood with its vivid hues of gold and scarlet and its smells of spice and dust. She knew with a certainty that was bone deep that Ravinder would never harm her. Hadn't he wanted her to stay with him? The complications of race and culture did not seem insurmountable when she lay in his arms.

And now, in her parallel world, everyone was on their guard. There was a new air of insecurity amongst the army wives. They travelled everywhere in groups and Amy knew that she would attract attention if she went out alone. She felt Maud Harris's snapping black eyes on her, the pinched little mouth smiling her approval as Amy accompanied her mother on the social round.

The strain began to tell on her. Amy's sleep was disturbed by vividly erotic dreams. She woke bathed in sweat, her head still full of confused images of long golden limbs, gleaming black hair, skin as dark and satiny as a ripe fig. The mouth she kissed was firm and male, then it changed to bruised-flower softness and was full and red as cherries.

Both Ravinder and Shalini seemed to have imprinted themselves on her senses. They were two sides of the same coin and their shared intimacy no longer horrified her. Rather it drew her towards them with invisible fingers, as insubstantial as smoke. She did not need to tell Ravinder that she knew that he and Shalini were lovers. The knowledge was there between them.

One morning she awoke to find that her hand was between her legs, her fingers rubbing gently at her moist, aroused sex. Even as she surfaced from the dream she felt the explosive release of an orgasm breaking over her.

'Ravinder,' she whispered. 'Oh God. Ravinder.'

Wrapping her arms around herself, she burst into tears.

More and more she felt as if she was living a dream and her reality was that which was denied her.

'Do you mind if I stay at the bungalow today, mama?' Amy said. 'I have a headache and I really can't face going to the dog show.'

'Poor dear,' her mother said, patting her arm. 'Have a lie down and a cool drink. You look paler than ever and there are shadows under your eyes. Perhaps I should get the doctor to look at you.'

'I don't need a doctor. I'll feel better after I've rested. Perhaps I'll go for a walk when it's cooler.'

'Very well dear. Don't forget your sunshade if you go out. You might take a stroll down to Maud Harris's house. She has a slight fever and would be glad to see a friendly face.'

Amy had no intention of visiting Maud. She had three precious hours before her mother returned and she had sent a message to Madeline, telling her that she would meet her at her house.

As soon as her mother's carriage was out of sight, Amy gathered her blue sprigged muslin skirts around her, sprang up, and reached for her sunshade. She decided to walk along the path which bordered the back gardens of the bungalows. Spreading fig trees and bananas provided shade from the merciless sun.

Amy's long skirts brushed against lush perfumed grasses as she moved. The pleasure of her own company and the prospect of seeing Madeline lifted her spirits and she began to hum softly to herself. An old woman sitting preparing vegetables on a back porch was singing a raga which blessed the rain. Her thin melodious voice soared in the still air. Amy smiled at her as she passed by.

A little further along the path Amy came to Maud Harris's bungalow. She saw that the cane blinds were pulled down around the back porch and assumed that Maud was taking advantage of the shady coolness while she recovered from her fever. Amy was about to pass by, when she heard the sound of faint moans and something – a cane, a belt? – striking flesh.

She stopped, hardly able to believe her own ears. Maud Harris was an acid-tongued wretch and a minor tyrant, but she hadn't credited her with beating her servants. But now that she thought of it, it did seem in character. She recalled the day on the parade ground when two men from Captain Landers' regiment had been beaten. Maud's enjoyment in their suffering had been pronounced. She remembered her glittering eyes and moist, parted lips.

Amy's mouth twisted with dislike. Maud was just the type to take pleasure in beating some hapless individual herself.

The moans were louder now and she could almost distinguish words. There was a pleading note to the voice, which was soft-pitched and hoarse, but the strokes continued, getting stronger if anything.

Before she realised what she was doing, Amy began striding down the path. Without hesitation she climbed the steps to the verandah. The voice came distinctly now.

'Please. Oh, please . . .'

It was a woman's voice.

A hot tide of anger rose up in Amy. She grasped the floor-length blind and pulled it aside, ready to step into the shaded outdoor room. The ready words of condemnation died on her lips. The sight which met her eyes was so unexpected, so bizarre, that she stood rooted on the top step, the ridged cane of the blind crushed between her fingers.

Maud Harris was bent over a carved wooden chest, her stomach pressed to the rounded top of it, skinny arms gripping the sides. She wore only her chemise, bright red petticoats and a stout red velvet corset, buckled with many small leather straps. The skirts of her beribboned and frilled petticoats were looped above her waist, revealing a surprisingly full and rounded bottom. Her skinny thighs were parted and trembling.

Neither Maud nor the young servant had noticed Amy. Both were too engrossed in each other. The slight noise of the blind being pulled aside was drowned by the sound of the cane meeting flesh and Maud's loud, theatrical moans.

Thin red lines bisected Maud's buttocks, startling against the soft white skin. The backs and insides of her thighs were flushed a deep rose-red, evidence that she had also received a spanking on the tender flesh there. She was moaning loudly, her head tossing from side to side.

'Yes. Again. Please. Oh, yes . . .'

'As you wish, memsahib.'

The young Indian, muscular, naked and sporting an

impressive erection, raised his arm and brought the thin bamboo cane crashing down onto Maud's bottom. The sharp sound as it connected hung on the still air. Maud jerked and arched her back, lifting her buttocks for the next blow.

The young man reached forward and ran the palm of his hand across the striped flesh. He caressed her slowly, gently, as if assessing the heat and soreness. Maud's buttocks quivered as he stroked them, his fingers sliding into the parted cleft and moving lower to pull at the lips of her sex which were prominent and well developed. When he parted the moist, pink flesh and thrust his fingers into her, Maud let out a hoarse cry and pressed against his hand.

'Beat me again. Please . . .' she whispered. 'Make my arse red and sore. Then fuck me. Push that strong young cock right inside me. Fuck me, until I beg for mercy. Lord, but I'm as a hot as a cat on heat.'

'As always, memsahib,' the young man grinned, extracting a finger which glistened with pearly moisture.

His thick cock twitched with eagerness as he raised his hand and brought the cane down squarely across the fullest part of Maud's bottom. A deep red stripe intersected the earlier marks and Maud let out a strangled moan.

Amy didn't know which stunned her most, the sight of Maud half-naked and showing the evidence of a sound beating, the richly coloured and frivolous underwear, or the stream of obscenities which was flowing from her thin lips. Maud spat out curses that a London carter would have been proud of.

For a moment longer Amy stood there, undecided as to whether to let the blind drop and move quietly away before either of them noticed her. She was tempted to let things be. After all, it was none of her business if Maud liked to be chastised in that way. But she could not help recalling Maud's many sly comments, the cruel way she had of judging others and her acid jibes about Madeline. Maud was loud in her condemnation of anyone who mixed with the natives – let alone made friends with them – and here she was urging a young Indian man to pleasure her and, by the look of things, not for the first time.

Amy felt sickened by Maud's hypocrisy. She couldn't let her get away with it. She was also overcome by a strong sense of the ridiculous. She felt a bubble of laughter rising inside her, threatening to erupt at any moment, and her anger and dislike dissolved. Oh this was just too rich. It was poetic justice, surely.

She began to chuckle and then to laugh aloud. Once she started, she found that she couldn't stop and all the tension of the last few days dissolved as she held her sides and rocked back and forth.

Maud went rigid with shock, her head whipping round to stare at the intruder. Her narrow face flushed darkly.

'What? You! What are you doing here?' she said.

'I . . . I hope I find you well, Maud,' Amy squeaked, still gulping with laughter. 'I see that you've recovered from your . . . fever!'

Scrambling to her feet, Maud pulled her petticoats down to cover herself and motioned to the naked young man.

'Go inside the house, Bhaiya. At once.'

He did so, silently and at speed. Maud's hands trembled and her thin lips were white with fury. She advanced on Amy, breathing hard. Her small breasts almost burst out of the top of the shaped corset and Amy saw that Maud had rouged her nipples. The big red circles looked so incongruous against her narrow chest and prominent collar bones, that Amy had to suppress another fit of the giggles.

Maud's small eyes narrowed with malice.

'How dare you laugh at me! You burst in here unannounced and have the gall to spy on me!' she cried. 'You wicked creature, poking your nose in where it isn't wanted. I know that you've the morals of an alley cat, but you've fallen low this time. I shall complain to your father. You'll be shipped home in disgrace. This is what comes of associating with undesirables. You're beyond the pale, Amy Spencer. You've been looking for an excuse to humiliate me, haven't you? You've always been jealous of me . . .'

Words failed her. She stood glaring at Amy, her fingers curled as if she'd like to rake her face with her long nails. In a voice that dripped venom, she said, 'I'd like to see you . . . horse-whipped for this! I'd do it myself . . . and gladly.'

'No doubt you'd enjoy that,' Amy said evenly. 'You're a hypocrite Maud Harris, of the worst type. How like you to try to blame me for your own sins. I wouldn't care one little bit what you did, if you weren't so eager to find fault with others. Well you can tell my father whatever you like. I'm sure he'd be very interested to hear about what you've been doing.'

Maud's eyes bulged and her small mouth worked impotently.

'You wouldn't dare!' she spat.

'Oh yes I would. And you know it. I think I might write a description of what I've just seen and go around pinning copies of it onto trees in the area.'

Maud took a step back. Her legs brushed against the wooden chest and she sat down abruptly. For a moment her face assumed an expression of blankness. She seemed to know that she was beaten. All at once the fight went out of her and her thin shoulders began to shake. She said tonelessly, 'What do you want to keep quiet? Money?'

Any pity Amy had felt, dissolved. Did Maud really think that she'd sink to blackmail? Suddenly she wanted to be anywhere but there. Madeline was waiting for her and she was wasting time bandying words with Maud.

'All I want is for you to leave me alone,' she said firmly. 'Don't comment on where I go or what I do. You keep your nose out of my affairs and I'll stay away from yours. But if you run telling tales to my mother or say another word against Madeline . . .' She left the sentence unfinished.

Maud's face cleared. Her pinched mouth lifted at the corners. There was a calculating glint in her hard eyes.

'I accept your terms. We understand one other then. We're more alike than you think. I'll keep out of your affairs, never fear, but you needn't look so superior. You can look down your nose at me all you like because I have your measure, Amy Spencer. You've been sitting on a hot coal since the moment you set foot in India and now you are following the path of the tiger. Have you heard that saying? It's the Indian equivalent of crying for the moon. Be very sure of what you want, because you might just get it. I wish you much pleasure with your Indian prince!'

She began to laugh and the sound of it made Amy feel uncomfortable. For, although she didn't like to admit to it, Maud Harris probably understood her best of all the army wives.

Before Maud could say anything else, Amy turned and descended the steps. Without looking back she continued on her way, Maud's mocking laughter ringing in her ears for some time.

Chapter Fourteen

Ravinder sat in front of the pink marble statue of Ganesha. Closing his eyes, he emptied his mind of everyday thoughts and concentrated on channelling the energy around his body.

Dusty sunlight poured in through the pierced windows and played over the erotic carvings which twisted and tumbled over each pillar. Ravinder was naked except for a loincloth of sky-blue silk. Oils of patchouli and cedar perfumed his body. He sat motionless, his back straight, staring straight ahead.

Here in the peace and beauty of the ruined temple, he was acutely aware of the power of the elephant-headed god – his master Ganesha – lord of the Tantric mysteries. In his presence Ravinder meditated on that most sacred temple of all, the temple of the body.

As the energy spread around his body, he reflected on the internal rivers, gardens, sanctuaries and gates, whereby the soul enters and leaves the bodily temple. The base of his spine felt warm and tingly and he drew the psychic fire of love upwards, concentrating until he felt the familiar pressure at the point between his eyebrows.

His breath left him in a long sigh as he absorbed the blessing of Ganesha. Refreshed and energised, he stood up slowly. He was ready now to meet with Amy.

She would be here soon. It was many days since he had seen her and he felt as excited and eager as a young man meeting his first love. Amy was special in so many ways. He had felt that the moment he laid eyes on her, but now he wanted to confirm for himself that she was indeed the soul mate he believed her to be.

How rare she was, his pale lotus. His art-woman, she whose yoni smelt of honey and musk. This time, when they made love, he would attune her to the rhythms of their joined bodies. In the West the energies produced by pleasuring the body were dissipated. But there were ways to harness sexual energy, ways too complex to put into words but he hoped that Amy would trust him enough to come willingly on a journey with him. And then, through the arcane knowledge which he would share with her, she would discover sexual ecstasy.

He already knew that he wanted Amy to stay with him always and be his lover and friend. There would be difficulties, of course – they came from such different cultures – but he would not allow doubt to shadow his mind. She felt the same, he sensed it from her letters, smuggled to him over these past two weeks.

Her writing was small and neat but she made complicated loops of many of the letters and he fancied that her warmth and sensuality was evinced by this. He was sure that her parents would not know that she corresponded with him. British rule was being challenged and news of more violent outbreaks reached him often. Death tolls rose daily. Reports of atrocities were rife. And now there was disease too.

In such a climate it was difficult to see past the divisions of race and culture. It amazed him that Amy did not consider him to be her enemy.

And he marvelled that she was so free-spirited, so

independent of thought. It was not a quality he had glimpsed in the other British women and not something of which the army approved. Armies functioned best when individuals did not question, but followed orders blindly.

His hunger for Amy was increased by their separation. He wanted to take her away from the hill station, where he was sure she wilted like a rose in a desert. In his arms, his pleasure palace, in the company of Shalini, she would find the oasis which her soul craved.

He needed to know everything about her, to explore her mind as well as her body. Already they had made a beginning towards mutual trust, without which there could be no commitment. And commitment was important to the Tantric mysteries, it was an integral element, an opening into mutual potency.

Ravinder cleared his mind of ugly and negative thoughts: killings, tortures, disease, these things had no place in the temple. He smiled as he recalled Amy's reactions to watching Shalini pleasure Madeline. It had not taken long for her to overcome her reticence and to appreciate and enjoy the beauty of two female bodies in the act of love.

Leaning back against the coolness of a marble pillar, Ravinder's eyes strayed to his groin, where his lingam was standing up straight and proud, pushing against the confinement of the blue silk. Thoughts of Amy's white body with the startling little plumes of red-gold hair, the delicate pink of her yoni lips, the lushly swelling curves at breast and hip, brought forth a strong sexual reaction from his body.

Pushing aside his loincloth, he clasped a hand around the golden shaft and began moving it gently back and forth. Smoothing back the skin which covered the fat red glans, he stroked himself, letting the sensations of pleasure build. He concentrated on building a mental image of Amy; her sweet oval face, her marvellous hair, the look in her eyes when she climaxed, the way she clutched at him with nerveless fingers when he thrust deeply into her hot, silky channel.

Ah, Amy was a tantalising mixture of wantonness and innocence, a sweet and fertile plain to be sown with seeds of Tantric wisdom. And soon, she would be with him. He thought of all the things they would do together, all the things he would show her, while the sensations of a satisfying climax spread like the petals of a lotus within his body.

Letting his head fall back he closed his mouth and opened his eyes wide, fixing them on the marble figure of Ganesha. With the index and middle finger of his left hand, he exerted pressure on an area over his right breast, at the same time letting out his breath. The words of his Tantric teacher came to him and he let them rise in his consciousness, holding back the moment when his orgasm would break.

'As your joy innate rises, you must glare as if angry, retain your breath, and contract your lower stomach. Visualise yourself in union with the goddess wisdom-energy and you will prevent the semen from moving outward.'

Ravinder had been a model pupil. The practices were now second nature to him. Pressing his tongue against his palate, he let out his breath in a series of harsh guttural sounds. The pleasure began to spread over him in waves, sweet and satisfying. His lingam leapt in his hand but he did not ejaculate.

His water of life, his camphor, was retained for the time when his lingam would absorb the essence of Amy's yoni.

In the quiet moment which followed the explosion of pleasure, Ravinder was aware that someone – a woman – was in the temple. His heart leapt, but it was not Amy, not yet. Ravinder recognised the footfall and the cloud of perfume which preceded his sister's appearance. Shalini was fond of the clean, sweet scent of ylang-ylang.

'How adept you are, my love,' Shalini said softly, approaching him, and he knew that she had been watching him from the shadows.

He smiled up at her, delighting in her dark beauty. They knew each other so well, each mood and nuance of speech so familiar to both of them. Shalini was part of him, the ties of their blood no less strong than the ties of flesh and spirit. She came closer, her body moving as sinuously and as naturally as her pet tiger.

'I thought I would find you here,' she said. 'You are waiting for your lotus woman, are you not?'

Ravinder nodded, reaching for her as she sank down gracefully next to him. His arm encircled her narrow waist and gathered her against him. Her high, firm breasts pressed against his naked chest as she lifted her chin and kissed him.

Her full mouth opened under his and she slipped her tongue into his mouth. She tasted of cumin and cloves. Her hand sought and found his lingam and she stroked it softly, her fingers sending a ticklish pleasure down the still firm shaft.

'I envy you, Ravinder,' she murmured against his mouth. 'Amy is lovely. I will be glad to welcome her into my house as a friend and companion. When can we share her?'

Putting her from him, Ravinder smiled and twisted a strand of her thick black hair around his hand.

'You are impatient, precious one. To suggest that too soon would frighten her away. She has many new ideas to learn and areas of her mind and body may need to be healed and released. Remember that the gift of pleasure must always be freely given.'

Shalini pouted prettily. 'But she desires me. I have seen the way she looks at me. She finds me as beautiful and fascinating as I find her.'

'That is true. When the time is right you shall prepare Amy and we will welcome her into our joint embrace.'

Shalini smiled, her full red lips curving voluptuously. 'Then let that be soon, my brother. My blood is hot and my yoni is eager for pleasure. The one of mixed race, Madeline, has fired my passions and now I am eager to caress the cool, white skin of your British passion flower. And to taste her essence.'

'If you are so eager, perhaps I should help you to release some of your sexual energy. But I do not wish to put my lingam inside you. You understand?' His deep-set eyes glistened. 'But I'm sure there is some way in which I can assist you.'

'Oh, yes, my dark star. There is.'

Letting out her breath on a long sigh, Shalini swayed towards him. She looked up at him through lowered lashes as her fingers began loosening the silk veils which were swathed around her lower body. He watched as her narrow waist, flaring hips and rounded thighs were revealed. In the dilute sunlight of the temple Shalini's dark skin had the bloom of purple grapes.

The gold and ivory of her anklets glowed against the rich colour of her dark skin. In the depression of her navel, the ruby glinted like red fire. Ravinder's blood quickened as Shalini ran her slim hands down over her hips. Moving her fingers in towards her groin, she toyed with the dark mass of curling hair which covered her yoni. The tip of one long, perfectly-manicured, hennaed nail slipped provocatively into the central groove of her sex.

'Your beauty always delights me, my sister,' Ravinder said huskily. 'I too am eager to see you embracing Amy. Should not ivory and ebony be joined and milk be laced with molasses?'

'It should be indeed,' Shalini grinned, sinking down onto the marble floor.

She allowed her thighs to fall apart, laughing softly when Ravinder's eyes settled on the slight swell of her lower belly. Putting her hands between her legs, she used her fingertips to open the lips of her sex, exerting pressure so that the tiny, nut-like protuberance of her pleasure bud was pushed into prominence, she smiled up at him.

'Your lingam is fully swollen again, my brother. And is that not a droplet that weeps from the tiny mouth? It seems that your lust was not sated by your act of solitary pleasure. Come close so that you may breathe in the perfume of my yoni. I have anointed my pubic curls with oil of saffron and placed sweet honey inside the opening of my yoni. And see here? Is this salty teat not a choice morsel for you to feast on?'

'Witch!'

With a soft groan, Ravinder positioned himself between Shalini's thighs. Placing his hands under her hips, he lifted her up so that her yoni was drawn close to his mouth. Savouring the warm, musky smell of her, he flicked out his tongue so that only the very tip of it brushed across the opened, dark-red folds.

Shalini trembled as Ravinder's hot breath teased her throbbing bud. His tongue tip stroked up either side of her bud and then pressed firmly against it. He felt the subtle texture of it, so similar to the inner flesh of Shalini's mouth. How he loved the way her lotus stamen pulsed under his tongue.

'Ah, brother mine. Drink from my fount of immortality. Imagine that I am your initiatress. Am I not your royal mother? Your formal wife and mistress? give me this caress as you will give the same to Amy.'

Shalini was so wise and generous. Without him asking her, she was making it plain that he did not have to fear her jealousy. He ought to have known that she wanted only his happiness. For what made him happy, enriched her also.

'Ah, ah . . .' Shalini murmured, her hand reaching out to stroke his long black hair.

With a sigh of delight and utter compliance, Ravinder opened his lips, took the tender, swollen morsel into his mouth and began to suck gently.

It was late afternoon by the time that Amy and Madeline arrived at the ruined temple. She had found it difficult to get away at all and had only managed it by telling her mother that she was going to visit Maud Harris.

'Maud's softened towards you lately, dear,' her mother said approvingly. 'I think she appreciated you looking in on her when she had that fever. Run along then. You'll be safe enough there.'

Amy had hurried to Madeline's house, where Madeline had two horses saddled and waiting. Hampered by her muslin day dress with its bunched-up skirts and petticoats, Amy managed to ride well enough. Cutting across country, they approached the temple under the shadow of the bamboo and banana trees, managing not to see anyone en route.

'I'm afraid, Madeline,' Amy said, as they rode abreast. 'It looks as if the whole of India will burst into flames. The mutiny has spread. The residency at Lucknow is under siege. Women and children are being murdered by their sepoys who they once trusted implicitly. There are reports of cholera and smallpox breaking out amongst those who are besieged. Where will it all end?'

Madeline's face was pale and drawn. There were violet shadows under her eyes. The tension and their enforced separation had taken its toll on her too.

'I do not know. The British women look at me with suspicion. I have heard them whispering about the deaths of women and innocent children and there is hatred in their eyes. My mother will not leave the house since she was spat at in the street. But what can we do?

This is none of our doing. I hate the killings and the torturing as much as the army wives do!'

'I know that, Madeline,' Amy said gently, distressed to see the tears glinting in her friend's blue eyes. 'I would never turn away from you. I feel torn in two by all this, as if I had a foot on both shores of a river which is widening by the moment.'

Madeline attempted a smile. 'Do not distress yourself, my dear friend. We must be patient and grasp what time together we can.'

Amy nodded. 'I know that you're right. But I've missed your friendship these past weeks. I've tried to be the person my mother expects me to be, but I just can't be. I don't see things in black and white as I'm expected to. I'm sure I shall go mad or do something reckless.'

Madeline threw her a sympathetic glance, then her eyes narrowed shrewdly.

'I know that set to your mouth. What are you going to do?'

'I intend to ask Ravinder's advice. Perhaps he will agree to speak to my father. I think he will offer the women his protection. Unlike the army wives, I do not believe that every Indian prince has set himself against us. Apparently Ravinder's father is unwilling to take sides and Ravinder himself has little power of his own. He can have nothing to do with the uprising. If I can prove that to my parents they might let me visit him.'

Madeline looked doubtful. 'And if they refuse to let you see him again – ever?'

Amy's lips thinned.

'Then I have a simple choice to make.'

At the temple they dismounted quickly and secured the horses' reins to a tree. Ravinder and Shalini came out to meet them. Framed in the decorated archway, with the great swags of flowering creepers overhead, they looked like Kama and Rati – the love god and his wife; the embodiment of sexuality.

Madeline had told Amy the story of the Hindu myth. Surely the characters who were central to the story looked like this brother and sister. She felt awed by their beauty and the force of their presence. Did she really think that they would welcome her into their midst?

'I'm . . . I'm sorry we're so late,' Amy said, her confidence ebbing, wishing that she hadn't given way to the impulse to see him again.

'It matters not. You're here now,' Ravinder said. His sculpted mouth lifted at the corners as he looked at her almost hungrily.

For a moment longer Amy stood still, unable to believe that he was actually there before her. The long days, hours, minutes fell away. Then Ravinder smiled and opened his arms and with a strangled sob she ran forward.

Fool. Fool, to have doubted him. She sensed his passion in the strength of his embrace and in the violence of his kiss. He gathered her close in such a way that she felt cherished, special. And she knew that he had suffered too.

'I didn't mean to do this . . .' she whispered against his mouth, the tears streaking her cheeks.

He put up a finger and trapped a single, shining drop.

'I would rather have this salt gem than a perfect white diamond,' he said, bringing the tear to his mouth.

Amy clung to him, pressing her cheek against his broad muscular chest, aware of the steady beating of his heart beneath his blue silk tunic. He wore loose white silk jodhpurs and knee-high boots of tooled leather, the toes turned up into points. His unbound black hair brushed against her hands where they rested in the small of his back.

213

'Come inside out of the sun,' he said, taking her hand.

Amy glanced over her shoulder to see that Madeline was following, her arm encircling Shalini's narrow waist. In the temple it was cool and shady. Amy smiled inwardly, recalling the first time she had come there and seen Ravinder and Shalini making love.

That seemed so long ago and she was no longer shocked by the image of their entwined naked bodies. So much about Ravinder and Shalini was unique but now it seemed right and natural to her.

Ravinder led her to a flight of stone steps which had been draped with thick woollen rugs. Silken cushions lay there too and in a wicker basket there was food and drink, packed in ice. Amy seated herself and Madeline sat nearby. Shalini poured drink and prepared food, serving it to them herself.

Ravinder lifted a hand and removed Amy's topi, laying the veiled hat aside. Her hair which had been pinned into a loose roll tumbled over her shoulders in a tangle of bright red curls.

'You are thinner, my dove,' Ravinder said to Amy. 'Those hollows in your cheeks were not there when you came to my palace.'

Amy's eyelids swept down to conceal her expression. He was so perceptive. Would it ever be possible to hide anything from him? She felt a sort of alarm but an excitement too. At that precise moment she dared not look at Ravinder.

In his dark, deep-set eyes, she had again glimpsed the promise of that challenging and unique intimacy. It was that which she both feared and craved. And she was reminded why she had thought of him at least a hundred times every day; why he haunted her dreams and why she had risked her family's shock and displeasure by smuggling letters to him.

Glancing up she saw that he hadn't looked away. He

214

was studying her still, with a look of such intensity that she seemed to feel the trace of it on her skin. Once, when she had been ill with a fever, her skin had felt peculiar – tender and bruised, with odd little chills that ran up her backbone. It felt like that now.

She realised that she was hungry – starving in fact – but it was not food she needed. And she saw the reflection of that same need, only intensified, condensed into something almost violent, in the expression on Ravinder's face. Without a word, he reached out his hand. She meshed her fingers in his and allowed him to pull her to her feet.

Shalini gave a throaty chuckle. 'It seems that we are to eat alone, Madeline.'

'I'm not very hungry either,' Madeline replied, her voice heavy with promise.

'Then come into my arms and let us share the sweet embraces of true sisterhood.'

Without a backward glance at his sister and Madeline, Ravinder pulled Amy behind the nearest pillar. She pressed her back against the erotic carvings, feeling stone breasts and arms and erect lingams pushing against her skin. Even while Ravinder began kissing her, he was raising her skirts. She helped him to pull up the many folds of pin-tucked muslin, the frilled petticoats, almost sobbing with her need for him.

There would be other times for tenderness, just now she wanted him inside her; hard, hot and demanding.

'I wanted to love you slowly but I cannot wait. Do you mind?' Ravinder said.

'No. I want it like this. Do it to me – now. I'm so ready for you. I've dreamt of this and thought of it until I'm sick with wanting.'

'Gods, Amy,' he moaned, kissing her mouth, her chin, her eyelids.

His hands found her thighs and she suppressed a groan as he pressed upwards and pushed his fingers straight into her. She was wet and ready and she worked her hips as he rubbed at her sex and pushed open the fleshy lips almost roughly. He seemed to be reminding himself of her physical geography, exploring and absorbing her through his fingertips.

He was uninterested in her breasts, buttocks, any of her anatomy except her sex – the scarlet, sweetly pulsing heart of her desire. She threw back her head and shuddered, contracting around his fingers as she came.

Oh God, this was just what she needed, nothing gentle or fancy, just a man and woman, lingam and yoni, thrusting and receiving. And more of it – much more. It was like that first time in the elephant house. She almost laughed as the echoes of her climax subsided only to begin to build again. Would they ever get past this hungry, almost primeval need?

'Your cock . . . lingam,' she whispered. 'Give it to me.'

Reaching for him, she ran her palms over his taut buttocks and then moved them down between their bodies. His hard flesh nudged against her hand. It was hot and pulsing with a life of its own. She plucked frantically at his belt, dragging his jodhpurs down over his lean hips.

His manhood sprang up between them and Ravinder made a sound deep in his throat as she closed her fingers around the firm stem. Cupping her buttocks with his hands, he supported her as she lifted her legs and wrapped them around his waist.

'Put it into yourself,' he said, biting gently at her bottom lip and then covering her mouth in a hard, demanding kiss.

Amy brought the moist, engorged head of his glans towards her spread sex. Keeping hold of his shaft she worked the swollen tip inside her, using the cock like an instrument for her sole pleasure. Ravinder moaned

216

as she rode him, fellating him with the firm, wet mouth of her sex.

At the same moment as she released his cock and allowed him to slide deeply into her, she pushed her tongue into the sensitive cavern of his mouth. Joined at mouth and sex, she surged against him, loving the feel of his big cock, the intruding force of him as he drove into her.

And all doubts about her being there, her secret worries that she was simply obsessed with his exotic beauty, fled from her mind. The reality of her feelings was borne in on her. She wanted all of him – body, mind, soul. But just now, oh God, it was his body which inflamed her.

In the midst of the most acute, almost mindless pleasure, she was aware that Ravinder fitted her as no other man had. His cock seemed to seek out new depths, new pathways to pleasure within her vagina. It was impossible, she knew, but that was how it felt.

Thrusting with long, slow strokes, he urged her towards another peak of pleasure. She climaxed for a second time, with Ravinder biting her neck gently. The tingles of ecstasy ran through her entire body and she felt her womb contract and release.

'And now you,' she whispered, when she could speak again. 'Do you not want to spend?'

'I satisfied myself earlier, so that I could bring you to the brink of many blissful peaks. I intended only to pleasure you and to absorb the essences of your yoni, while retaining the semen within my body.'

Was that so? She thrust against him, feeling the big cock-head nudge against her womb. She imagined her soft pink walls, sucking at his sensitive glans and worked her inner muscles milking him. Smiling wickedly at his indrawn breath and his expression of almost pained pleasure, she murmured, 'And do you still intend to do that?'

Ravinder gasped, making no attempt to stop her moving or to draw free from her enclosing flesh. Amy worked her hips, sheathing herself on his cock, ramming her pubis against the nest of curly hair at the base of his penis.

Now that her own sexual tension was somewhat appeased, she enjoyed the shift in power between them. Now she was in control, she was the instrument of Ravinder's pleasure. The pearly juices seeped out of her, lubricating the shaft which she rode with total abandon.

Ravinder threw back his head, exposing the strong golden column of his neck. Amy licked his skin, tasting the faint salt of his sweat. She loved the signs that Ravinder was losing control. This beautiful man, so adept in the ways of love, such a master of sexual self-control, was allowing her to draw down the pleasure from his body.

When he came, Ravinder closed his eyes tightly and clenched his teeth. Amy wrapped her arms around his neck and kissed him tenderly. She was touched by his vulnerability. Spent and gasping he laid his head on her frilled bodice.

Was it not the ultimate pleasure to see a strong man made weak by his lust for her?

Chapter Fifteen

'I can't believe that you have been so indiscreet as to discuss army business with a potential enemy! You little fool. Men have been court martialled for less.'

Amy's spirits sank as she listened to her father's booming voice which rang through the house and could, no doubt, be heard down the street.

Madeline had warned her that it would do no good to talk to her parents about Ravinder or to pass comment on the rights and wrongs of the uprising, and her friend had been right. Ravinder's unconditional offer of protection for the women and children, should the need arise, had been turned down out of hand.

Her father finally stopped pacing the room and placed himself in front of her. For a moment Amy thought he might hit her. She had never seen him so angry. His usually high-coloured face looked almost puce.

'Father I – ' she began.

He held up his hand. 'Be silent. I've heard more than enough. I forbid you to have any contact whatsoever with that young man or that half-caste girl. You've done enough harm between you. You're not to leave this house. I'll decide what's to be done with you later.'

Amy pressed her lips together. There seemed nothing for her to add. Later, when her father had left the house and gone back to the barracks, she tried to reason with her mother, but on this occasion it was no use.

'Your father's word is law in this house. I shall abide by what he says.' Her mother's tone was cold, although it softened a trace as she went on, 'I'm sure you spoke in good faith, Amy, but you ought to have known better. We never discuss army business with outsiders. Never. It is quite impossible to accept Ravinder's invitation. How would it look if we women were to go scuttling off to skulk like cowards in some prince's palace? British army women are made of sterner stuff. The men know that we are loyal subjects of the queen and support them fully.'

'I should think the men would be glad to know that their families are safe from any possible harm,' Amy said sulkily.

Her mother tapped her foot in irritation. 'You haven't been listening to a word your father said, have you? Do you never think of anyone's wishes but your own? To go sneaking off like that, when I asked you not to see Madeline. And to have exchanged letters with the prince's son. Obviously my trust in you has been misplaced. You really are the most impossible, selfish, obstinate, stubborn . . .'

'Copy of my father?' Amy said helpfully.

Her mother made a sound of exasperation and swept across the room with a rustle of silk skirts, leaving a faint smell of Devon violets in her wake. At the door she paused and looked over her shoulder.

'I wash my hands of you. Go to your room, Amy. I think you may assume that you'll be leaving for England within the month. How could you do this? You have compromised yourself and your family. I thought better of you.'

Her mother's tone of voice, soft and heavy with

disappointment, hurt Amy far more than her father's angry shouting. Perhaps she was selfish and headstrong, but she wasn't a hypocrite.

Lifting her muslin skirts, she stormed off to her room and flung herself across her bed. Tears of impotent anger stung her eyes. It was pointless now to bring up the subject of her feelings for Ravinder. She had admitted only to writing to him with a request for his help. Her parents would have had apoplexy if they knew what she had actually been doing in Ravinder's pleasure pavilion.

She needed Ravinder, wanted him with all her heart and soul. And now she would not be allowed to see him again – ever. To salvage the family's honour she would be sent back home to Sussex where a suitable marriage would be arranged as soon as possible.

She drew her knees into her chest and hugged herself miserably. The thought of never again seeing the golden beauty of Ravinder's face, never touching him, never lying with him, brought her actual physical pain. A life without him would be unbearable.

She felt as if she stood on the edge of an abyss. It was better to grasp at a chance of happiness than to let it pass by – wasn't it? It would serve them all right if she did something desperate. But what a dreadful scandal it would cause. She would be an outcast, a pariah.

But she did not really have a choice. There was only one course of action open to her now. She felt sick and afraid but she was also aware of the hot core of need and excitement within her. If there was a heavy price for taking her destiny into her own hands then she was prepared to pay it.

Having come to a decision she wiped away the tears that were drying on her cheeks. She would need help to get away. After this latest escapade she couldn't imagine her mother leaving her alone for a moment.

Then it came to her. There was one person who could

help her. One person whom her mother trusted implicitly and whose discretion she could count on. Crossing the room, she sat down at her writing desk and smoothed out a fresh sheet of embossed cream paper. How ironic that it was her one-time adversary to whom she turned now.

Dear Maud, she began writing. *I need your help. I must speak to you – alone . . .*

A few evenings later, Amy sat in the drawing room setting small stitches into a cross-stitch sampler. She was pale but composed, her eyes downcast. There was an uncomfortable silence in the room. No one spoke as her mother and father prepared to go out for the evening to a regimental dinner. She could smell her father's lemon hair oil and the gardenia perfume her mother wore. Such ordinary smells that usually brought her feelings of well-being.

The rustle of silk skirts and starched petticoats seemed loud in the stillness. Amy wished that she could go to her mother and embrace her but she knew that if she did she would begin to weep and that would delay them leaving.

When Maud Harris arrived, her mother feigned surprise. Amy hid a bitter smile, knowing that it had been arranged between her parents for Maud to be her unofficial chaperone.

'Do come in, Maud,' her mother said brightly. 'We have to go out, but Amy will entertain you. It will be pleasant for her to have some company. She is indisposed at the moment and will not be accompanying us to the dinner.'

Maud smiled, playing her part perfectly. 'Then it's just as well that I decided to call. We'll be company for each other. I'm sure that we have a lot to talk about.'

Amy stood up and walked over to her mother who

222

was buttoning her evening gloves. She leaned over and kissed her mother's cheek.

'Goodbye,' she said softly.

Her mother looked at her closely, gave a wistful little smile, and shook her head. She patted Amy on the arm and then made her way to the open front door. Amy's father strode out to the waiting carriage without a backward glance. The sound of horses' hooves and jingling harnesses faded into the distance.

Amy turned to Maud. 'Thank you for coming,' she said. 'I didn't know who else to turn to.'

Maud's small mouth pursed. 'I think I prefer it when you act all high and mighty. Humility doesn't suit you.'

Amy ignored the jibe. 'I just wanted you to know that I appreciate you coming. You could have refused.'

'And missed the pleasure of seeing the back of you! I shall sleep easier knowing that you're taking my secrets with you.' Maud's pinched face lit up when she laughed.

Amy laughed too, coming close to liking Maud. You had to admire someone who was so consistently unpleasant.

'Did you pass my message on to Madeline?'

'I did. Your friend is aware of what you are going to do. No doubt she approves wholeheartedly. Well, if you're packed and ready, you'd best be off. No sense in waiting to be caught. Is Ravinder sending transport for your things?'

Amy nodded. 'He's coming himself. He'll be waiting out on the back road that passes our garden. I'll . . . go then. Goodbye Maud.'

'Goodbye Amy. I know that we've never liked each other, but I wish you well. Truly.'

A lump rose in Amy's throat. Now that the moment had come, she felt full of misgivings. Was she doing the right thing? She glanced back at Maud and saw the glint of unshed tears in her eyes. Hesitantly she took a step towards her.

'Maud – '

'Will you get going, Amy Spencer, before I make a complete fool of myself!' Maud said sharply, dashing the back of her hand across her eyes. 'This is no time to be indecisive. Do you think that I'd hesitate for a single moment if I had the same chance as you?'

Gathering her long skirts about her, Amy ran through the bungalow and out across the back verandah. She steeled herself not to look back at all the familiar things she was leaving behind, but set her eyes on the figure who waited in the shadows beyond the garden.

She ran into Ravinder's arms unable to stop the tears welling up inside her. As he bent his head to kiss her forehead, a strand of his unbound black hair caressed her cheek.

'You're sure about this now?' he whispered.

Amy laid her cheek against his chest. Under the black silk of his tunic his muscles felt firm and warm. The force of his persona seemed to surround and enfold her. His smell of patchouli and clean maleness intoxicated her, soothing and arousing her senses at the same time.

Her last remaining doubts were swept away. 'I've never been more sure of anything in my life,' she said against his mouth. 'It's just . . . so hard to leave like this. I wish that things could have been different.'

'In time, your family will come to accept your decision.'

'Perhaps. I've left a letter for my mother, telling her how she can contact me if she wishes to.' She couldn't actually imagine her parents understanding or forgiving her actions, but anything was possible, and she knew that her mother at least would wish her well.

'Come. Let's go to my palace. Shalini awaits you. She has planned a special welcome. Something which will drive all unpleasant thoughts from your mind, for a time at least.'

Shalini waited impatiently for Ravinder to return with Amy.

She had prepared a chamber for her and hung it with rich silks and brocades. Pierced copper lanterns cast a lacework of patterns over the sleeping dais which was covered with a red cloth and strewn with cushions.

She hoped that Amy would like the gifts she had assembled. There was jewellery, choice food, carved rosewood cabinets. In the garden there was a tiger cub and a pair of young peacocks. Shalini had chosen them to divert Amy's thoughts from regret or guilt about leaving her family.

Her mind turned to more immediate things and she cast her eyes around the dimly-lit chamber. There, laid out on a low table, were the substances necessary for the ritual of honouring the Shakti – or female principle. After this night, Amy would truly be one with Ravinder and herself.

Shalini loved the procedure of decorating the body for sacred sexual rites. There was an art in such preparation. She had painstakingly mixed the oils and cosmetics herself, using sandalwood powder, rice paste, tumeric, ground conch shell, soot from camphor and many other rare and costly elements. After her servants had bathed and oiled her body she had applied the cosmetics to her skin.

The soles of her feet and the tips of her fingers were reddened with henna and she had anointed the different regions of her body with fragrant oils and coloured dyes. Her mirror of polished bronze showed her the image of a seductive, sloe-eyed temptress.

Her dark skin had a smoky bloom to it, her painted mouth was full and cherry-red. In the centre of her forehead was a mark, depicting the third eye. She knew that she looked her most beautiful. This was a mark of respect and her gift to Amy. She looked forward to honouring and readying Amy for her first shared night of pleasure – the first of many to come.

She would use all her skills in esoteric body adornment, knowing that the pale lotus whom her brother loved would respond to the seductive pleasure of being prepared for the sex act. What woman could resist being cherished, pampered, and made beautiful while her handsome lover watched appreciatively?

Shalini remembered how much Amy had enjoyed the massage after her swim. The British woman was unusually receptive for a Westerner. She would prepare her slowly, giving her time to become aware of the changes which would come over her. And then, when Amy was relaxed, her senses fired by the potent and intoxicating oils, Ravinder, Amy and herself would bind themselves together with sensual pleasures.

For it was written that when a man makes love with two women, who love him equally, it is known as the united position. And all three will benefit from the flow of circulating energy.

Both Amy and herself would honour Ravinder as Lord Shiva, while stimulating and invoking the innermost Shakti – or primordial woman-power – of the other. The sexual union they would share would bring each of them the gift of ecstasy.

Shalini shivered, her rouged nipples drawing together into hard peaks. There was a sense of warm anticipation in her lower belly. Her yoni pulsed and trembled. Amy was so beautiful with her white skin and her red hair. She desired her strongly. She wanted only to honour her with pleasure and to receive Amy's blessing in return.

She meditated for a while, reciting a mantra and concentrating on the Tantric union of three. Then, confident that she had cleared her mind of negative thoughts, she placed fresh flowers in vases around the chamber and touched a taper to the cones of scented charcoal in their brass dishes.

There was a noise outside and Shalini straightened. Ah, they had arrived. Shalini rose gracefully, her silk robes of coral and amber flowing out around her as she went to welcome her brother and his new consort.

Amy closed her eyes and gave herself up to the ministrations of Shalini's male servants. Their strong expert hands smoothed a paste made of wheat and cream over her exposed lower body, removing even the slight down that covered her limbs.

She pushed away all thoughts which were not centred on her body. Time enough for worries later. The strain of planning her elopement and the guilt over betraying her parents had drained her. Now that she was actually in Ravinder's palace she felt swamped by lethargy. Ravinder and Shalini had planned to make her first night with them into something special and she resolved to do justice to the many sensory delights which they offered.

This chamber, later to be her own private room, was bathed in a rosy glow giving it a womblike, erotic quality. At one end of the chamber Ravinder was reclining on a low divan, smoking a hookah. He looked mysterious and beautiful in his black silk robes. His long black hair was clasped at his nape and rubies glistened at his ears.

There was a watchful stillness about him as if he had leashed all his vibrance and male energy within himself. He smiled as he caught her eye and she saw the pride mixed with desire on his face as Shalini's servants drew the final garments from her upper body.

Straightening her back, so that her full breasts with their small pink nipples stood out proudly, Amy threw Ravinder a glance from lowered lashes. She knew that this ritual of cleansing and body preparation was a prelude to the sexual pleasure that they would share. Part of Ravinder's pleasure was to watch her, to absorb the signs as the desire accumulated within her layer upon layer.

How refined were his responses. He took delight in simple things, the line of her brow, the neatness of her ear lobes, the slenderness of her feet. She had never known any man like him. Ravinder was much practised in the arts of love. Compared to him she was an innocent.

A little shiver rippled down her back as she imagined his hands on her, caressing, stroking, exploring, seeking out new areas to imbue with erotic longings. The hands of Shalini's servants could have been *his* hands; their touch on her skin was a prelude to the pleasure that was to come.

She raised her hands, lifting the heavy fall of red-gold curls, and stretching luxuriously. The shock of being naked in the presence of others had quite worn off. She felt wanton, glad of Ravinder's eyes on her and proud that he considered her beautiful.

After the servants plaited her hair and pinned it high on her head, Amy stepped into a large shallow bath made of beaten metal. Warm water was poured over her skin and a pad of abrasive fibre used to buff her entire body to a pink and shining smoothness. After she was dried, Shalini waved away the servants. Silently they left the room, pulling a large tapestry over the door space so that Amy was alone with Ravinder and Shalini.

'I will attend to you myself, newest sister,' Shalini said, holding a gilded tray which held jars and boxes filled with scented oils and coloured pigments. 'The arts of Tantric decoration are not for the eyes of everyone.'

Lifting her hand to her shoulders, Shalini unwound the silk veils of coral and amber and dropped them to the marble floor. Amy tried not to stare, but the Indian woman looked particularly beautiful and provocative. Her glossy black hair hung down her back in a single plait. A jewelled chain decorated her parting and her face was skilfully painted.

Amy's eyes travelled downwards. A deep collar of jewel-encrusted metal adorned Shalini's upper chest. Hanging down from the centre of the collar was a shaped tongue of metal which passed between her bare breasts and continued under them, separating and supporting the swelling dark flesh.

The effect of the garment was startling. It forced Shalini's large breasts into greater prominence and emphasised the narrowness of her tiny waist. Slung low around her swelling hips, Shalini wore a sort of beaded apron. Matching armlets and anklets decorated her limbs.

Amy found the thought of wearing such garments exciting. What would be Ravinder's reaction when she was dressed like a goddess?

'You find me beautiful?' Shalini said with a trace of pride. 'I will make you beautiful too. This night we shall honour each other's bodies when we share pleasures with Ravinder.'

Amy hid her shock, lowering her eyes against the frank approval and desire in Shalini's slanting eyes. They were *both* going to make love with Ravinder – and with each other? Amy let the idea take hold, realising that this moment had been inevitable. She weighed the composition of her emotions and found that she was eager for the exchange. It was only hearing Shalini say it aloud that had prompted her surprised reaction.

She knew that she desired Shalini in a different way to Ravinder. Ravinder had once spoken of the *Sakhis* who shared the lives and beds of certain Indian women; such unions strengthening their mutual femininity. It seemed right that Ravinder was to be her lover and Shalini would be her *Sakhi*.

Shalini bent her head, her eyes shadowed by a trace of doubt. With only the slightest hesitation, Amy reached up and pulled her close. Their lips met gently, tentatively at first, then they kissed with passion. Shalini slipped her tongue into Amy's mouth and Amy sucked at the tender tip, collaring it with her own pursed lips.

Shalini drew back first, her eyes glazed with passion. She smiled, her full berry-red mouth trembling slightly.

'How far from your own world you have travelled to meet us,' she whispered. 'It is truly extraordinary. I never expected to share Ravinder with such a pale lotus flower. But he is my heart and his wishes are my own.'

Amy knew that Shalini referred to the great chasm between their two cultures. She knew that she had much to learn, new ideas to encompass, but all this seemed to be less of a problem with each second that passed. Shalini's love and friendship would make the journey to come very much easier.

'And I never expected to find my personal *Sakhi*,' Amy whispered, enjoying the play of slim dark fingers over her skin as Shalini rubbed her body with oils.

She was rewarded by Shalini's wide grin of delight. 'How quickly you learn, my sister.'

After a while Shalini began applying body make-up. Amy was aware that Ravinder watched with silent intensity as Shalini outlined her eyes with kohl and painted her eyebrows and lips. His deep-set eyes were shadowed in the tinted gloom, but light fell on his straight nose and sculpted mouth. Tendrils of perfumed smoke drifted from his parted lips.

Whenever Amy glanced at him, she saw that he was wearing a half-smile or nodding with approval. She longed for him to approach her, to feel the light tracery of his fingers against her skin following the path which Shalini's hands made.

But she knew that he was aroused by watching Shalini stroke oils over her. Perhaps it was her acquiescence that drew him, while he contemplated all the movements she would make later – the involuntary shudders, the boneless clutching of her hands as he drove into her moist and willing centre.

Locking eyes with him, she let him see her pleasure as Shalini coaxed her nipples into hard, aching peaks. The oily fingers plucked and pinched, moving over her skin like fluttering birds, and Amy squirmed as little darts of pleasure-pain radiated through her.

The pungent, heady scents of the preparations made her feel light-headed. Shalini smeared some kind of grey powder across her forehead, drawing lines on her skin. Smoothing her hands down Amy's sides, Shalini rested her palms on the outswell of her hips. Amy held her breath as the slim, dark fingers moved inwards, spreading oil onto her stomach and then moving lower. Dipping her fingers into a box of red powder, Shalini rubbed at Amy's pubic curls.

'You do not really need to be anointed in this place,' she smiled, 'for your hair is the colour which stimulates the male sex centre. But I think that your yoni really must be anointed. Does it not ache for such attention?'

With a wicked glint in her eye, Shalini slipped her hand lower still, spreading more of the red powder over the closed lips of Amy's sex. Her touch was gentle and she did not probe further, although the circular rubbing motion was maddening.

Tendrils of heat spread through Amy's body in the wake of Shalini's touch. They seemed to centre in her groin where a pulsing pressure was gathering. She moved her hips, trying to change position so that the little bud which ticked so strongly against the imprisonment of her flesh would be eased somewhat.

231

The sexual tension inside her was becoming unbearable. The soft female touch seemed to underline the fact that strong, male fingers waited to stroke her.

'Relax, fair one,' Shalini said huskily, removing her hands from between Amy's thighs. 'There is no hurry. You will have all night with Ravinder and many nights thereafter.'

She drew lines with ash-coloured paste on Amy's forearms, thighs, chest and across her naval. Amy almost groaned aloud with frustration. Surely Ravinder would join them soon. She imagined his mouth crushing her, his tongue thrusting strongly into her mouth. Her quim fluttered and she felt the warm wetness gathering there.

'Let your arousal find its own level,' Shalini said, her voice softly soothing, but somehow only serving to excite Amy even more. 'Concentrate on the tides within you. Let this powder with cinnabar, datura, nutmeg and other intoxicating substances work their magic on your senses.'

The potent aroma of the oils and cosmetics cast a powerful spell over Amy. A spiralling excitement rose inside her. She was conscious of every inch of her skin. It seemed that her whole body cried out to be caressed and her yoni was like a furnace. She felt powerful, yet yielding, and wholly female.

She heard a sound from somewhere far away and realised that she had uttered a soft moan. The rosy light in the chamber seemed to grow more intense and to reach out and surround her. She was sinking into the heart of the redness, her body dissolving into pure sensation. The sense of power within her was stronger, centred.

She had an image of her secret place swelling, opening like the petals of an exotic orchid. The petals were of moist, pink and receptive flesh. Pearls of creamy moisture dripped from the heart of the orchid. Ravinder's lingam was a red lotus stem, a swollen dart to be sent to the heart of her womanly crevice.

For a moment she was afraid. Was this magic? She seemed to be outside herself, looking down.

Then strong hands encircled her waist and she felt her back rest against a smooth, broad chest. A clean-shaven cheek pressed against her jaw as she turned her head. Of course, he was there, at the moment when the strength of her desire had made her afraid. In the future he would always be there. A great wave of happiness rose up inside her.

Ravinder's breath caressed her neck, then his lips moved in a line up to her ear. Just that simple touch was so intense that she cried out, her eyes pricking with tears. It must be the intoxicants mixed with the oil which affected her so. She had never felt so sensitive to every external stimulus.

She felt Ravinder smile as he brought up his fingers and stroked her exposed nape.

'Come with us now, my love. You are ready to be opened, for, according to our teaching, every woman is a virgin until she has passed through this ritual. It is time that we shared the ultimate pleasure.'

Somehow Shalini had crossed the room and was lying on the red-draped dais. Ravinder placed Amy gently down on the soft red fabric and lay beside her, Shalini took up a similar position on her other side.

Both of them were still clothed but Amy was completely naked. Her vulnerability and the fact that she was the focus of both of their attention made her a little anxious but she was too aroused, too cocooned by their proximity, for real alarm.

Ravinder picked up a carved wooden box. Opening it he held up an object. Amy saw that he held a beauti-fully-carved phallus of some smooth pale stone.

'Behold the Shiva lingam,' Ravinder said. 'With this

sacred object, my love, you will be deflowered. Do not be afraid. Your pleasure will be great.'

Amy's eyes opened wide. The phallus was long and thick. Did Ravinder really mean to put that object inside her while he and Shalini watched? The thought of it filled her with a sort of dread. How shameful to have to lie there while he did that to her.

Yet the shame added a new dimension to her pleasure. Oh God, her pleasure bud burned and throbbed. What had Shalini done to her? She felt desperate to come. Just the thought of having the marble lingam pushed into her made her grow wetter. It was as if her yoni was salivating. It was horrible to admit it to herself, but she was almost past caring what they did to her.

Was that a mouth on hers; fingers plucking at her breasts? She couldn't tell what was reality. Such sweet torture. Her mind and body clamoured for release. Arching her back she clutched at Ravinder's shoulders, her breasts straining towards him.

'Please . . .' she whispered. 'Do it to me.'

Shalini gave a soft laugh and began to stroke Amy's cheek. Her lips brushed Amy's damp forehead.

'She is ready brother. More than ready I would say.'

Amy groaned when Ravinder's mouth covered hers in a firm, demanding kiss. She strained against him, pushing her tongue into his mouth, tasting the cinnamon on his breath. The kiss was almost violent and she revelled in it, loving the invasion of his tongue, knowing that soon her yoni would be treated to a similar delight.

She felt Ravinder slip his hand under one of her thighs and Shalini mirrored his action. Gently they drew her legs apart and up so that her hips were tipped in towards her belly and her yoni was exposed, pouting and swollen.

Fingers stroked over her belly and she no longer

knew nor cared which of them caressed her. Ravinder, Shalini, they seemed part of one body – male and female energy in tandem.

Someone parted the lips of her yoni and circled the hard bead of her pleasure bud, tapping it gently. A moist finger stroked over her anus, rocking against the tight orifice and causing it to pulse with ticklish delight. Amy let out her breath on a sigh as lips closed over her nipples. The sweetly pulling sensation was exquisite.

She began moving her hips back and forth, lost in the world which had narrowed to this red glow of pleasure. She wanted something more now; to be penetrated, pushed into, pierced by something hard and male. Ravinder must have sensed that the time was right.

The cold marble nudged against her entrance and all the time the caresses and kisses continued. Warm hands stroked her and the coldness of the lingam probed her vaginal opening, stretching her gently, wonderfully. Pushing her inner lips aside, the big glans began sliding smoothly in. It must have been oiled, she thought dimly, awash with the sensations of a singular, indescribable pleasure.

The marble phallus slipped inside more deeply. Fraction by fraction it nudged against her hot inner walls, making her shiver at its delicious coolness. Amy moaned softly. Her sex pulsed around the shaft and she surged forward, impaling herself fully.

Someone kissed her mouth, someone licked her sex, mouthing the wet pink skin which was stretched around the base of the marble phallus. Amy bucked helplessly when a tongue flicked against her bud, so painfully erect and all pushed out by the pressure of the phallus within her, so that it stood proud of her wet pink folds.

Now lips nuzzled her pleasure bud, nibbling and suckling at the firm, salt teat. She felt long hair brush across her thighs. A wet finger slid across her distended anus, smoothing around the damp, sea-anemone shape of it and slipping just inside the entrance.

Amy tossed her head from side to side, unable to stand the dual pleasures of mouths and lingam – the many subtle caresses of every orifice. Surely she would break, melt, dissolve, but Ravinder and Shalini would be there to gather her up again and make her whole.

When she climaxed, she screamed, the sound reverberating around the draped chamber to be absorbed by the embroidered red tapestries. For a moment everything faded and she lost consciousness. Figures loomed up before her – Ganesha, the elephant-headed god and his consort Siddhi. The god was smiling, his ruby eyes glinting with approval. Amy reached out a hand to him, but he was fading already. The black behind her eyes gave way to the flickering scarlet light of the chamber.

She felt Ravinder withdraw the Shiva lingam slowly, the now warm marble slipping out onto the dais. Cleaning the stone phallus with oil, he wrapped it in silk and replaced it in its box, then he lay beside Amy.

With a small dry sob, she turned into Ravinder's embrace.

'Cry if you wish,' he whispered. 'An initiation is always emotional.'

He held Amy in his arms, stroking her hair away from her damp forehead. Amy laid her head on his broad chest, a sense of peace washing over her. He was her love and her life. She would never regret making the decision to leave the life she had known. This place was her home now.

She had reached a new state of being. Sometime, in the last months, she had cast off the cowl of her Western upbringing and allowed Eastern thoughts and values to enter her life. The experience of the long night of love had confirmed in her own mind the fact that she had been right to come to Ravinder. It didn't matter that her family would never understand. She knew, and perhaps Madeline alone knew, that this was right for her.

'And now my pale lotus, you belong to us,' Ravinder said against her mouth.

'And we belong to you,' Shalina said, stretching out her arms to enfold them both.

In a little while the caresses began again and this time it was Ravinder's hard, hot lingam which Amy welcomed into her body. While he plunged into her from behind, holding her tightly around the waist, she kissed Shalini's full mouth.

Later, Amy marvelled that she felt no jealousy while watching Shalini receive Ravinder's lingam into her body. The generosity of them both, the care they took to nuture her feelings, made it impossible to feel envy. There was no need, for she knew that she was valued equally by them both and they would all enjoy each other many times over.

She was glad that she had found the courage to follow the path of the tiger. You were wrong about crying for the moon Maud, she thought. Anything is attainable if you want it badly enough.

BLACK
lace

NO LADY
Saskia Hope

30-year-old Kate dumps her boyfriend, walks out of her job and sets off in search of sexual adventure. Set against the rugged terrain of the Pyrenees, the love-making is as rough as the landscape.

ISBN 0 352 32857 6

WEB OF DESIRE
Sophie Danson

High-flying executive Marcie is gradually drawn away from the normality of her married life. Strange messages begin to appear on her computer, summoning her to sinister and fetishistic sexual liaisons.

ISBN 0 352 32856 8

BLUE HOTEL
Cherri Pickford

Hotelier Ramon can't understand why best-selling author Floy Pennington has come to stay at his quiet hotel. Her exhibitionist tendencies are driving him crazy, as are her increasingly wanton encounters with the hotel's other guests.

ISBN 0 352 32858 4

CASSANDRA'S CONFLICT
Fredrica Alleyn

Behind the respectable facade of a house in present-day Hampstead lies a world of decadent indulgence and darkly bizarre eroticism. A sternly attractive Baron and his beautiful but cruel wife are playing games with the young Cassandra.

ISBN 0 352 32859 2

THE CAPTIVE FLESH
Cleo Cordell

Marietta and Claudine, French aristocrats saved from pirates, learn their invitation to stay at the opulent Algerian mansion of their rescuer, Kasim, requires something in return; their complete surrender to the ecstasy of pleasure in pain.

ISBN 0 352 32872 X

PLEASURE HUNT
Sophie Danson

Sexual adventurer Olympia Deschamps is determined to become a member of the Légion D'Amour – the most exclusive society of French libertines.

ISBN 0 352 32880 0

BLACK ORCHID
Roxanne Carr

The Black Orchid is a women's health club which provides a specialised service for its high-powered clients; women who don't have the time to spend building complex relationships, but who enjoy the pleasures of the flesh.

ISBN 0 352 32888 6

ODALISQUE
Fleur Reynolds

A tale of family intrigue and depravity set against the glittering backdrop of the designer set. This facade of respectability conceals a reality of bitter rivalry and unnatural love.

ISBN 0 352 32887 8

OUTLAW LOVER
Saskia Hope

Fee Cambridge lives in an upper level deluxe pleasuredome of technologically advanced comfort. Bored with her predictable husband and pampered lifestyle, Fee ventures into the wild side of town, finding an an outlaw who becomes her lover.

ISBN 0 352 32909 2

THE SENSES BEJEWELLED
Cleo Cordell

Willing captives Marietta and Claudine are settling into life at Kasim's harem. But 18th century Algeria can be a hostile place. When the women are kidnapped by Kasim's sworn enemy, they face indignities that will test the boundaries of erotic experience. This is the sequel to *The Captive Flesh*.

ISBN 0 352 32904 1

GEMINI HEAT
Portia Da Costa

As the metropolis sizzles in freak early summer temperatures, twin sisters Deana and Delia find themselves cooking up a heatwave of their own. Jackson de Guile, master of power dynamics and wealthy connoisseur of fine things, draws them both into a web of luxuriously decadent debauchery.

ISBN 0 352 32912 2

VIRTUOSO
Katrina Vincenzi

Mika and Serena, darlings of classical music's jet-set, inhabit a world of secluded passion. The reason? Since Mika's tragic accident which put a stop to his meteoric rise to fame as a solo violinist, he cannot face the world, and together they lead a decadent, reclusive existence.

ISBN 0 352 32907 6

MOON OF DESIRE
Sophie Danson

When Soraya Chilton is posted to the ancient and mysterious city of Ragzburg on a mission for the Foreign Office, strange things begin to happen to her. Wild, sexual urges overwhelm her at the coming of each full moon.

ISBN 0 352 32911 4

FIONA'S FATE
Fredrica Alleyn

When Fiona Sheldon is kidnapped by the infamous Trimarchi brothers, along with her friend Bethany, she finds herself acting in ways her husband Duncan would be shocked by. Alessandro Trimarchi makes full use of this opportunity to discover the true extent of Fiona's suppressed, but powerful, sexuality.

ISBN 0 352 32913 0

HANDMAIDEN OF PALMYRA
Fleur Reynolds

3rd century Palmyra: a lush oasis in the Syrian desert. The beautiful and fiercely independent Samoya takes her place in the temple of Antioch as an apprentice priestess. Decadent bachelor Prince Alif has other plans for her and sends his scheming sister to bring her to his Bacchanalian wedding feast.

ISBN 0 352 32919 X

OUTLAW FANTASY
Saskia Hope

On the outer reaches of the 21st century metropolis the Amazenes are on the prowl; fierce warrior women who have some unfinished business with Fee Cambridge's pirate lover. This is the sequel to *Outlaw Lover*.

ISBN 0 352 32920 3

THE SILKEN CAGE
Sophie Danson

When University lecturer Maria Treharne inherits her aunt's mansion in Cornwall, she finds herself the subject of strange and unexpected attention. Using the craft of goddess worship and sexual magnetism, Maria finds allies and foes in this savage and beautiful landscape.

ISBN 0 352 32928 9

RIVER OF SECRETS
Saskia Hope & Georgia Angelis

Intrepid female reporter Sydney Johnson takes over someone else's assignment up the Amazon river. Sydney soon realises this mission to find a lost Inca city has a hidden agenda. Everyone is behaving so strangely, so sexually, and the tropical humidity is reaching fever pitch.

ISBN 0 352 32925 4

VELVET CLAWS
Cleo Cordell

It's the 19th century; a time of exploration and discovery and young, spirited Gwendoline Farnshawe is determined not to be left behind in the parlour when the handsome and celebrated anthropologist, Jonathan Kimberton, is planning his latest expedition to Africa.

ISBN 0 352 32926 2

THE GIFT OF SHAME
Sarah Hope-Walker

Helen is a woman with extreme fantasies. When she meets Jeffrey – a cultured wealthy stranger – at a party, they soon become partners in obsession. Now nothing is impossible for her, no fantasy beyond his imagination or their mutual exploration.

ISBN 0 352 32935 1

SUMMER OF ENLIGHTENMENT
Cheryl Mildenhall

Karin's new-found freedom is getting her into all sorts of trouble. The enigmatic Nicolai has been showing interest in her since their chance meeting in a cafe. But he's the husband of a valued friend and is trying to embroil her in the sexual tension he thrives on.

ISBN 0 352 32937 8

A BOUQUET OF BLACK ORCHIDS
Roxanne Carr

The exclusive Black Orchid health spa has provided Maggie with a new social life and a new career, where giving and receiving pleasure of the most sophisticated nature takes top priority. But her loyalty to the club is being tested by the presence of Tourell; a powerful man who makes her an offer she finds difficult to refuse.

ISBN 0 352 32939 4

JULIET RISING
Cleo Cordell

At Madame Nicol's exclusive but strict 18th-century academy for young ladies, the bright and wilful Juliet is learning the art of courting the affections of young noblemen.

ISBN 0 352 32938 6

DEBORAH'S DISCOVERY
Fredrica Alleyn

Deborah Woods is trying to change her life. Having just ended her long-term relationship and handed in her notice at work, she is ready for a little adventure. Meeting American oil magnate John Pavin III throws her world into even more confusion as he invites her to stay at his luxurious renovated castle in Scotland. But what looked like being a romantic holiday soon turns into a test of sexual bravery.

ISBN 0 352 32945 9

THE TUTOR
Portia Da Costa

Like minded libertines reap the rewards of their desire in this story of the sexual initiation of a beautiful young man. Rosalind Howard takes a post as personal librarian to a husband and wife, both unashamed sensualists keen to engage her into their decadent scenarios.

ISBN 0 352 32946 7

THE HOUSE IN NEW ORLEANS
Fleur Reynolds

When she inherits her family home in the fashionable Garden district of New Orleans, Ottilie Duvier discovers it has been leased to the notorious Helmut von Straffen; a debauched German Count famous for his decadent Mardi Gras parties. Determined to oust him from the property, she soon realises that not all dangerous animals live in the swamp!

ISBN 0 352 32951 3

ELENA'S CONQUEST
Lisette Allen

It's summer – 1070AD – and the gentle Elena is gathering herbs in the garden of the convent where she leads a peaceful, but uneventful, life. When Norman soldiers besiege the convent, they take Elena captive and present her to the dark and masterful Lord Aimery to satisfy his savage desire for Saxon women.

ISBN 0 352 32950 5

CASSANDRA'S CHATEAU
Fredrica Alleyn

Cassandra has been living with the dominant and perverse Baron von Ritter for eighteen months when their already bizarre relationship takes an unexpected turn. The arrival of a naive female visitor at the chateau provides the Baron with a new opportunity to indulge his fancy for playing darkly erotic games with strangers.

ISBN 0 352 32955 6

WICKED WORK
Pamela Kyle

At twenty-eight, Suzie Carlton is at the height of her journalistic career. She has status, money and power. What she doesn't have is a masterful partner who will allow her to realise the true extent of her fantasies. How will she reconcile the demands of her job with her sexual needs?

ISBN 0 352 32958 0

To be published in December . . .

DREAM LOVER
Katrina Vincenzi

Icily controlled Gemma is a dedicated film producer, immersed in her latest production – a darkly Gothic vampire movie. But after a visit to Brittany, where she encounters a mystery lover, a disquieting feeling continues to haunt her. Compelled to discover the identity of the man who ravished her, she becomes entangled in a mystifying erotic odyssey.

ISBN 0 352 32956 4

PATH OF THE TIGER
Cleo Cordell

India, in the early days of the Raj. Amy Spencer is looking for an excuse to rebel against the stuffy mores of the British army wives. Luckily, a new friend introduces her to places where other women dare not venture – where Tantric mysteries and the Kama Sutra come alive. Soon she becomes besotted by Ravinder, the exquisitely handsome son of the Maharaja, and finds the pathway to absolute pleasure.

ISBN 0 352 32959 9

WE NEED YOUR HELP . . .
to plan the future of women's erotic fiction –

– and no stamp required!

Yours are the only opinions that matter.

Black Lace is the first series of books devoted to erotic fiction by women for women.

We intend to keep providing the best-written, sexiest books you can buy. And we'd appreciate your help and valued opinion of the books so far. Tell us what you want to read.

THE BLACK LACE QUESTIONNAIRE

SECTION ONE: ABOUT YOU

1.1 Sex (*we presume you are female, but so as not to discriminate*)
Are you?
Male ☐
Female ☐

1.2 Age
under 21 ☐ 21–30 ☐
31–40 ☐ 41–50 ☐
51–60 ☐ over 60 ☐

1.3 At what age did you leave full-time education?
still in education ☐ 16 or younger ☐
17–19 ☐ 20 or older ☐

1.4 Occupation _____

1.5 Annual household income
  under £10,000 □ £10–£20,000 □
  £20–£30,000 □ £30–£40,000 □
  over £40,000 □

1.6 We are perfectly happy for you to remain anonymous;
but if you would like to receive information on other
publications available, please insert your name and
address

_____

_____

_____

_____

SECTION TWO: ABOUT BUYING BLACK LACE BOOKS

2.1 How did you acquire this copy of *Path of the Tiger*?
  I bought it myself □ My partner bought it □
  I borrowed/found it □

2.2 How did you find out about Black Lace books?
  I saw them in a shop □
  I saw them advertised in a magazine □
  I saw the London Underground posters □
  I read about them in _____
  Other _____

2.3 Please tick the following statements you agree with:
  I would be less embarrassed about buying Black
  Lace books if the cover pictures were less explicit □
  I think that in general the pictures on Black
  Lace books are about right □
  I think Black Lace cover pictures should be as
  explicit as possible □

2.4 Would you read a Black Lace book in a public place – on
a train for instance?
  Yes □ No □

SECTION THREE: ABOUT THIS BLACK LACE BOOK

3.1 Do you think the sex content in this book is:
Too much   ☐   About right   ☐
Not enough   ☐

3.2 Do you think the writing style in this book is:
Too unreal/escapist   ☐   About right   ☐
Too down to earth   ☐

3.3 Do you think the story in this book is:
Too complicated   ☐   About right   ☐
Too boring/simple   ☐

3.4 Do you think the cover of this book is:
Too explicit   ☐   About right   ☐
Not explicit enough   ☐

Here's a space for any other comments:

SECTION FOUR: ABOUT OTHER BLACK LACE BOOKS

4.1 How many Black Lace books have you read?   ☐

4.2 If more than one, which one did you prefer?

4.3 Why?

SECTION FIVE: ABOUT YOUR IDEAL EROTIC NOVEL

We want to publish the books you want to read – so this is your chance to tell us exactly what your ideal erotic novel would be like.

5.1 Using a scale of 1 to 5 (1 = no interest at all, 5 = your ideal), please rate the following possible settings for an erotic novel:

Medieval/barbarian/sword 'n' sorcery ☐
Renaissance/Elizabethan/Restoration ☐
Victorian/Edwardian ☐
1920s & 1930s – the Jazz Age ☐
Present day ☐
Future/Science Fiction ☐

5.2 Using the same scale of 1 to 5, please rate the following themes you may find in an erotic novel:

Submissive male/dominant female ☐
Submissive female/dominant male ☐
Lesbianism ☐
Bondage/fetishism ☐
Romantic love ☐
Experimental sex e.g. anal/watersports/sex toys ☐
Gay male sex ☐
Group sex ☐

Using the same scale of 1 to 5, please rate the following styles in which an erotic novel could be written:

Realistic, down to earth, set in real life ☐
Escapist fantasy, but just about believable ☐
Completely unreal, impressionistic, dreamlike ☐

5.3 Would you prefer your ideal erotic novel to be written from the viewpoint of the main male characters or the main female characters?

Male ☐ Female ☐
Both ☐

5.4 What would your ideal Black Lace heroine be like? Tick as many as you like:

Dominant	☐	Glamorous	☐
Extroverted	☐	Contemporary	☐
Independent	☐	Bisexual	☐
Adventurous	☐	Naive	☐
Intellectual	☐	Introverted	☐
Professional	☐	Kinky	☐
Submissive	☐	Anything else?	☐
Ordinary	☐	_____	

5.5 What would your ideal male lead character be like? Again, tick as many as you like:

Rugged	☐		
Athletic	☐	Caring	☐
Sophisticated	☐	Cruel	☐
Retiring	☐	Debonair	☐
Outdoor-type	☐	Naive	☐
Executive-type	☐	Intellectual	☐
Ordinary	☐	Professional	☐
Kinky	☐	Romantic	☐
Hunky	☐		
Sexually dominant	☐	Anything else?	☐
Sexually submissive	☐	_____	

5.6 Is there one particular setting or subject matter that your ideal erotic novel would contain?

_____

SECTION SIX: LAST WORDS

6.1 What do you like best about Black Lace books?

_____

6.2 What do you most dislike about Black Lace books?

_____

6.3 In what way, if any, would you like to change Black Lace covers?

_____

6.4   Here's a space for any other comments:

_____

_____

_____

_____

*Thank you for completing this questionnaire. Now tear it out of the
book – carefully! – put it in an envelope and send it to:*

Black Lace
FREEPOST
London
W10 5BR

No stamp is required if you are resident in the U.K.